I KILLED STALIN

By Sterling Noel

COMPLETE AND UNABRIDGED

WILDSIDE PRESS

PRINCIPAL CHARACTERS

JAN MILES

American secret operator whose life is in greatest danger when he sees in his gunsight—the figure of Joseph Stalin!

COLONEL JANUS

Undercover man for the mysterious "Bureau K." One night in Nevada he acts as an executioner to save Miles' life.

RITA BARSTOW

Beautiful Communist agent. She uses her physical charms to lure unsuspecting F.B.I. men to their deaths.

GENERAL GODOVISKY

High official in the dread MVD. He poses as an innocent clerk at Russia's UN headquarters.

DOROTHY JANUS

In love with Miles. A severe beating by Red agents can't force her to reveal Miles' true identity.

CAPTAIN PETSKY

MVD hatchet-man. He has long been searching for the man who caused the death of many MVD members—but doesn't know Miles is the person he seeks.

AND

MARSHAL JOSEPH STALIN

who, although he does not have a line of dialogue, is the most important character in this book!

Published by Wildside Press LLC
www.wildsidepress.com

1 Now in this May of 1959, in the ninth month of the shooting war between Russia and the United States, readers of this document will become informed for the first time of the full story behind the death of the Red Tsar, Joseph Stalin.

Although this is in no way an official account, nonetheless it is presented with the tacit permission of the International Intelligence Agency, familiarly known as Bureau-X (or Bu-X), which was disbanded upon completion of its primary function. It is hoped that such approval will be deemed adequate by the United States and other Allied Governments, and that censorship will not withhold it from the public.

The death of Joseph Vissarionovich Dzugashvili, alias Stalin, which was the cause of such unbounded rejoicing when it was announced to the free world late in December of 1958, was brought about through years of labor and planning by Bureau-X. Of necessity, the path that Bureau-X charted for its assassin, to approach within gun range of the world's most closely guarded person, led through blood, but I should like to stress that we of Bureau-X were at war, and that there never is logic in the killings of wartime, wherein the cut and color of a man's uniform are sufficient cause for his murder.

It was no accident that the Communist dictator's death coincided with the Soviet Union's atom-bomb attack upon eight principal cities of America.

For Stalin was executed. He was executed as the first war criminal of World War III, on the day that he started the conflagration that is now engulfing so much of the world.

I know this to be true because I was his executioner.

I put a bullet through the heart of the mad-dog dictator of the Kremlin at 3:38 P.M. of August 18, 1958, as he sat down to luncheon on the terrace of his new summer palace in the Crimea, between the towns of Simeiz and Alupka.

2 For me, it was a long time between wars. Beginning late in 1945, after I left the Navy, I knocked around on five continents, doing everything from smuggling

3

out of Tangiers, to gun-running up the Orinoco, to acting as assistant chief of police of Tabriz at the special request of the shah for reasons which concern no one outside of Iran. I was waiting and hunting all the time for someone or something— like as not, my destiny. An ample inheritance removed the problem of financial necessity, and also deprived me of that fiduciary spice that makes so many of life's activities palatable. But I'm not complaining about it; I mention it merely so that one may better appreciate the general aimlessness and lack of motivation of my actions.

I suppose I inherited a primary urge for peregrination from my father, who was a Russian and one of the very few Old Bolsheviki who escaped with a whole skin, to die of natural causes in his own bed. But compared to his, my life was adventurous only on a minor-league scale. He fought through two wars and a revolution, he was a Cheka ax man, and later, for many years, the most sought-after fugitive of the succeeding Ogpu; he was gunned more times than an iron rabbit in a shooting gallery, and his blood had stained the sod of five free countries and a satellite; he was the toughest, most irascible, most wary and most lovable old guy I've ever met, and he taught me most everything I know, including five languages, a score of dialects, and a reasoned dislike for Communism and all its works. He amassed and squandered several fortunes in the free world and, happily for his survivors, he was approaching the acme of his fifth and largest when coronary thrombosis laid him low, in 1941.

I was born Alexis Ivanovich Bodine in Brooklyn on a snowy February night in 1921. Twenty years later I possessed an M.A. from Columbia University and a ticket to an archeological expedition to the Upper Nile, when my dad's death and Pearl Harbor combined to set my feet on the path they have followed ever since. I went to Navy boot camp in Norfolk; in two years I had a commission as an ensign and an assignment from Navy Intelligence behind the lines in the Balkans. In two more years I had killed, for one reason or another, some eleven N.K.V.D. men, among others, and I was myself, like my father before me, a favorite quarry of the Russian secret police.

Now, with the passage of another fourteen years, I am putting the final touches on what I hope will be my last association with violence.

It was a long and devious road from my Master's thesis to my present home upon a closely guarded and nameless island in the Pacific. I shall conduct you over only the latter part of it,

4

which concerns my assignment as assassin, and then you will understand why my government believes it necessary to isolate from me the evil and the hate of the totalitarian world that would have my life at all costs—today, tomorrow, or the day after that. . . .

I gave up my name of Alexis Bodine in 1945, discarding with it all of the associations and some of the physical characteristics of that identity, as a prelude to leaving Navy Intelligence and returning to civilian life. There was nothing melodramatic about it, although such an unusual action might appear so. The fact of the matter was that my Balkan activities, which had become so fatally involved with the Russians, who were our allies only when such a pose was advantageous to them, had caused much consternation in the Communist-loving high places of Washington. It was deemed advisable to have me vanish. This was not accomplished simply; first I was reported officially as "missing in action" and, a year later, "presumed dead." The place where this presumed demise took place was in Italy, in the Arno River area, where I was supposed to have gone as an artillery observer on loan to the Army to demonstrate some new electronic gadgets. No fuss, no mess, and no body to dispose of—and I emerged with a new name, a new nose, the scar on my forehead covered over, and a new profession, that of airplane jockey.

The Navy had had the foresight, some years before, of having taught me to fly, and my new identity was that of an Army transport pilot by the name of Steve Ellery who had been discharged from the service because of a collection of heebee jeebies called war nerves. . . . But forget the name of Steve Ellery. I've got a new name and identity coming up, and that's the one that's important to this account.

3 Well, back in 1954 and not long after my hitch in the Tabriz police force where, incidentally, I acquired a new scar on my forehead, but lower down, over the left eye, I found myself in the bedroom of a plush layout on New York's Park Avenue, playing pigeon in the oldest swindle of history—the badger game. How I became involved with this Cora Dorsey dame and her alleged husband, who went under the impossible name of Colonel Frank Rittenhouse Grubb, is

5

not pertinent nor particularly amusing, so I'll skip it. Anyone with better than 4-20 vision might have fallen for this apprentice Jezebel, for she had more curves than the Simplon Pass; anyway, why should I explain? I was free, white, and 33, which is a sufficient age for any man to make a fool of himself.

I have no doubt that this Cora and her Grubb traced my bank account through the usual rent check I gave her and found it fat enough to go into action. Anyway, there I was in this bedroom with a scantily clad babe hiding her shame, or whatever it was, and an outraged "husband" baying at me in the doorway and waving around a .38 Colt that might have been loaded. This was enough to stir up my Russian dander, and if you don't think that's considerable dander, you've never read *Pravda*.

So I waited until he got close enough for me to grab, and I grabbed. When I departed this Park Avenue hive, leaving a prone Grubb and a screaming Cora, and reached the corner of Sixty-first Street, I was still burning. Me, such a sucker!

I got into this cab on the corner and I said to the driver, "Take me someplace where I can get a ticket to Florida. Drive slow so I can cool off."

"How about Penn Station?" he asked.

"Sure, anything," I said. "You be the doctor."

I settled back in my seat and resumed feeling sorry for myself. I thought of a lot of appropriate names for Cora and the Colonel, but I was losing my head of steam about them because her curves kept intruding, and finally I hit on the word luscious, which was the word for Cora, and at the same time I became aware that the driver's name was Joseph Hogan and that his number was 13,586. I leaned forward in my seat.

"Hiya, Joe," I said.

"Hi," he said.

"How's business?" I asked.

"O.K."

"Carry many people this time of the year?"

"Sure. Lots."

"Many people besides me?"

There was a pause. He took a quick look at my face as he coasted through a light that had just turned at Thirty-eighth Street.

"You a wise guy?" he said.

"Sure I'm a wise guy," I said. "And I'm getting sick of riding in your damned cab."

6

"You want to get out here?" he asked, putting a hand on the meter.

"I'll get out when I get to the station," I said. "Meanwhile, maybe you'll tell me why I've got your cab three times today."

"Oh, that," he said. "Probably coincidence."

"It's no coincidence," I asserted, "and besides, no cab driver is going to use a seventeen-cent word like coincidence. What's the racket?"

"No racket," he mumbled. By this time the light had changed and we were under way again down Park Avenue.

I got to thinking of other things and didn't attach any significance to the fact that we turned east on Thirty-fourth Street and then took the East River Drive going south. I know where Penn Station is as well as anyone. But along about Grand Street I woke up and asked him where the hell he thought he was headed.

"I just wanted to stop down here and get some gas," he said. "I won't charge you for the extra ride."

"Damned right you won't," I agreed.

"I get it four cents cheaper down here," he said. He had a loose, English bulldog face and I found it difficult to dislike him.

We stopped at a gas station, across from a dock, that had a big sign on it announcing it was run by a couple of veterans. Joe Hogan got out and went into the station. While one of the veterans gassed the cab, I saw him phoning. It didn't take long. When he came back, he got under way in a hurry, without paying the gas man, and headed south again.

I pushed forward in my seat so I could talk into his ear. "Do you just feel like going sightseeing, or do you think they've moved Penn Station down to Wall Street?" I asked.

"Keep your shirt on," he said.

"How do you like that?" I said to myself, but to him too. "This son of a bitch thinks he's taking me for a ride."

I wasn't worried. Not only was it broad daylight in the midst of a busy city, but there wasn't one person in New York, or in the entire world, for that matter, who knew me back beyond 1945. A guy by the name of Steve Ellery was a menace to no one.

"I'll take the West Side Highway back uptown," he said. "And you better watch that nasty tongue of yours. You're liable to get a tire-iron along the side of your fat head."

7

"Pull over," I said, "and we'll try out which head is the fattest—yours or mine."

He went about a block farther without further comment, then suddenly swerved to the left and stopped just north of a dock entrance. He made the mistake of turning his face toward me, and I reached through the partition and let him have it on the nose. Then I opened the door and got out, and wiped the blood off my hand with my handkerchief. I looked in at him and he was shaking his head, like a box fighter coming up from an eight-count. Then he put the cab in gear and moved away fast, leaving me standing there in a fine rage.

At the dock entrance there was a circle of pickets, plodding around with placards on their backs and signs held aloft and making a lot of racket. I stood there and read their signs and figured them for Commies. They were picketing about an "Imperialist War" and such hogwash, but there was no indication that any of the stevedores or other shipping people were paying any attention to them. I was about to move on when I noticed in the picket line a big, rugged ape who walked with a slight limp and who could be none other than Dingdong Kelley.

Now this Dingdong Kelley was a celebrated character during much of World War II. He was principally a labor agitator and organizer, and he got himself elected to the City Council during the war, where he earned a reputation with salty rhetoric and party-line contortions. He had received a wide, if unfavorable, press.

What was not known about him was that he was a mainstay of the F.B.I. anti-Communist activity. Also, and incidentally, he had been a close friend of my dad, who had originally coached him on Communism, and he had known me since I was a kid.

While I stood there contemplating Kelley and wondering if I should speak to him, the battle started. A bunch of rough, tough longshoremen came out of the pier entrance in a flying wedge and landed on the pickets with fists, cargo hooks, and odd bits of lumber. I couldn't get out of the way. It happened too fast and all around me, and before I had a chance to choose sides I was helping Dingdong to his feet and fending off a four-quarter pine club with a mad Polack on the wielding end.

Dingdong and I were doing not too badly, with some help from a couple of the others who had been able to stay on their feet, when the cops moved in. I got a nightstick on the back of my head and that's the last I saw of South Street.

8

I came to in the pie wagon, and beside me, propping me up in the seat, was Kelley. He had a cut over his left eye, and there was a trickle of dried blood down his face. He was grinning.

"How you doing?" he asked when I opened my eyes.

"Not too bad," I said. I felt the back of my head. It was mushy and sticky.

"It was good while it lasted," said Dingdong.

I looked around the wagon, which was bouncing along much too fast with a whistle screaming and a horn tooting. This was after the New York police had abandoned sirens so as not to confuse the people on air-raid alarms. I counted seven others besides myself. The light was dim, from a small grating up front and the steel screen door in the back, guarded by a large bluecoat, so I couldn't see clearly, but all the occupants looked the worse for wear.

Kelley leaned over and whispered in my ear, "Just nod yes or no. Don't I know you?"

I nodded yes.

"You carry a card?" he asked. That would mean only one thing to a Communist—was it a so-called red card?

I shrugged. I took my checkbook and pen out of my pocket and wrote across the face of a check, "John Hamilton." That was a cover name Dingdong had used when he visited us. I tore the check out, folded it up, and slipped it into Kelley's pocket. He nodded at me, then turned away and began talking to a big ugly ape across the aisle.

This character didn't answer Kelley. He was bent over, rubbing his shin. Then I butted into the conversation.

"They hurt you?" I asked him.

He stopped rubbing and raised his head. I could see his eyes flash in the gloom.

"Is it any of your business?" he demanded nastily.

"No," I said, "but I'd just as soon make it my business and bust that other leg for you."

He started to get up and go for me. Several hands grabbed him. Dingdong reached out a long arm and pushed him back in his seat.

"Take it easy, Alex," he said to him, "this guy was fighting on our side."

The cop standing at the back door told us to pipe down.

"Never saw him before," said the sullen type without looking at me, and he went back to his rubbing.

We arrived at the Third Precinct Station and were led in

9

through the front door and up to the lieutenant's desk. Ding-dong had hold of my arm and he jockeyed me to the end of the line and a few feet from the nearest man, as we faced the desk.

As the first man started to give his pedigree and all attention was on him, Kelley bent over to my ear and said quickly and urgently:

"How do you know John Hamilton?"

He hadn't seen me since my operations and change of identity and he was obviously puzzled. There was something he did recognize as familiar—perhaps my voice, or my walk, or the way I swung my fists. I had no fear of trusting him, but this wasn't the place.

"You've known me since I was a kid," I whispered back. "I'll use the name of Hamilton."

"O.K." He nodded.

We moved back to the others, and I was wondering idly what Kelley's play was going to be, when the sullen monkey with the aching shin, who was in the middle of the line, spoke up and dropped the bombshell.

"My name," he said in an oratorical voice, "is Alexis Ivanovich Bodine."

4 Like all Russians, my dad was a fatalist, and I suppose I inherited—or acquired—much of this same attitude. Along with this fatalism goes patience, and along with patience goes the faith that you will find a solution for all problems, if you wait long enough or hunt hard enough.

Well, I was willing to wait, but not too long, for the answer to this imposter who had adopted my discarded but real identity.

What was uppermost in my mind, as I stood there before the police desk with my mouth open, was that this was no coincidence, that it all had been carefully planned, and that what I did next, what my reactions to this situation would be, would determine the next move of these master tacticians who had entered into my life.

So I closed my mouth and did nothing. I needed time to think. I stood there and smiled at Kelley, and it took no great genius or insight to arrive at the conclusion that Joe Hogan

10

and Dingdong were in it up to their ears and that something critical was well along on its way to happening to me.

The big question, of course, was whether this "something" was benign or dire. Which side of the street was Kelley playing—the Communist or F.B.I.? Was Hogan friend or enemy? I wasn't too worried about my sanguinary past, although it was still a certainty that the M.V.D., which had inherited all the hates of the Ogpu, would have considered it a great triumph to have eliminated the Alexis Bodine who was for so long the top man on the list of Enemies of the People.

My protection from that menace resided in the carefully executed shift in identities, which was known to no man then alive. This had been no mere official matter conducted on the level of ordinary military secrecy. Far from it. I had been placed in the hands of an expert, a retired navy captain who had spent most of World War I as a trusted aide on the Kaiser's general staff. He had reported to no one what identity I was to adopt or how it was to be done. I spent many months with him, traveling and covering up trails, getting my operations, shifting bank accounts and other financial holdings, changing Navy records, even down to fingerprints. . . . Four years later he died, and I lost a true friend.

It was unthinkable that the Communists could have penetrated that veil, even if they did have access to every other secret of our government. But if not the Communists, then who else?

I decided to play along with Kelley, whom I felt I could trust, and find out. And I also decided that there was one Bodine too many in this crowded world and that, come hell or high water, I would rectify this imbalance at the first opportunity.

My turn came for the police lieutenant to take my pedigree, and I told him my name was John Hamilton, that I was an unemployed airplane rigger, and that I lived in Hempstead, L. I. I offered to go bail for the crowd, if he would make it reasonable, and pulled a wad of mad money out of my pocket that made his eyes goggle. He asked $50 a head and I got it down to $30 and paid up, and we were all released in Dingdong's custody for appearance in magistrate's court the next morning. The charge was disorderly conduct, inciting to riot, assault, battery, and a few other meaningless legal dodges.

We were all allowed to clean up in the station washroom. A kindly sergeant put a temporary bandage on the back of my head. As we started out the front door, I edged over to this

11

phony Bodine—with Kelley all the time breathing down my neck—and I told him I was sorry I'd cracked at him in the wagon.

"Yeah?" he said.

"This is John Hamilton, an old friend of mine," said Kelley, making an introduction.

Bodine thawed slightly and handed me a damp hand, which I shook with enthusiasm.

"Glad to know you," I said. "I've heard a lot about you."

By that time we were on the sidewalk in front of the station-house. He turned a mean, searching look at me and demanded, "Where?"

"Oh, around," I said. "Here and there."

"Where?" he insisted. His voice was low and nasty.

"In the war," I replied airily. "I was around the Med and I heard all about how you were driving the Russians crazy."

"Oh," he said. He shrugged and we all started to walk west. Dingdong, who had resumed his iron grip on my arm, suggested we go to a nearby dog wagon and get some coffee. Bodine refused at first, then capitulated to Kelley's urging.

Five of us sat around a table in this place on Front Street and I started in on Bodine again.

"I thought you were killed," I said. "Somebody told me you got it somewhere in Italy."

"No, I wasn't killed," he replied with a slight, tight smile. "I was damn' near, though. Had my head busted and was captured by the Germans. Lost my memory for nearly three years."

"That was convenient," I said.

He jumped up from his seat, upsetting his coffee cup with a crash.

"What the hell do you mean by that?" he demanded.

"Take it easy," soothed Kelley, putting a big hand up to his shoulder.

"This son of a bitch makes too many cracks," said Bodine, pointing a finger at my nose. His voice was low and dangerous.

"I was just commenting," I said. "I was just thinking how I would have liked to lose my memory—for some of those years."

"Yeah?" said Bodine. He relaxed slightly.

"Yeah," I said. "I could have forgot it all, and I wouldn't have missed it a bit. . . . You seem to be awful touchy for a guy who was in Navy Intelligence."

12

"What the hell do you know about Navy Intelligence?" he shot back. But he sat down, just glaring at me.

"I don't know anything about it—but I wouldn't trust any of those bastards who were in it," I replied.

He stewed over that for a few minutes and ordered another cup of coffee.

"You seem to know a hell of a lot about me," he said, finally. "How did you know I was in Intelligence? No one knew that. My assignment was Top Secret."

"Oh, I get around," I said. It was evident to me that I had him where I wanted him. He had to know more. He had to know about me and how much I knew. I had no fear of not seeing him again, and under the circumstances that would be most desirable—alone. I turned my attention to Dingdong.

Kelley was a different breed of Indian. I knew well that I wasn't going to lead him around by the nose as I had done my impersonator. Dingdong was by far the most astute operator ever developed in the F.B.I.

"I saw a friend of yours in Tabriz," I said.

"I haven't got any friends," said Kelley. "In this business, the whole world is after your scalp, for one reason or another."

"You have your comrades," said Bodine severely.

"Yeah, of course," said Kelley. "But only a damned fool would trust them in any personal matter."

"That's bourgeois sentimentality," interposed another man at the table, who went by the name of Block. "Personal matters are for the bourgeoisie."

"This guy," I said, ignoring the ideological miasma, "spoke very highly of you. He said he was once your teacher—that he taught you Communism. I disremember his name."

Kelley looked at me with a slight smile at the corners of his mouth. "My teacher, eh?" he said. "Well, that adds up."

And that's all I could get out of him.

Finally Bodine got up and we all followed, and then we were back on the sidewalk in a group, telling each other we'd meet in the morning in court.

Bodine motioned me aside and said he'd like to see me later that night, if I wasn't doing anything.

"Sure," I said. "Where, when?"

"I got a little hideaway up on West Fifty-fourth Street," he said. He wrote down an address on a match cover and shoved it into my coat pocket. "Drop up about nine and we'll have a drink."

13

"I'll be glad to," I said. Then I felt Kelley's hand on my arm.

"Better not make it tonight," he said. "We got business."

"It can wait," I said shortly. "This is more important."

"No, it isn't," said Kelley. "This is party business."

"Oh, well," said Bodine, "another night, then. Make it tomorrow."

"O.K.," I said.

Bodine and the others walked away and I stood there with Kelley, looking after them.

"Give me that address," said Dingdong.

"Don't be silly," I replied.

There was a cab at the curb and I walked over to it. Kelley followed.

"Look, guy," he said pleasantly, "I don't want to jump you on the street, but I will if I have to."

"Let's get in this cab and go somewhere and forget about jumping people," I said. "Lower Manhattan is beginning to depress me."

I had the cab door open and I was leaning in when I saw that the driver was the inevitable and omnipresent Joe Hogan. I said, "Oh, no!" and started to back out, when the lights went out.

It was a sap, on the back of the head—again.

5 It was all very much like the first time. Same place on my battered skull, and when I came to I was riding fast over a rough street. But no horns or whistles. I was lying on the bottom of the cab. I felt nauseated and I remained as still as I could until it passed. I raised myself up on an elbow, then grabbed the seat and eased myself into it. I rolled down the left window and the fresh air dispelled some of the fog.

Joe Hogan turned around and grinned at me. "Don't try anything," he warned in a pleasant tone. "Stay in the cab. We'll be there in a minute."

"Where?" I asked.

"Just around the corner," he said. He pointed and then took a left turn and another left and drew up to a couple of large doors that looked like the truck entrance to a warehouse. I took a fast look up and down the street and guessed it was

14

about Washington Street, still in Lower Manhattan. I didn't recognize any landmarks, and the street sign at the corner was turned askew. Joe raced his motor a couple of times and the doors were opened by a shabby character in overalls. We drove in, to a vaulted garage with a half-dozen cars and a couple of trucks in it. There was a guy to the left of the door dozing over a tommy gun that lay across his lap. He seemed to be dozing, but maybe he was just looking down so a nosy visitor couldn't see his face.

Joe opened the door for me and helped me out. "Sorry about that bash on the head," he said, "but we were pressed for time, and I'd already been on that street too long."

"Whatever that means," I said. "What the hell are you talking about, anyway?"

"Skip it," he said. "Go up those stairs and I'll follow you." He pointed to a flight of cement steps that led to a door in the side wall. I walked up and tried the door. It opened on a long hallway, softly lit, with a row of solid oak doors on each side.

"Third door on the left," said Hogan. "Go on in and sit down. I'll be outside, so don't get any ideas."

I went into a square room, about twenty-five feet across, also softly lit, and furnished with a divan, end tables, a desk in the far corner, and a half-dozen easy chairs. There was a deep pile carpet on the floor, neutral beige; filing cabinets lined the wall on each side of the door I had entered. There were no windows. I stretched out on the divan, closed my eyes, and waited. I'd lain there maybe ten minutes when the door opened. I sat up and a girl came in, dressed in a nurse's uniform and carrying a tray with a basin of water, some bottles, and a roll of bandages. She nodded a greeting, put the basin on an end table, and asked to see my head. She knew it was my head, and she knew just what part of my head.

"You people are quite efficient," I said.

"Thank you," she said.

"It's a nice day, isn't it?" I said.

"Quite," she said.

She washed and dressed the wound and asked me if I felt all right.

"Quite," I said. "Nice of you to inquire."

Then she spoke to me in Russian. She asked me where I was born.

"Come again?" I said. I had to stall for time. This was too sudden.

15

She repeated her question, very fast and with an accent that only an American could achieve.

"You people are damnably clever, as well as efficient," I said. "Just what is that gibberish you're tossing at me?"

"That's Russian," she said haughtily.

"My, my," I said, "and what ever made you think that I could understand Russian?"

"I am following orders," she replied, her face turning brick red.

"You blush very prettily," I said.

She gathered her stuff together on the tray and started for the door with angry steps.

"Your accent stinks," I said, "and if you really want to know, I was born in Afghanistan."

She tossed me a tentative smile and closed the door softly behind her. I went back to the divan and sat down, and a couple of minutes later Joe Hogan opened the door and ushered in a tall, gray-haired man of about fifty who walked with a stoop to starboard, as though he were ducking away from a kidney punch.

"This is Brigadier General Garson," Hogan said to me. "He's the Marine Garson who was in China."

He didn't have to tell me any more. This Marine espionage ace had been a boyhood hero of mine, and I knew of his exploits from Peiping to Tokyo. So I got on my feet.

"I am pleased to meet you," said the general, sticking out a lean, hard hand. I shook it and mumbled, "Ellery, sir."

"I didn't get the name," he said.

"Ellery," I repeated. "Steve Ellery."

"Fine," he said. "Now first, Ellery, I want to apologize for the beating you've taken today. I regret it exceedingly, but it appeared the only thing to do under the circumstances, which are, I might add, critical. Won't you sit down?"

I went back to the divan, and he took one of the chairs, turning it to face me. Joe Hogan wandered around and finally settled behind a desk in a corner and fiddled with a row of buttons on a panel.

"I presume this joint is wired for sound," I said, more to myself.

"But of course," said the general. "Colonel Janus has just switched on our recorders." He nodded toward Joe.

"What a hell of an appropriate name, Colonel Janus!" I said. "Well, just what would you like to record?"

"Your voice, generally, and speaking Russian, German,

16

French, and English," he said. "We are particularly interested in your Russian accent, and in some of the several dialects at which you are adept."

"And the purpose of all this?" I asked.

"Why, so we can identify you, old man! What else?"

"May I ask another question?"

"Why, certainly. Ask as many as you wish."

"Well, who the hell are you—all of you here? What sort of a trap am I in?"

Garson laughed, and Joe Hogan—Colonel Janus—looked wise and nodded "I-told-you-so" to him.

"Suppose we can't tell you that?" countered the general. "Suppose we refuse to tell you?"

"Well, then I just don't take a hand in your game," I said. "I doubt very much any of you have anything I want to buy anyway."

"Oh, don't say that," exclaimed Garson, with genuine concern. "We've so depended upon you—that is, if you are who we suspect you are. . . . You must go along with us. I will give you my word that you will never regret it—my solemn, sworn word as a gentleman by act of Congress and proclamation by the Secretary of the Navy." He smiled wryly at this last.

"Whom—who do you suspect I am?" I asked.

Garson looked at me long and searchingly, then turned to Joe. "Shut that thing off, Colonel. I suppose we've got to tell our mulish friend a thing or two. What do you think?"

Joe pressed a couple of buttons, then got up and came over to the general's chair.

"I told you about him," he said. "I told you he'd be a tough, stubborn monkey."

"Well, we're taking a bigger chance than he is," declared Garson. "We've got a whole hell of a lot more at stake than any one person."

"Not more than my neck," I interposed. "Look, you've pushed me around more in this one day than the whole damned German Army did in four years, and I don't like it a bit. I've tried not to show my resentment with any violence because I'm curious and I've got other things on my mind. But I'll tell you this, and it's no big-mouth talk: don't push me any further or I'll tear your whole damned trap apart and you with it—and me too, if that's necessary."

Joe nodded his head in agreement. "He'd make a try at it," he told Garson.

17

The general lit a cigarette, took a long puff, and looked me in the eye. "We think," he said, "that you're Alexis Ivanovich Bodine, of Brooklyn, New York."

"And I think," I said, "that you're nuts. . . . Why, I just met this Alexis Bodine you speak of today, and you know that as well as I do."

"What did I tell you!" said Joe. He laughed.

"You people are off your rockers," I said. I got up and walked around and the two of them followed me with their eyes. "My name is Steve Ellery and I was born in Fargo, North Dakota, and I served a hitch in the Army Air Force and I can prove every word I say. My fingerprints prove it, my Army Discharge proves it. . . . Why, I've got more damned identification than the Koh-i-noor diamond, and you sit there and tell me I'm some tramp by the name of Bodine!"

"Yes, we know," said Garson.

"Well, who the hell are you, then?" I demanded.

Garson suddenly looked resigned. He reached in his pocket and took out a long Manila envelope. He opened it slowly and extracted therefrom an official document and handed it to me.

On the top of it was the Great Seal of the United States, and the signature at the bottom was that of the President. What it said is not important, but it was ample for their purposes and for mine.

6 I stayed in that Bu-X layout—it *was* on Washington Street—for the next six months, on and off. I missed my appointment in court the next day on the disorderly conduct and other charges, but Dingdong Kelley fixed that. More important to me, I missed my appointment that night with the phony Alexis Bodine. The matchbook cover with his address on it, which I never did see after it was placed in my pocket, had been lifted by Kelley when he sapped me, and all I remembered was West Fifty-fourth Street. But that was a purely personal affair, I thought, so I put it out of my mind while I did what was required of me by this Bureau-X. But I vowed to myself that I would take care of Bodine when the appropriate opportunity offered.

I passed the language and voice tests, to re-establish my true identity, which proved a lot easier than I had anticipated.

18

As corroborative evidence, I recounted a number of intimate details about people still alive whom I had known in my Bodine days, and all of this was checked down to the last minute detail. One of the clinchers, for instance, was an unrepeatable account of a night in Algiers with an assistant chief of staff of ComNavNaw, who later was made admiral, and who had entertained picturesque but erroneous notions about Arab women. I had helped to acquaint him with the facts about the female True Believers. . . . That was the kind of story they checked.

After taking innumerable physical and mental examinations, I was put next in the hands of a Frenchman, a *capitaine de vaisseau* who shall remain nameless because he is one of my Bu-X associates who is still alive. (Those whose names I use are all dead, from one cause or another.)

From this Frenchman, I learned about a number of things that were never studied, analyzed, or compiled in this world before. Most of it was senseless from the standpoint of the uses to which knowledge ordinarily is put, but for me these facts—all the thousands of them—were to make the difference between life and death; success and failure. I can tell you, for instance, how much salt the obscure but all-powerful General Igor Godovisky, chief of the dread M.G.B., takes in his soup; I can tell you how fast the elevator rises and descends in the nine-story yellow brick building on Furkasovsky Alley, between Dzerzhinsky and Little Lubyanka streets,. in the heart of Moscow, which is the headquarters of the M.V.D. and all the rest of that secret-police alphabetical setup; I can recognize at a glance and duplicate the signatures of half the members of the Politburo, and I can imitate perfectly and with no study or hesitation the complete handwriting and the "B" signature of Marshal Beria; I know all of the revealed personal and public habits of Joseph Stalin, right down to his favorite brand of tooth powder, how fast he walks and how fast he drives, and what kind of jelly he likes with his tea. (It's strawberry.)

To list all of these items of special knowledge would take several volumes and could be of very little interest to anyone except such persons as this erudite and encyclopedic Frenchman, who loved all of these bright little facts for themselves— a true collector. He had that rare type of mind that thrives upon the specific and the detailed and abhors the generalities that so often pass for thinking and for knowledge in this confused world of ours.

When the Frenchman got through with me, after months

19

of sixteen-hour-a-day sessions, I was passed on to a Commander Fornshell, a crusty old sea-dog who was, among other things, a mnemonist, psychologist, philosopher, gourmet, and, to hear him tell it, a hell of a hand with the ladies. What he taught me was how to think straight and when (there are times when it can be fatal to be logical) and, most important of all, how to remember. What I learned to remember specifically was what the Frenchman had taught me. You'd think, and so would I, that I should have taken Fornshell's course first, but that was not the way Bu-X did it, and I must concede that Bu-X was never wrong.

If you are acquainted with the latest gimmicks in psychology, it might interest you to know that I had a thorough course in every discovery and theory of mental dynamics from Joseph Breuer to Fritz Osterkamp, and not omitting such as Freud, Semen, Jung and the like, on the way. And finally, toward the end, I was moved into an apartment on the east side of town, where I spent many hours with a number of experts on various subjects, from the latest Communist apparatus in America, Yugoslavia, and Siam, to all of the recently devised variations in the more fatal aspects of Judo. Among my teachers there—all of whom were only indirectly associated with Bureau-X—was the aforementioned Dingdong Kelley. He and I resumed the friendship of my boyhood, and so you will understand when I tell you that I will never recover from the heart-sickness that was mine over his death in the Grand Central riots of 1957. But that comes later—how and why I killed Dingdong.

7 There were five of us. I will tell you about them briefly, but I will not mention them again in this account. Our paths crossed from time to time, and toward the latter stages of my assignment, in Moscow, a couple of them were of some slight help in putting me in touch with the underground and passing on information that made the success of my job possible. But their stories are their own, and not for me to tell. I am not concerned in writing a history—only in telling you how I was able to assassinate Joseph Stalin.

There was Sam Laskey, a Russian-born Jew and one of the world's foremost atomic technicians. It was Laskey who discovered and fabricated the secret alloy that would isolate the

20

rays of uranium, plutonium, and other such radioactive elements. All I know about it is that part of the principle was temperature control, and that this alloy, in sheets as thin as tinfoil, enabled him to transport the parts of an atomic bomb, assemble it, and plant it for explosion without fear of detection by any known electronic instrument. Laskey carried these parts of an A-bomb into the Kremlin in Moscow in the winter of 1957-58, while Stalin was on the Crimean Peninsula, and he assembled it and placed it in one of Napoleon's cannons in the Museum of Armor and Antiques, which adjoins Stalin's office and living quarters. The bomb exploded all right, and on the correct date, but Stalin was still out of Moscow, so all it did was to destroy the Kremlin and most of the heart of Moscow and kill a lot of Russians.

Sam Laskey is dead.

There was Milo Peters, the explosives expert. Milo was a White Russian, brought up in China after the Revolution of 1917, and he, like myself, joined the M.V.D. He rose to the exalted position of engineer, furnace man, and janitor of the Red Tsar's country palace, or château, on the northwestern outskirts of Moscow. Milo, who knew more about dynamite than Nobel himself, planted enough of the stuff in and around the château to blow it to hell, which, eventually, it did—but Stalin wasn't there, either.

And Milo Peters is dead.

There was Constantine Fordor (known naturally as Ford), who could hit a dime at fifty yards with anything that would shoot, including a water pistol. Ford had designed and built a high-velocity .25 caliber pistol that he could hide completely in the palm of his big hand, and he could do things with it that I won't mention because you won't believe them. He was a native of the Caucasus and the best horseman I've ever known. He got down to Stalin's summer palace on the Black Sea, and he knew about that hideout long before I did, but he missed his only shot at the dictator through the intervention of an M.V.D. guard, a colonel by the name of Zalaskorne.

Constantine Fordor is dead—with more holes in him than a Swiss cheese.

There was Waller (first name unknown), who had at one time headed up one of the Soviet espionage organizations in America. This Waller, I suspect, was too intense for his own good; he was a somberly sincere, crusading type and he did some wonderful work in organizing the Russian underground, especially in the Ukraine, but he rendered himself almost use-

21

less to Bureau-X and its primary objective through this extracurricular activity. He was devoid of emotion and humor, as are most Communists and many Russians, and although I saw him many times in Moscow and later in the Crimea, I never knew him to smile or make the slightest gesture of friendship or human feeling. Waller got to Simeiz, on the Black Sea, and within walking distance of Stalin's summer fortress, but he was seized by the M.V.D. on August 17, 1958, which was one day before the Russian attack on America.

Waller is dead, by his own hand.

There was John, or Jan, Miles, a Roumanian national, seaman, dockwalloper, saboteur, and, you would say, a born killer. . . . That was me. My specialties included the rifle, at long range, or anything close up, from shivs to bar stools. I made it. I got Stalin in my gunsights on the appointed day, and I squeezed the trigger.

I'm alive, and I aim to stay that way.

8 My chief sponsor in the Communist Party in America was Waller, who had been in Bucharest in 1940 and had known this original Jan Miles. It was he, I suspect, who had produced this identification for me in the first place. He vouched for my attitude and my associations, and he was supported by a couple of Maritime Union types who were dug up by some Bu-X contact. They said they had sailed with me on voyages in the Mediterranean.

I was assured by Bu-X that all of the data in my papers was verifiable and I was told all I needed to know to establish the identity of Miles under all foreseeable circumstances. My induction into the C.P. was the first occasion when this data was investigated, but far from the last. I think that there are few Communists in the world who were subjected to as searching a series of investigations as were launched on me from time to time.

My induction took place in 1955, when the generally hardening view against the C.P. and all Marxists in America had driven the Communists pretty well underground. It was not yet a formal underground movement, as was set up later, but the suspicion with which all recruits were regarded was in the best underground tradition. You may recall that in those days,

22

after we had rid ourselves of most of the Washington whistle-heads who had refused to accept the reality of Russian enmity, it had suddenly become unpopular to identify oneself with Communist-loving Liberals and the Left, and all of the government paternalism and planned economy that went with them.

The first rule of the C.P. apparatus for such a secret operation is to divide the membership into the smallest of cells and to keep these cells isolated. It is not important to this account who my cell members were, so I will skip names and descriptions. I integrated myself with them, and I was handy and efficient with all party business. Our cell chairman, who had been much impressed by an account of the guerilla activities of Jan Miles (on the side of the Soviet, naturally) following the Roumanian attack on Russia in 1941, took me with him on several occasions as a sort of bodyguard when he visited unfriendly areas, and from time to time I was permitted brief views of the wider aspects of C.P. activities. For me it was a matter of waiting, and I had nothing but time. What I was waiting for was for them to discover what a jewel of a stooge they had picked up in Jan Miles. It took them several months.

I was living in celibate isolation in a hotel in the Chelsea section, in a room as grim as a monastery cell, and I had even put out of my mind the most important of all personal businesses—the liquidation of the phony Alexis Bodine. I was seeing no one and making no friends. Bu-X people checked with me every once in a while—I had a schedule of contacts for the next five years in case there was ever anything that I needed—but these meetings were no friendly associations with my own kind. In fact most of them, to any observer, no matter how interested, were merely cases of one guy stepping on another guy's foot and begging his pardon, or something similar. Let me tell you about one of them as an example: An old gent's hat blew off as he was crossing Twenty-third Street at Eighth Avenue and I picked it up. I handed it to him. He thanked me. He walked away. In my pocket I had $500 that I hadn't had before. Oh, sure, it was my own money, out of my own bank account, but I had to get it some way, didn't I?

One Sunday afternoon while I was luxuriating in this Chelsea trap and dozing over Volume II of Stalin's *Problems in Leninism,* which was my homework for that week, there came a knock at my door. I opened up and admitted the cell chairman and a small, hard, round-looking Slav, about my age and with a deep scowl of animosity creasing his brow, who was introduced as William Nichols. After the introduction the chairman

23

took a quick powder and Nichols roamed about the room, critically examining the walls, ceiling, and closet, and finally looking behind the genuine steel engraving of Paul and Virginia that defaced the wall over my bed.

"It's not much, but I call it home," I said.

He grunted and went over to the window and pulled down the shade on the scenic beauties of West Twenty-second Street. Then he occupied my single stuffed chair with the built-in backache, lit a cigarette, and motioned me to sit on the bed. These Communists were never bashful about letting you know what they wanted.

"I presume that we can safely talk here?" he asked in Russian.

"Yes," I replied, also in Russian, "but how did you know that I speak your language?" I affected a strong Bessarabian accent, which went with my claim to Roumanian nationality.

"Oh, we know about you or I wouldn't be here," he replied. His manner had become quite friendly and he smiled when he said it, which was a rare thing with a Communist. I put it down to the fact that we were talking Russian together; it is essentially a language of confidences and friendship when spoken on foreign soil—but I guess most any language would be under that circumstance.

"This is party business," he said. "You have been recommended to us by your chairman, and in every other way you seem to measure up to what we are looking for."

"It is most welcome to hear you say that, comrade," I replied.

"Your height seems to be right. How much do you weigh?" he asked.

"One eighty-five," I replied.

"That is exactly right," he said. "How are you with firearms —pistols and rifles and machine guns?"

"One of the best," I said modestly.

"Do you know the Thompson and the Browning guns?" he asked.

"All of them," I said. "I made that a hobby once."

"We'll see," he said. "We'll give you a chance to show us. Can you drive automobiles and trucks?"

"Any make," I said. "Drive them, fix them—anything."

"Have you a driver's license?"

"No," I replied, "but I can get one easy enough."

"We can get that for you," he said. "Now about ships; are you acquainted with the engine rooms of the ships you have sailed on?"

24

"Oh, yes," I said. "Mostly I signed on as A.B., but I've also sailed as fireman and water tender and I used to have those papers."

"Ah, so?" he said. "Can you read blueprints? Would you be able to follow a marine construction blueprint, for instance?"

"Sure," I said, "I've done that, for repairs and for installations on stand-by jobs."

"Ever been in trouble with the police?" was his next question.

"Not here—in America," I said.

"They've never photographed you or taken your measurements?"

"Never. I've never been arrested, except once for disorderly conduct last year, and they didn't mug me."

"Where was that?"

"Here in New York. I got mixed up in a fight over at an East River pier. Nothing ever came of it."

"You told them your name was Hamilton," he said.

"That's right," I replied.

"You never showed up for the hearing," he said.

"I went out of town," I said.

"Where?"

"That's my business."

He thought that over. He crushed out his cigarette on the window sill and threw the butt in a corner. I don't have ash trays. This damned Jan Miles character didn't smoke, much to my pain and disgust.

"Where did you go?" he repeated.

I shrugged at him.

"I've got to know," he insisted. "Either you tell me or you lose out on this assignment for me."

"It's why I came to America," I said slowly. "It was to hunt for the son of a bitch that killed my sister back in Galati. He was an Iron Guard officer. I got a tip he was in Detroit."

"You find him?"

I shook my head. "It was the wrong guy. Same name, but not him. So I got to hunt some more."

That seemed to satisfy him, for the moment.

"Who fixed up that charge against you in court?" he asked.

"You mean the disorderly conduct?"

"Yes."

"Guy by the name of Kelley. He used to be a city councilman or something."

25

"You know Kelley?"

"Just to talk to. I see him around at the piers."

"The M.V.D. doesn't care too much for Mr. Kelley," he said. "You know what the M.V.D. is?"

"Sure," I replied. "Who doesn't?"

He pulled a metal disc, about an inch in diameter, out of his pocket and showed it to me. It was engraved on the upside in Russian letters with "KOVOL" and a thumb print under the name. He turned it over in his hand. On the obverse was the Russian character "B" in a script I knew very well—"B" for "Beria."

"Know what this is?" he asked me.

I shook my head.

He put it back in his pocket. "I am the commandant of the M.V.D. in this area," he said. "I am telling you this because I trust you. Do you understand the importance of that trust?"

"Maybe not completely," I said, putting on my best and glummest Communist face. "But I appreciate it."

"It means," he said solemnly, with a hammy gesture of hand over heart, "that you are one of us."

That effort seemed to call for another cigarette. He lit up and continued:

"But you may as well know that you are on probation. You are with us only on a temporary basis."

"I realize you have to be careful," I said, helping him out. "After all, you don't know much about me."

"Oh, we know quite a bit," he said. "We've been checking. After all, Roumania is now a part of Russia. There are many people there who remember Jan Miles when he fought for the Soviet."

I made a mental note to keep out of Roumania.

"Then why am I on probation?" I asked naïvely.

"We have our most important work to do in America," he said. "It is a question of whether you have the ability to help us. It is a question of whether you can take orders and follow them."

"I will take orders and I will follow them," I said.

"Good," he said, getting up. "We will try you. Come to this number on East Eighteenth Street tomorrow at noon." He wrote the number down on the edge of a *Daily Worker*—297. "Come to the top floor and walk to the rear. On the right, at the very back, you will see a door with the number 8 on it. Knock three times very slowly. Announce my name when you are asked who is there. Understood?"

26

I repeated the instructions and satisfied him that I knew them. Then I tore the number from the *Daily Worker* and burned it with a match.

"I remember everything," I said.

He nodded approval and let himself out the door. I read, ate, slept, and ate again and got to my first M.V.D. rendezvous at one minute after twelve. I was admitted to a comfortably furnished apartment in a renovated brownstone. The living room, where we went, was in the back, overlooking a courtyard, and was lined with books. There were deep leather chairs and floor lamps, an Oriental carpet, and in a corner was a drawing board, with T-square and triangle on top of a half-finished plan. I took a fast look at the books while I waited for Nichols (or Kovol, as I had filed him in my own mind) and saw that most of them were technical books—engineering, physics, architecture, and such.

He came in from the hallway lighting a cigarette and motioned me to a chair by the window. He plunged right into the middle of it—where he had left off the day before.

"So you say you can take orders?"

"That's my specialty," I said.

"Tell me what you know about the engineering department of ships. What's the proper temperature for West Coast oil?"

"About two-eighty," I said.

He asked me a number of technical questions and then came up with, "Where is the main oil pump on a C-12?"

"Never been on one," I said.

"Where would you look for it?"

I pointed to his bookcase. "You got a marine-engineering handbook that looks like a late edition. Maybe it would be in there."

That answer seemed to please him and I saw him smile for the second time.

"All right," he said. "Now we get down to business. I would like to have a special preparation, which I will supply you, put in the bearings of the main oil pumps of three C-12's that are now being loaded at Hoboken. What do you think of that?"

"Consider it done," I said. "Just give me the names of the ships and let me look at that handbook."

"The C-12 isn't in there," he said, "but I have a plan over here that's almost finished that will show you what you have to know."

27

9 I ran into no trouble sabotaging the ships. That's elementary stuff we had all learned back in World War II. In addition, our docks, piers and vessels were not on a wartime basis in 1955, and security, where it existed at all, was very lax. But just to make certain that I would not be picked up by some remote accident, I asked for and got some help from Bu-X. In fact, they offered to do the whole job for me, but I didn't accept their generous proposal. It took me only two weeks, and then I reported back to Kovol-Nichols, but not at his apartment, just in case some government agency had put a tail on me. We met at a rooming house in the Village, on Christopher Street, and I made sure that I came alone. This was a place known as Christopher House. It had a sign on it, "Rooms and Board," and a smaller sign under that, "No Vacancies." It was the B.O.Q. of the E.K.U. section of the M.G.B. division of the M.V.D. in New York. If you want a rundown on these initials, it's like this:

B.O.Q. means Bachelor Officers' Quarters; E.K.U. translates itself into Ekonomicheskoe Upravlenie, which means Economic Section. The M.G.B. is the designation for the old State Security Commissariat of the N.K.V.D., which commands espionage and counterespionage activities at home and abroad, as well as giving orders to all Soviet citizens who travel. M.V.D. is the over-all designation for the organization that started out as the Cheka, then became Ogpu, then N.K.V.D. In this account, I'm going to ignore, as far as possible, the organizational distinctions and refer only to the M.V.D., or secret police, because there are many more sections and divisions than those listed, and it would lead only to confusion. Also, who cares?

I had kept my hotel room in Chelsea when I moved to Hoboken; now my meager possessions were installed in a small room in Christopher House, on the second floor. That had all been done for me while I was away the two weeks.

I was in business. I was a member of the M.V.D.

Nichols, who was waiting for me in the "parlor," came up to my room with me and I gave him a complete report on the C-12's. He was satisfied but not enthusiastic. He disapproved of some of the chances I'd taken, but he brightened up considerably when I mentioned that I had avoided Dingdong Kelley, who was at one of the docks when I was making a preliminary sortie.

28

"I remembered," I explained, "that you said the M.V.D. did not like him."

"That is very good," he said. "You are to be commended. . . . I don't know what it is about that man, but I cannot feel right when I deal with him. It is instinct more than reason."

"He's a loud mouth," I said. "I can't understand why the Americans put up with him."

"That's it!" he exclaimed. "He is too loud, too apparent, too obvious. That is not the way we have to conduct our business these days."

I felt sorry for Kelley. This might well have been the preamble to liquidation that we were discussing—but that was his lookout. If he were disliked and suspect, he would be more harm than use to the F.B.I. If he were eliminated, he would have no one but himself to blame. Certainly I was in no position to do anything about it. I had a job that could be jeopardized by no human feeling; that was more important than the work or the life of any other person in the espionage business.

Kovol-Nichols and I talked communism for the next hour—and I won't bore you with that. I am sure everyone in America is well enough acquainted today with the excruciating contortions of Soviet ideology to make any exposition here superfluous. Nichols was raking over my intellectual fields hunting for possible seeds of deviation or other heresy, and particularly as it concerned morality, but he turned up nothing to disturb his trust. It is remarkably easy to mislead these people, as it would be to mislead anyone who substituted dogma and slogans for beautiful, free cerebration. All you have to do is to learn their dogma and slogans.

"You know," he said, finally getting down to cases, "that there is a great shortage of dollars. These embargoes by the imperialists in Washington against U.S.S.R. goods have seriously hampered us."

"I have heard such reports," I replied.

"That is a condition that I have been called upon to rectify," he said. He produced a professionally drawn plan from his pocket and spread it out on my bed. We both bent over it. It was the floor plan of a building, and he pointed to a room in one corner. "Right here," he said, "we can get two million dollars. It is all capitalist funds, from banks and railroads and other such enterprises, and it is there waiting for us, neatly stacked in bundles. All we have to do is to go in there and take it."

"By 'we,' you mean myself and some others," I said.

29

"That's it. You are quick to draw the correct conclusions."

"And that is," I continued, "why you have been inquiring into my morals?"

He nodded assent and picked up the plan and folded it, replacing it in his pocket.

"I will be frank with you," he said, sitting on the edge of my bed. "Although we have known each other very briefly, I feel that I can trust you, and I am never wrong about that feeling. I am only surprised that you, with your background, have not joined us before."

"Lack of opportunity," I said. "I've spoken about it to several people from time to time, on board ships and here in America, but I never met the right people, I guess."

"And in Roumania?"

"I fought against the Iron Guard, and then the Germans, and for a time I fought with the Russian army when they came in to liberate us, but the commissars never asked me to join them."

"There must have been a reason."

"I came from a bourgeoise family. I don't blame them for being suspicious of my motives."

He nodded and lit a cigarette. I knew well that all of this information had been, and was being, checked, probably by a dozen M.V.D. men, and that I was not telling him anything he did not know.

"The plan I showed you is of the second floor of a building in Chicago," he said. "This building is the chief collection point for the Banks Express Company, and all of the money they collect in any given period, no matter what its destination, passes through that room.

"We have been reliably informed of all the details of that building and that room, and we will be informed further of the exact time when we will find the greatest amount of money in it that will coincide with the most convenient time for a visit. All of the details that will have any bearing whatsoever upon this operation will be known and considered. There will not be the remotest possibility of failure, nor will there be the least danger of any subsequent arrest or questioning. All such eventualities have been foreseen.

"We have selected ten of our most trusted party members for this work. Of all of them, you have been with us the shortest time, but I have faith in you and so I am naming you the tenth man."

I reached out and shook his hand warmly. "I am honored,"

30

I said. "You can depend upon me to the fullest of my ability."

"I know that," he said solemnly. "Now wait here a minute and I will be right back."

He went out the door and I finished unpacking my one bag and hanging up my good suit. He came back in about five minutes with another M.V.D. man, whom I'd seen when I first came to Christopher House.

"This is Solovene," he said, introducing us. "Solovene is one of our ten."

"Glad to meet you," I said, shaking his hand. He was a big man, about my own height and age. He had a flat Slavic face and very light blue eyes. He spoke Russian with a slight Polish accent.

I invited them to take the two chairs in the room and I sat on the bed. Nichols and Solovene lit cigarettes.

"He will take you to our first rendezvous, in about a week," Nichols said. "You will drive and he will show you the way. It's about two hours from here, up the Hudson. Mr. Solovene is our gunnery instructor, and he will acquaint you and the rest of your group with the various arms that you will use. Are there any questions?"

"It's all very clear up to this point," I replied.

Through all of this, Solovene was sitting there blowing smoke and staring at me through half-closed eyes. Finally he said:

"I have seen this man before. I have seen him somewhere."

"That could be," I said easily. "I've been around."

"No, it was many years ago," he said. "Either I have seen you or you look much like someone else. I never forget a face."

This was an old secret-police method, never to accept a new man without suspicion and to try, in one way or another, to put him on the defensive. The I've-seen-your-face-before routine was so corny that I didn't give it much thought. But just the same, I decided that I'd have Bu-X look him up. There was always the chance that he *had* seen me before.

It was just as well that I did. Solovene did prove to have an uncanny memory for faces and a sixth-sense insight into human characteristics. The Bu-X report I got on him a couple of days later stated that he had been one of the Ogpu men assigned to track down the original Alexis Bodine, back in 1944. Small world, what?

31

10 Solovene and I went to a farm in Putnam County, in the back country east of Highway 22 and not far from the Connecticut state line. I found him a dull traveling companion, and part of the way up he sat hunched over the radio speaker vent, listening to an impossible soap opera that he was evidently following. I heard some of it despite myself, and it was a hospital sequence and several times I heard the word "codeine" used. When Solovene turned the radio off finally, on a concert of jive recordings, he mumbled to himself, "Codeine, Bodine." Then he turned to me and he said:

"I was thinking of one Alexis Bodine. You remind me of him, for some reason. Have you ever heard of such a person?"

"Yes," I said, "I met one who called himself that last year."

"You did!" he exclaimed. "Where?"

"In New York," I said. "I got involved in a fight on a pier, and this Bodine was in tow of a character known as Dingdong Kelley."

"Oh, that one," he said. "I know about him."

"That's all he said, and I didn't know whether his remark referred to Kelley or Bodine. But I decided right then that he was no one to have prying around my personal business.

After an hour and a half of steady driving, we reached this large working dairy farm with a herd of some ninety Guernseys, a large milking barn with all modern improvements, and a two-story relic of Colonial times that had been renovated recently into a comfortable modern house. There were a couple of hundred acres of rather mean, rocky land and many stands of scrub growth and, back below a hill, an artificial lake about half a mile long. Extending from the house over this hill and bordering on one side of the lake, there was one good tractor field of nearly thirty acres, and to the left of the private road as you entered the property there was another cultivated field nearly as large. The residents were a couple of glum-faced Yankee Communists, a leather-skinned, stooped farmer of about fifty and his sour, dried-up spouse of like age. There were three "hired men"—but not hired in any capitalistic sense, you understand. They had as many rights as the couple, and the only benefits I ever saw derived from this arrangement was a constant debate over the division of labor. The debate kept them all from becoming too introspective.

Solovene and I arrived there ahead of the other ten, and we

32

had a choice of bedrooms on the barracks-like second floor. We selected a couple of adjoining cubicles in the rear of the house, over the kitchen. We unpacked our belongings, and I took a bottle of Bourbon into his room and we had a couple of drinks together, so that I could make certain he was unarmed. Then we went for a walk over the place. He had been there before and he knew his way around.

"This lake," he said, "has many bass in it. If we are here long enough, perhaps we can fish."

"Fishing bores me," I said. "I've never had the patience for it."

"It is good for the nerves," he said.

"I haven't got any," I replied.

"I have noticed that about you," he said. "Most of the people in our work are like that, but not so much as you. It is a valuable trait."

"I suppose it is," I said. "I wouldn't mind going swimming, though."

"It is dangerous," he said. "Very deep."

"I take it you don't swim?"

"No," he said.

We were walking along on the bank and there were a couple of boats there. One was a large canoe with paddles in the bottom.

"We could go for a boat ride," I suggested. I had a half-formed plan in mind, and it seemed like a good idea to get him out in the middle of the lake while we talked.

"Do you handle a boat?" he asked.

"Sure, hop in the canoe and I'll take you for a spin." He complied and took a seat in the bow. I shoved off, got in the stern, and paddled leisurely to the center of the lake. He showed some uneasiness when we got out there, as though he were reading my mind. He was anything but relaxed.

"You should keep closer to the shore," he said.

"What's the difference?" I said. "Nothing can happen. These canoes are safe."

"I am not used to boats," he said.

The lake was surrounded by low hills and nestled against a dense growth of saplings and a few larger oaks and gums that came up to each side of the field. This cleared land sloped upward and disappeared over the rise, which hid the house and barn from our view. I examined the trees and the field. There was no one in sight.

33

"You know," I said, "there is one thing I would like. Have you a cigarette?"

He pulled out a pack and stretched it to me. I crawled over to him and took one. I lit it and took a deep, satisfying drag.

"I thought you didn't smoke," he said.

"Well, ordinarily I don't," I said. "Just once in a while—times like these. You'd better light up too." I moved back to my seat.

He sat looking at me. He lit a cigarette but he didn't take his eyes off me while he did it.

"What is this?" he said finally.

"I want to ask you some questions," I replied.

"Go into shore," he commanded.

"We'll stay here," I said.

"I am ordering you," he said, glowering at me. "It will go hard with you if you disobey me."

"We'll just skip that," I said. "What I want to know is, have you told your suspicions about me to anyone?"

"Don't be stupid," he said. "Why should I discuss that with you?"

"No reason," I said. "If you won't, you won't. Now, one other question. What did you plan to do about me?"

He sneered at that. "Nothing—now," he said.

"And later, after our Chicago operation?"

"That would remain to be seen," he said. His face had become white and tense, and when he spoke he bared his teeth like an angry dog.

"Well," I said, "the primary rule of this business is to take advantage of the opportunities as they are presented."

"What are you going to do?" he demanded. His voice was almost a wail, but I honestly didn't hear him—not until later when I thought back on that scene. For at that moment I got up, stepped on the side of the canoe, and tipped it over.

I dived deep and came up on the far side of the canoe and trod water, looking for him. He came up twenty feet from me, on the other side of the boat, screaming, and his arms thrashing wildly. He went down again almost immediately, the water cutting off his scream. I stroked over to the spot and dived. The water was clear and I saw him ten or twelve feet down, still struggling but more feebly. I grabbed him by the hair and came to the surface, but holding him under. I started for the shore, swimming carefully to keep out of reach of his arms, and set up a yelling for help. About twenty-five yards

34

along he stopped moving and I grabbed his wrist in such a way that I could feel his pulse.

It had stopped beating.

Well, what's one M.V.D. man more or less?

11 Naturally there was hell raised over the death of Solovene, and I came in for plenty of criticism, along with praise for my heroic attempt at rescue. One of the farm hands had been working at the house end of the big field, over the rise, and he had heard Solovene's scream and my subsequent cries for help. He called the others, and by the time I reached the bank, swimming with Solovene in an approved rescue hold, all four of the men were waiting for me. So there was ample testimony by competent witnesses that I had done all humanly possible to bring Solovene ashore and save his life.

What upset them all, and especially Nichols, when he and the rest of the ten arrived shortly afterward, was that the police and the coroner would have to be called in because of the death. That, and the fact that now we were one man short and would either have to alter our plans or dig up another robber.

"It is carelessness," Nichols stormed at me while we walked back to the house. "I hold you responsible because you never should have permitted such a stupid accident to happen. We cannot afford to deal with people who become involved in accidents."

"I agree with you," I said. "The damned fool wouldn't sit down. We had a couple of drinks and he got exuberant."

"That's not like Solovene," said Nichols, puzzled.

I shrugged. "Couldn't hold his liquor, I guess," I said.

"He has for years been one of our most dependable men. It makes me sick—now we have lost the key man for our entire operation."

"Perhaps I could step in," I suggested. "As I once told you, I am an expert on firearms."

"That will remain to be seen," he said. He was still too upset to be reasonable.

The nine of us left for the Chicago job were mobilized outside the house by Nichols and were ordered to return to New York. The farmer, who knew the state police of the

35

Brewster barracks, was instructed to inform them of the death and give appropriate testimony with the help of his fellow workers. We got into a couple of cars and I drove one, loaded with five of the group.

They were all big and obviously had been selected for size. None of them talked; they were a glum and humorless lot and they merely grunted or ignored me althgether at my several attempts to brighten up the trip. Finally I turned on the radio and forgot them. In New York I distributed them to various subway stations, after fixing a rendezvous with them for three days later, when we were to return to the farm. I drove our car to the C. P. garage at Seventh Avenue and Morton Street and then started to walk to Christopher House.

It was then that I remembered the phony Alexis Bodine and decided I could be doing something about him during this wait. I had three days to kill, so I figured I might as well include him. I went to a Bu-X contact point at one of the entrances to Macy's on Thirty-fourth Street and waited for a girl in a red dress to get out of a cab and go into the store. Finally a likely one did just that and I followed her into the book department on the main floor. While I stood next to her and looked over titles at a counter marked "Rare Books" I told her, "I want a match-book cover with an address on it. They'll know. I'll be at the northeast corner of Twenty-third and Seventh in an hour." She looked at me as though I had made an indecent proposal to her and moved away quickly. In addition, I got a nasty glare from the salesgirl behind the counter.

So an hour later, on the Twenty-third Street corner, there was this same girl again and she tripped over my feet as she squeezed by me in the crowd and dropped her handbag. I picked it up and handed it to her and got another dirty look. Then, as I walked uptown, I put my hand in my pocket and felt a match-book cover that hadn't been there before. I went into a coffee joint a couple of blocks up, ordered coffee, and read it. It wasn't the address. What it said was: "Lay off. He's a plant."

That made me sore. I remembered Bodine had said his place was on West Fifty-fourth Street, so I went up there and started a patrol from Fifth Avenue west to Tenth. It was a long walk and a dull street, and you will not believe me when I tell you that for three days, from seven in the morning until midnight, I did not see one face I knew in all that distance.

It was a rainy Saturday when we all gathered again at the farm, and the smell of cow dung and roasting beef was heavy

36

on the air. Kovol-Nichols was in better humor—he told me the police affair had been a breeze and that Solovene was already buried—and the farmer, *Frau,* and comrades all greeted me with a deference a hero deserves. I went up to my room and Nichols came with me.

"Now you will get a chance to show me what you know," he said as he sat on my bed.

"That's fine," I said. "That's what I've been trying to do."

"You will be the leader of this group," he said. "You will train these men in their duties and you will take orders only from me. Understood?"

"Yes, sir," I replied. "I am honored."

"Call them together in the hall and I will address them," he said.

He waited in my room while I went out and rounded them up. I found some of them in their rooms and a couple of them below in the living room. They assembled with alacrity when I told them it was at Nichols' order. I counted them, checked below and outside to make sure we would not be disturbed, and notified Nichols.

"Where are the farmers?" Nichols asked me.

"The woman is in the kitchen," I replied. "The rest are outside, at the barn and other places."

"Very good," he said. He turned to the men. "Comrades," he intoned in his stilted English, "first I want to tell you that Comrade Miles is your superior officer, and you will receive all orders from him. He will instruct you in your duties and he will lead you in the operation we are planning, which you all know about. In our organization and under such conditions as these, comrades, I must warn you that your superior officer has the power of life and death over you. That is our discipline. It is for the greater glory of the Soviet Union. If you do not wish to accept such discipline, speak now. It is your last chance. Any questions?"

There were none. Eight hard-bitten faces were turned to us, and their eyes showed no wavering.

Nichols turned to me. "Do you wish to say anything, comrade?" he asked.

I turned to the men. "I know we will have no trouble," I said. "Thank you."

I could describe them all to you and tell you their names, but no useful purpose would be served. As I indicated earlier, they were all—including myself—picked first for size. They came from C.P. cells from Baltimore to San Francisco and they

37

were all sincere, even fanatical, Communists, steeped in the lore of slogans and ready to cut a throat or betray their country for Joe Stalin, their only god. One, the most vicious of the lot, was a youth of twenty-three who came from a minister's family in Kansas and had found in the party, I suspect, a proper outlet for his sadism. He was the only one who gave me any trouble, but a clout on the head straightened him out and he was a lamb thereafter. All of them had attended various Soviet "schools," and most of them were accomplished saboteurs. Two of these nine, in fact, were responsible for blowing up the Boeing plant in Seattle a couple of years later, which you no doubt remember reading about.

Nichols decided that we would operate with only nine, and he changed our plans accordingly. He turned these plans over to me and told me in clear, succinct Russian just how I was to drill them and how long it was to take.

Under the big barn there was a huge subcellar, with at least a four-foot-thick roof of earth over it, and this was the rifle, pistol, and machine-gun range. First I demonstrated, to Nichols' satisfaction, that I could use these various instruments; then I drilled the men. I taught them how to use sawed-off shotguns at close range, how to shoot .45's and .38's at rapid fire, and how to use the Thompson submachine gun. There were a dozen Thompsons on the place, all the cast-steel prewar models made by Colt. Later I had Bu-X check the numbers on them for me, but that proved nothing. They were part of several thousand such guns sold to various buyers for the A.R.I.R. back in the Twenties.

It was two weeks later and the end of September that I pronounced my charges ready. We put on a demonstration for Nichols, who was in and out of the farm during that time, and he complimented me on my thoroughness.

Another routine we had practiced was walking in formation along a strip marked off as a hallway, and stopping five times where we would encounter doors. We did this, too, for Nichols, and he made one change.

"You cannot go through first," he said to me. "You are the leader and you must be guarded at all times."

He picked the tough minister's kid to precede me. I had no objections.

The next day we left the farm and I set a rendezvous for them a week later at an address on West Madison Street, in Chicago. I instructed them to go to Chicago separately and I gave each one a route and a schedule which I had typed up.

38

I went back to New York with Nichols and when we parted, down in the Village, he gave me a package with nine rubber Halloween masks in it.

The robbery itself, which took place on a Saturday night three weeks later, you all know about from your newspapers and magazines, as well as radio and television, so I won't repeat the details. You will remember that eight men wearing Halloween masks, and all of a height and weight and all dressed in Navy pea jackets and uniform caps, entered the Banks Express Company main offices on Wabash Avenue on this Saturday evening in October, walked through five doors that should have been locked, got a guard to open the money-cage door at the threat of submachine guns, tied up the five men in the cage with lengths of rope that they carried, and finally walked out with $1,800,000 in currency, each man with a sack of it on his back. A ninth man, you will recall, waited below in a large limousine, and two others, who did not wear masks or pea jackets, drove up in a new Ford truck just as the eight emerged and parked their truck so that the money sacks could be loaded. Then the two vehicles drove away.

And that was the last seen of the men or the money or the limousine or the truck, except that what might have been parts of this truck were found a couple of months later, cut up with a torch, in an automobile-scrap dump on the outskirts of Evanston.

What you might be interested in reading at this late date are some of the details that are unknown and have so successfully baffled police, both local and state, the F.B.I., and countless insurance and banking investigators—everyone, in fact, except Bureau-X, which knew all about it but couldn't do anything for fear of compromising me.

Practically all of our information about the Banks Express Company—the layout of the offices, the schedules of the armored-car drivers, the habits and vulnerability of the men in the money cage, and even down to the types of locks on the five doors—came from an executive of the Banks Company who was beyond and above suspicion and was a member of the C.P. I will not name him here; he was to have been taken care of and probably has been by this time.

The mystery of the Jackson Boulevard Bridge, which our limousine and truck used for the getaway: The reason this bridge was late getting up when the police ordered all of them raised to isolate the Loop was that the bridge tender was also a member in good standing of the C.P. and was following our orders. It is proper that he was fired, but he should have been jailed as well because it was he himself who sabotaged the warning system so that he would not have to comply with the police orders until we had passed over his span.

The Ford truck: This was stolen, as police have suspected. But the owner of it "arranged" for the stealing. He too was a C.P. member.

The $102,000 in registered Federal Reserve bills. These were not burned or otherwise destroyed, as most everyone has guessed. They were sent back to Russia, where experts changed the numbers, but they have not yet been put into circulation, so far as I know.

The getaway: We went north on Wabash to Wacker Drive, took the lower level to Lake, then over to Franklin and south to Jackson. There we turned right and crossed the bridge. The truck went to a garage a couple of blocks west, where it was unloaded and the dismantling started. We went to a second garage just beyond the Union Station. The limousine was taken to a paint shop in the basement, and we went to the top floor, where there was a large room set aside for us with a change of clothing for each man.

All of this was done like a similar job in Boston some years earlier, in which I had no part.

12 The end of the year 1957 had been tentatively set for me by Bu-X as the most propitious time for my debut behind the Iron Curtain, and I was given three years, beginning in 1954, in which to achieve it. Bu-X figured that the Russians could be expected to attack anytime after that winter. The methods by which I was to achieve my goal were outlined only in a broad way; all specific activities were left to my own discretion, and the Bureau remained ready at all times to supply me with any assistance I required. I could call upon them for anything from money to the condoning of murder, so long as it furthered my ultimate success. They were naturally interested in my progress, but they made no move ever to contact me. It was I who had to call on them, and the elaborate system of contacts which had been set up was designed to cover any possible needs I may have had.

I never knew who the Bu-X operatives were, outside of those I actually met for one reason or another. For instance, it was not at all beyond the realm of possibility that Kovol-Nichols himself worked for them as well as for the M.V.D. There was never any hint of this, nor did Nichols ever, in our long association, commit any act that was in any way suspicious. Naturally he wouldn't. But I mention this possibility to illustrate what an involved and intricate system had been implemented by this international network. Their tentacles reached everywhere, into all the capitals of the world and into the lives of many thousands of persons who, in one way or another, might have fitted into their scheme.

I have no knowledge of the over-all objective of Bureau-X beyond that in which I was engaged, but I presumed they had other activities. One of these I was to learn about with no little sorrow to myself, on the M.V.D. assignment that followed our Chicago caper.

I met Nichols in New York, at Christopher House, after I had dispersed the Banks Express Company group and had tied up a couple of loose ends in transportation of the loot and disposal of the masks, pea jackets, and caps. He was patiently pleased with me and he told me that some day I would doubtless be a credit to his organization.

"When our investigation of you is complete," he said, "then we can talk about taking you in."

"Still on probation?" I asked.

He nodded. "But you will continue to work with us," he said. "I have made arrangements to disassociate you with your cell and to destroy all trace of your connections with the party."

"There is no work I would like better," I said.

"Now, on your next assignment," he said, "I want to warn you that there is great danger and the need for the utmost secrecy. The only person who can possibly pull this off is one who speaks English with no accent and can pass as an American. In addition, he must have no nerves and he must be an excellent shot. Am I right in believing that you fit these requirements?"

"Completely and precisely," I replied.

So he gave me instructions for the next several days, making me repeat my lessons over and over for many hours a day, and at the end of it he gave me a stack of papers that would identify me as one John Becker, a semidisabled war veteran of World War II, and a roll of bills large enough to choke an aardvark. What I was to do was to go to Yorktown, Virginia, and get a

41

job as a shell loader in the U.S. Naval Mine Depot there, which is actually a munitions factory and manufactures many kinds of explosives.

It also manufactures the trigger mechanism for a certain type of atom bomb. Nichols wanted one of the mechanisms.

Although there was no union among the workers at the mine depot, the Communists had enough contacts with foremen and others, apparently, so that I was promised a job. I had to wait for clearance by the F.B.I., and I sat in a motor court on the outskirts of the town for a week until they checked down the past of this John Becker. A young, pink-faced agent from Richmond came down the peninsula to question me and he was very sincere and not too bright.

I'll give you an example. My papers said I was born in San Francisco and that I had lived and worked there most of my life. I had a plausible story about coming to Virginia—relatives who lived nearby—and I had the answers to all of his other questions. But I didn't ever speak with that peculiar slow accent of the native San Franciscan, which I've got to know well since my return to this country from Russia, and not once did he wonder about my accent, or lack of it. I don't say this to criticize the F.B.I., because generally they're on the ball a lot more than most people suspect. But I do criticize this one agent, a dope by the name of McCarthy.

Well, I started to work on a Tuesday, loading 1,000-pound bombs in one of their "candy factories" spread over several hundred acres of woodland. This place where I worked was a one-story concrete building off by itself in the woods, with walls about four feet thick, and inside of it there were more walls four feet through that separated the various compartments, or rooms. In one of these was a large mixing machine, run by electricity, that looked like a candy mixer and gave the place its name. In this the explosive was mixed. Then it was poured onto large, flat pans and allowed to dry, in sheets about an inch thick, four feet long, and a couple of feet wide. When it was dried, it was broken into chunks with a rubber hammer—that was a job I never wanted—and then these were placed in the shell casings by this very careful John Becker, who was me. When the shell casings were full, I poured in some liquid explosive of the same brand to fill up the cracks and such, and I did it for five months and I never got used to it. On that job, I discovered I did have nerves. . . .

Near the entrance to the mine depot, on the right of the main gate as you went out, there was a large warehouse-type

42

building with a railroad siding running along one side of it, that was my objective. That's where they assembled the trigger mechanisms for this atom bomb, and the casual stroller had as much chance getting near it as he would getting into Farouk's personal harem. There were Marine sentries on four sides of it on twenty-four-hour watch, and there were a couple of extra ones at the building's only open entrance, and all of them had fixed bayonets and ample ammunition.

However, the C.P. did have one guy inside, and he was the one I was going to work with to get a trigger out when the time came to try it. He was a squat little man, almost as broad as he was tall, and he went under the name of Cligget. He worked on an assembly bench for one of the many precision parts of the instrument, but even he didn't know what the finished product looked like or how it operated.

The gimmick was that this Cligget was a member of the volunteer fire detail at the base, and after I had been there five months he got me a place on the fire brigade.

This brought us to March 1956. We had a number of clandestine meetings at Cligget's farm on the river, a couple of miles from the mine depot, and we worked out a time-table for a moonless night at the end of the month.

On this day, about four o'clock in the afternoon, a pickup truck going along the road beside the depot broke down just as it reached a spot opposite our trigger-assembly building. There was a ten-foot wire fence separating this road from the depot. Next to the fence were the railroad tracks, and adjoining them was the building.

The driver of the truck got out, opened the hood, and tinkered with the engine, but apparently he couldn't fix it. One of the Marine guards moved over to the fence and watched him (I learned later) and finally ordered him to get his vehicle towed out of there. The truck driver said he would and started to walk toward town and a garage.

At 4:00 P.M. I had finished my daily stint loading shells and by 4:30 I had my clothes changed and was walking the mile and a half toward the main entrance.

At 4:50 a tow truck parked behind the stalled pickup, which was facing away from town. The pickup driver and the garage man both looked under the hood and tinkered, for maybe fifteen minutes. The Marine sentry watched them all this time but he didn't say anything.

At 5:05 I was in the vicinity of the firehouse, which was off to the right of the main road, beside the administration build-

43

ing. Just about then there was a hell of a blast from the direction of the trigger factory. I stopped where I was, and a couple of scores of others along the road and in that area stopped too.

In about thirty seconds the fire siren went off with an ear-splitting wail and I sprinted for the firehouse. The main doors were open when I got there, and the engine of the big chemical truck had just caught. I grabbed a helmet and rubber coat from a hook to the right of the door and climbed aboard.

There were about ten or twelve others on various footholds when we swung out of there with our own siren wailing. We sped around to the right and skidded to a stop at the main entrance of the warehouse. We all piled off the engine and grabbed chemical extinguishers and axes. By this time smoke was beginning to pour out of the factory door and through it came tumbling the figures of the workmen, coughing and gasping for breath.

I ran around to the other side of the building, lugging a fifty-pound extinguisher and an ax, and didn't notice, until I had got up to the loading platform on the railroad side, where one of the big loading doors had been blown out, that I wasn't alone.

"This looks like the source of it," I yelled to my companion. "Let's get inside and see what's burning."

"O.K.," he yelled back at me.

We climbed up on the platform and he picked up his extinguisher and ran inside. I took a quick look around. The Marine guard who usually covered that side of the building was at the far end helping his buddy to shoo away a gathering crowd. A couple of kids were outside the fence looking in, but they were no menace. Beyond the fence was the pickup truck, with its engine running and the driver standing alongside it. The tow car behind it was just starting to back off.

I turned back to the blown-out door and saw Cligget staggering toward me through the smoke, with a stained wood case in his arms. It was about three feet across and half as thick and wide, and it had no markings on it. I took it from him and he jumped off the loading platform. Then I leaned down and handed it to him. It weighed about fifteen pounds, I should judge.

I remember wondering whether he would be able to heave it over the fence as I turned back to the building and started to go in through the smoke to keep any nosy intruder occupied.

Just as I got inside the door, this other fireman came hurtling toward me. I dropped my extinguisher and threw a football

44

tackle around his legs—or thought I did. I tripped him but didn't hold on, and while I was picking myself up I heard a gun go off, close to my ear. This fireman was on his knees. He had a .45 in his hand, and he had just dropped Cligget by the fence with a big hole in his head and the atom-bomb trigger still in his arms.

It was too late for me to do anything. I started back through the blasted door and into the smoke, when there was another shot. It got me on the backside and knocked me flat on my face.

13 Of course it had to be a Bu-X agent who shot me. He was a character by the name of Mike Crosby, and if you're a sports fan you may recall the name and understand why I hadn't dropped him with my football tackle. Mike had been the defense mainstay of the University of Oklahoma Eleven for three years back in the forties, and I couldn't have wanted a nicer guy to put a slug in the part I sit on. His Bu-X assignment was to see that no atom-bomb triggers made at the Yorktown Naval Mine Depot ever got into the wrong hands, and that's exactly what he did.

I was taken to the depot infirmary, and a Navy surgeon probed for, and removed, the bullet within an hour. Then I was taken to a private room and placed under guard, both inside and outside.

Were they happy! Here was a plot cracked wide open on their own doorstep! Medals were sure to be passed out, and behind that snide remark is the sincere conviction that whoever got them deserved them. . . . We were playing for keeps, just as they were. Me, I was doing a job that had certain aspects I couldn't be proud of.

Well, I had to get out of that place and fast, before I was mugged and otherwise rendered useless to my Communist cohorts. My whole back hurt, from my shoulders down to my thighs, and I was so stiff I was certain I couldn't stand up. Besides, I had been given a large dose of sedative—possibly morphine—and I could keep awake only for brief periods.

I didn't know until later that Bu-X was involved in guarding this operation, but during one of my brief periods of wakefulness I decided I'd have to contact them and ask for their

45

help or my entire assignment would go up the flue. But how? There had been no contacts arranged for Yorktown, Virginia.

I told the Marine guard that I wanted to speak to the commanding officer of the base, and he gave me a good imitation of a Marine horselaugh.

"No lousy son-of-a-bitch-of-a-spy is going to tell me what he wants," the Marine said succinctly.

The next time I woke up I repeated my request, and got a similar reply, but with several more picturesque but less printable adjectives.

"Listen," I said patiently, "things are not always what they seem. Will you please get word to your commanding officer that I will make a full confession—to him. To him alone."

This was the kind of language the Marine understood, and he agreed to send out word.

I went to sleep again.

It must have been about 2:00 A.M. when I woke up and looked into the cold gray eyes of a four-striper sitting on a chair alongside my bed. Behind him stood the Marine.

"I'm sorry I was asleep, sir," I said.

"What did you want to tell me?" he asked. There was no warmth or sympathy in that voice. It was like steel pig-stickers.

"My name is Miles," I said. I spelled it for him. "Will you please call Admiral B——— in New York, Cortlandt 6-1739, and tell him my name."

The captain got up from his chair, and his face was flushed with anger. "What is this damned foolishness?" he demanded.

"It is not foolishness," I said patiently. I repeated the admiral's name and the phone number. "Call him and find out." I felt myself beginning to doze off again. I managed to start another sentence. "The situation is desperate . . ." I said.

I was out. I came to again and it must have been hours later. The first light of dawn was graying the sky outside my window. I looked around the room and there was no Marine guard. I sat up slowly and painfully and turned on the light beside my bed. My clothes were laid out at the foot. I picked up the pants and looked at them. There was a hole in the seat, on the left-hand side, but all of the blood had been cleaned off.

I turned off the light and got dressed. It was a painful process and I passed out twice getting on my shoes and socks. Then I saw a bottle on my bureau, by the window, and a glass beside it. It was Scotch, and I poured myself a stiff slug. After that it was easier.

46

I limped out into the hallway, carrying the bottle, and saw no one. I negotiated the stairs to the main floor, went out the front door and on down to the road. There wasn't a soul in sight. I passed the firehouse and the administration building and got to the main gate. The sentry house was empty, and the gate, always closed at night, was slightly ajar. I walked through and saw parked outside the gate a black Buick sedan. I started to walk by it, when my ear caught something. The motor was running. I looked inside and it was empty. There was a piece of paper stuck to the steering wheel. I opened the door and got in. I turned on the dome light and read the note. It said: "Leave the car parked anywhere in Richmond."

I took another long drink, leaned far over to my right to get comfortable, and started out. It wasn't too bad. I was in Richmond by noon and I left the car in front of the main post office. I took a cab to the airport and I was in New York by 4:00 P.M., riding in from LaGuardia and smoothing out the details of my story of escape.

It was a good story, borne out in most of its aspects by newspaper accounts printed in the first editions of the morning papers. It earned the commendation and, I do believe, the respect of Kovol-Nichols, who was not too greatly saddened by the failure of my mission, the death of Cligget, and the arrest of the pickup-truck driver.

"After all," said Nichols philosophically, "the chances of succeeding by such methods in such a closely guarded place are very remote. I sometimes miss the days of our happy hunting when all we had to do to get such secrets was to ask for them from the officials in charge in Washington." He thought over this for a moment and then sighed deeply.

14 I don't want to give the impression that American security in the fifties was particularly good or that we kept any important secrets from the Russians. Generally we didn't. For each failure, such as the affair in Yorktown, there were a dozen successes, but most of them, I must admit, were on a level higher than violence. Our government had not fully recovered from left-wing "liberalism," and a number of misguided but dangerous persons of high estate were still going about the country telling Americans that there was a difference

47

between the well-educated "idealists" with leftist political leanings and the avowed dirty-shirt Communists.

Now I don't mean to oversimplify this problem, and I am well aware that it is not in some aspects merely a question of black and white—or white and red. But it was no time, either, to be "open-minded," and only a pathological idiot would attempt to apply reason and logic to a condition that affected the survival of his own country. Either you were for survival or you were against it. That was black and white. And if you were for survival, then you didn't quibble over the shades of pink and red, or the degree of viciousness, of those who would destroy you.

This idea has been thoroughly discussed by many writers, but I want to underscore it here because, as a trusted and somewhat efficient operative for the Russian M.V.D., I was in a good position to judge the effectiveness of the disservice performed against America by the spy network on the one hand, and my own countrymen on the other. Let me state that the Russians were at times highly appreciative of the mischief promulgated by the soft-headed segment of the self-styled intelligentsia, who didn't learn, actually, until the Soviet planes were dropping their atom bombs on American cities, that it was too late to conduct reasonable debates on academic questions of loyalty. I don't mean to libel these folk, whose worst fault was probably only foggy thinking, for they all showed unquestioned patriotism and loyalty themselves when the chips were down, but I don't think the American people should ignore the fact, either, that the Russians, at times, loved them.

I never operated on the higher echelon of intellectual treason, principally because it was no part of my job, but I did become a contact man, and for a short time the chief, of the Soviet spy corps in Nevada, following the Yorktown debacle. Kovol-Nichols considered that I was too hot for the East, despite my assurances that I had not been mugged or otherwise measured for identification by the careless Navy authorities before my escape.

I rested at Christopher House for a few weeks until the wound in my backside healed, then took a train west and settled in a small apartment in Las Vegas, overlooking the downtown gambling area and the upcountry flashes from the atom-bomb testing grounds at Frenchman Flat. This apartment house I went to was owned by one of our comrades and was a rookery for the elite of the sabotage and spy contingent that had flocked to the new A.E.C. atom test laboratory from all over the world.

48

The comrade-landlord also supplied liquor and women to his guests in accordance with the general mood of Las Vegas, and as a result there was a continual house party in progress on the two upper floors, which was considered good for morale as well as good bait for any testing-ground workers that got to wandering around hunting for relaxation.

It was bad for my sleep, but I stuck it out in that house because there turned out to be a mystery of a sort connected with one of these females who came a-visiting to the house party, and I was never in a position to ignore any puzzles.

I had a Bu-X contact schedule for Las Vegas, and I put this into operation before I left New York. My first meeting turned out to be with a very shapely brunette who sold lingerie in a store on the main drag. She was so attractive, in fact, that I was tempted to violate a couple of rules and date her, which didn't look too difficult. But I got hold of myself in time and confined myself to business, which consisted of telling Bu-X to lay off our espionage operation, just in case some joker should get the silly idea of cleaning out the Russian atom-bomb spy network. The message was in code, naturally, and read like a demand for money from a long overdue debtor, plus maudlin regards to his sister. It made just enough sense to get by in the clear, but just the same, it was hardly the kind of message an M.V.D. espionage agent would send to anyone, ever.

Now these Bureau-X contacts didn't necessarily know for whom they worked. In the case of a babe like this Las Vegas dish, it was almost certain that she was not aware that she was connected even with a government agency; that she probably believed, if she gave it any thought at all, that she was transmitting messages for some secret gambling syndicate or other such illegal setup. What she looked like was a dame with nothing more on her mind than a man and a pleasant evening.

About a week later I caught a fast glimpse of her as I was leaving my apartment. She was on her way to the revel aloft with a couple of blondes. She saw me and hesitated, waiting for me to speak, I guess, but I turned fast and went down the stairs. I went to a gambling hell and spent fifty dollars on several one-armed bandits, and while I was pulling the levers, I thought.

I was far enough along in my M.V.D. work to be particularly wary and not to take any chances, no matter how remote. I knew the M.V.D. had no spies in Bureau-X, and that they didn't even suspect that such an organization existed, but it was a cinch that if this dame worked for Bu-X and was friendly with the Russians she was a potential menace.

49

What I had to find out was who and how smart she was and for whom she worked. Not only my assignment but my neck might depend on it, so I accepted the landlord's next invitation and went up to the top floor of the building and joined a half-dozen hard-drinking comrades and their hard-eyed molls. She wasn't there. I drifted to the floor below and back again several times and finally resigned myself to my fate and got stiff on Scotch. I hadn't been doing any drinking for about three years then, and it hit me hard and fast, and tasted much better than I had remembered. I had always been able to hold my liquor, within reason, and I was gratified to discover that I retained this ability, so far as I could judge.

I felt only slightly hangoverish the next day, ate a big breakfast and a bigger lunch, and about 5:00 P.M. I joined the party again. A couple of hours later this brunette came in, with a frumpy, frilly femme in red hair, and I went over and spoke to her.

"Hello," I said, "I remember you."

"Why, hello!" she exclaimed, with a real happy smile. "I had no idea I'd see you here. I want you to meet a friend of mine—this is Margie Collins, Mr.—er—ah . . ."

"Harrison," I said. "John Harrison. It's a pleasure." I shook the redhead's hand and took them both by the arm and steered them to an unoccupied divan. On the way over, she whispered in my ear, "My name's Sonia."

I asked them what they wanted to drink, filled up three glasses at the makeshift bar on a dining room table, and came back. By this time a large, intoxicated comrade, who blew up things with dynamite, was moving in on the redhead. I gave her her glass, let her go, and turned to the brunette.

"Sonia," I said. "Sonia what?"

"Markham," she said.

"Pretty name," I said. "Live here in Las Vegas?"

"For now," she replied. "I come from Los Angeles. Where are you from?"

"New York, last," I said. "I came out here for the slot machines."

"You must have gone broke fast," she said.

Point No. 1: She knew when I had arrived.

"No," I said. "I just didn't have much money to start with. I came away suddenly."

She tossed off her first Scotch in a hurry and asked me to get a refill. When I came back she was standing up talking to a little comrade from San Francisco by the name of Selig

50

Abeles, who was my nominal boss. Selig was a perpetually smiling, gnome-like person with the most vicious tongue west of the Pecos. He was a good organizer and he had an insatiable curiosity about people—any people, but more particularly the individuals who worked with and for him.

"I see you have met Sonia," he said when I came up. "She is the prize cat of our zoo."

His smile made it seem like a pleasantry, but it wasn't.

"We've met," I said noncommittally.

"Be careful of her," he said. "I think she's a spy."

Sonia laughed. "I work for the Russians," she said.

"Well, have fun," said Selig, walking away. Then he added a very filthy and personal remark to Sonia. She laughed again.

"He's my dream-boy," she said to me.

We drank and talked and wandered around from floor to floor until something after nine, and the only things I learned for sure were that she was a pleasant companion and that Selig Abeles had what might have been a yen for her, the way he looked at us from time to time when we got in his vicinity.

She was either very cagey or slightly stupid, and my vote went for the former because, on the subjects that she wanted to avoid, she was never obviously uncommunicative, and the way she skirted around the edges and skipped the holes was an expert performance. For my part, I acted drunker than I was and gave her all the rope I had.

"How about going out to dinner?" I asked finally.

"An excellent idea," she said. "I was wondering when you were going to feed me."

We stopped by my apartment on the way down while I got a hat, and coming out the door I kissed her. It was good. What I mean is, it was good but hardly ladylike. But then, you don't meet ladies in my business.

We dined at the Flamingo and after dinner we spent an hour and nearly all of my own cash at a dice layout. She had one streak of seven straight passes, but she pulled down all but the original bet after each win, so she didn't make very much.

Point No. 2: She wasn't in Las Vegas to gamble.

I had business for the M.V.D. at the Flamingo, and at eleven o'clock, while we had shifted temporarily to roulette, I excused myself and went to a room in one of the wings. I picked up some carefully sketched plans of an atom-bomb warhead for a torpedo, which was good stuff for the Russians. I got them

51

from an Army sergeant, who was shot for treason the following year but not because of me.

I gave him $1,500 for the plans and we had a fast drink together before I left his room. He thanked me and then he said:

"The money means nothing. I just can't stand imperialists."

"That'll make Uncle Joe happy," I said.

I went back to the roulette table and stood beside Sonia, who was working on her last five chips. I waited until they were gone, then I suggested a walk. She agreed, and we went out and wandered around the elaborate grounds and finally found a bench facing the moonlight.

"Have you known this Selig Abeles long?" she asked me.

"No," I said, "only since I got here."

"Know anything about him?"

"Nothing," I said. "He's just a guy who lives in the same house as I do and attends parties."

"He's a man of mystery," she said, as though she had just made a big discovery.

"So are you," I said. "That is, a girl of mystery."

She laughed. "Why, there's nothing mysterious about me," she exclaimed. "I'm just a poor working girl, trying to make a living."

"Why was I sent to you?" I asked.

"Were you?" she said. "I didn't know about that."

"You know about it," I insisted. "I was sent to you and I gave you a message—asking for money."

"You know as much about it as I do," she replied. "It doesn't make sense, but it helps to make dollars, which are what I need."

"Then I take it," I said, "that you'll do just about anything for money."

She looked at me long and hard. Then she put her arm through mine and snuggled up to me.

"You're so right," she whispered.

We got a cab and went to my apartment and she spent the night with me.

Point No. 3: She was no professional.

I didn't hear from her or see her for two days, and that gave me forty-eight hours to wonder about her. When we did meet again, up on the top floor, she was wearing a heavy veil and she was talking to Abeles. She greeted me warmly enough, and Abeles, smiling as usual, said, "Hello, Don Juan."

52

"Now that you mention it," I said with a straight face, "I suppose a person like yourself would consider me with some envy."

He stood there glaring at me through his smile, which is no easy thing to do, and finally he said, "You forget yourself."

"That's a pretty weak comeback, for a person of your reputation," I said. "Just don't twit me and I won't twit you."

"Come, Sonia," he said, and the two of them walked away from me.

I got quietly plastered, or nearly so, and roamed about the two floors talking to this one and that one but not to Sonia or Abeles. After a couple of hours I got one fast word with her alone as she came from the ladies' room. What she said was, "Hi," in a very warm, low voice. Then she lifted her veil slightly and showed me one of the most beautiful shiners I've ever seen.

Point No. 4: She was Abeles' woman.

Point No. 5: She liked me and she undoubtedly had kept quiet, so far, about my odd message; but she was not to be trusted.

15 The question was whether to do the job myself or turn it over to Bu-X. We were both about equally well equipped out in that country. But it occurred to me that if too many people got bumped off in my immediate vicinity, sooner or later the M.V.D. might begin to wonder. So I took a fast trip to Los Angeles in Abeles' car, which he loaned me reluctantly, and made a Bu-X contact in a Pacific Electric trolley going through the Third Street tunnel. This was a guy who poked me in the ribs as he walked by and apologized in French.

We left the streetcar together, took a taxi back to Abeles' car, and drove on out Sunset to the beach. Somewhere around Malibu, in a parking lot alongside a restaurant, I told him what he'd have to have done and who would "finger" them for him.

"You might as well get this Abeles as well as the girl," I said. "I have no exact idea how much he knows, but it's probably too much. You won't have any trouble finding them together. This is the car they'll be driving. They go out to a ranch in the back country together nearly every weekend."

53

We returned to Los Angeles then and I let him out at a bus stop on Wilshire. I went on to the Towers Hotel and finished up some minor M.V.D. business which had been my excuse for the trip, then drove back to Las Vegas that night.

I kept away from the parties and saw Abeles only briefly and officially a couple of times the next week. He was about as abrupt and nasty to me as he figured he could get away with, and I was nasty right back. I had the jump on him in that department; he was afraid to go too far because of my size, and I didn't let him forget it.

All of the time I was expecting him to ask me about my first meeting with Sonia in the lingerie shop and the message requesting money. Sonia was one colossal and dangerous boner, on my part as well as on the part of Bu-X, and I was really on the hot seat waiting for them to get around to her and to Abeles.

It finally happened, but it took Bu-X ten days to do it and that gave me plenty of time to regret having left the job to them. Ten days can be ten years when so much depends on each minute. And the way I figured it, any one of those minutes might have been the one that this Sonia dame popped off to Abeles about me and my mysterious "contact." I was never sap enough to believe her apparent liking for me meant a thing beyond what she thought she could get out of me.

It was a Saturday night and the party was going full blast overhead. I was stretched out on my bed, reading a detective story and sipping a lonesome Scotch and soda, when there came a gentle rapping at my chamber door. I knew who it was as certainly as if I could see through the panels. I opened the door, pulled Sonia in, and closed it.

The veil was off and there was no discoloration around her eye. Both of her eyes, in fact, sparkled at me, and then she covered them with their lids and turned her mouth up to be kissed. I kissed it. When we were through with that, she pushed me away and said breathlessly:

"I've only got a minute, or I'll be missed. I had to see you."

"I've been wanting to see you too," I said. "But what is this —are you married to that guy?"

"Oh, no!" she said and laughed. "Are you jealous?"

"Of him? Don't be silly."

"He's jealous of you."

"Probably," I said. "So what?"

"I want to get out of here," she said, her face becoming serious. "I've got to get away from him and I need your help."

54

"What help?" I asked.

"Either you take me or lend me some money," she said.

"I'll do both," I said, "but not right now. Wait about a week."

"I can't wait," she said. "I've got to go now."

"I haven't any dough that would interest you right now," I said. "And I can't leave here for another week at least."

"How about that message you sent? You could get some more money from them, couldn't you?"

"Oh, that," I said. "No, there's no more money there. That was just a gambling debt and the guy promised to pay me off when I got out here."

"Do you expect me to believe that!" she exclaimed. There was a mean, petulant droop to the corners of her mouth, and I was surprised that I hadn't noticed it before.

"Listen," I said, "go back upstairs and have fun. I'll see you Monday in the lingerie shop and we'll arrange everything."

"Then you won't send for more money tonight?" she asked. "You refuse?"

"There isn't any more," I said patiently. "I told you what it was—just a gambling debt. Now go back up and tell your friend Abeles what I said, that it was a gambling debt, and tell him, too, while you're at it, that I suggest the both of you keep your noses out of my business."

She swung at me then, a vicious swipe with her beaded handbag, but I ducked and caught her arm. I opened the door with my other hand and eased her out into the hall. She was furious. She called me a nasty name.

"Beat it," I said.

I closed the door and went back to my reading. I half expected Abeles to come in next, but he didn't show. Sometimes he acted very smart. About one o'clock I turned off the light and went to sleep. About two-thirty there was a loud banging on my door and I got up, put on a dressing gown, and opened up. It was one of Abeles' men, an old-time Ogpu terrorist by the name of Gordon who had been "retired" to this soft touch on the desert.

"Get dressed in a hurry," he said in a stage whisper. "There's been an accident."

I invited him in, closed the door, and motioned him to my Scotch bottle. I put on my clothes and was ready in five minutes, but I had to wait until he finished his second slug.

He had a car waiting below, and I got in beside him and he sped off across town and out Highway 99 going south. About

55

two miles out we came to a lot of red lights and flares and people and a hell of a smashup. A two-and-a-half-ton truck had tangled with this sedan, both of them apparently going at high speed, and there wasn't enough of the sedan left to keep off the rain.

Beside it were two bodies, by this time stiff and cold. Side by side they lay, together in death as they had been in life—Selig Abeles and Sonia Markham.

Down the road a piece was the truck, and it stood on its four wheels. There were scratches on it, on the right-hand side, but no dents. I tapped on the body as I walked by it, and it seemed to be made of very heavy-gauge steel. In fact, it was like tapping on the turret of a battleship. The driver was down in the road talking to a couple of cops. There was a red gash across his forehead and blood stains on his wind-breaker.

This driver was talking earnestly and explaining that the sedan had swerved suddenly to the left and right into his truck just as he pulled even to pass it. The driver was none other than Colonel Janus, back in his Joe Hogan role as a driver of vehicles.

Could he drive!

16 Don't get any idea that the deaths of Sonia and Selig solved my problems or finally removed the threat of M.V.D. probing for that phantom menace to their operations which suddenly had deprived them of a couple of top people. These killings always start up a chain reaction, and you're not through with them until you've reached the last link of the chain and the final man is safely under his allotted six feet of sod. Usually this last man is pretty high up in the hierarchy. In my case, he was tops. He was Joe Stalin himself. You might ask what was the connection between Solovene, Abeles, and Sonia Markham and Joe Stalin? The connection was that these were some of the corpses I had to climb over to get to my objective, and if these people hadn't been dead I never would have reached it. It's as simple as that.

Now this Gordon—Sam Gordon, of Odessa, the Ukraine, and Alameda, California. He was no dope. He had been Abeles' confidant, and he had a very active imagination and a great intellectual curiosity. It was no accident that he came to

56

my apartment first when he heard of the smashup out on Highway 99.

He followed me around out at the wreck scene, he listened while I berated Joe Hogan and demanded of the police that they arrest him for homicide, and he helped me make the arrangements to have the bodies taken to a mortuary in Las Vegas. He was there, and wherever I was from then on, he was there. He didn't say much, and he never indicated by any word or action that there was anything amiss or that he was suspicious in any way, but you could practically hear him thinking. I am certain that he didn't have a thing to go on, but he was certainly hunting for it. That first Bu-X contact of mine, through Sonia, might well have worried Abeles, principally because his woman was involved in it, which would make it necessary for him to find out exactly what it was. But that interest could hardly have been inherited by Gordon, who was ten years past the age of any woman. He just stayed close to me for reasons of his own—because he was curious; because I just happened to be in the same general area when his boss and friend was killed.

Because he didn't like me.

Sam Gordon hated my guts, and that's the way it was.

I took over temporarily as chief of the Las Vegas and Frenchman Flat activities for the M.V.D. and boss of sundry lesser representatives of the U.S.S.R. and I made Gordon my chief aide. I wanted to keep my eye on him, too. There's only one way to combat enmity and suspicion when you're playing for blood. Get as close to it as you can and make damned sure you strike first.

I stayed on that job for two months more and broke in my successor, who was a skinny, clerklike guy with pimples whom I'd seen around Christopher House. He went under the name of Edgar Worth, and he usually worked as an auditor in companies handling critical defense contracts. He had asthma, and it was considered that the dry air of Las Vegas would help him. I guess it did.

Worth brought me word from Nichols that the heat was off me in the East and that they wanted me back there for some strong-arm work. That was his expression, said with ill-concealed contempt.

Did I tell you this Worth was a disagreeable little twerp? "Nichols needs some muscles," he said. "He's got some strong-arm work that doesn't take too much brains."

"That sounds dangerously like deviation to me," I said with

57

a straight face. "That sounds like a cheap, bourgeois criticism of the glorious proletariat."

That sent him into a fit of sneezing.

"I shall certainly report your attitude to Nichols," I continued.

Sam Gordon was there, of course. And he naturally took Worth's side.

"This is hardly the time and place for such ideological discussions," Gordon said severely. "We have important work to do and I don't think you should take up our time quarreling with Comrade Worth."

"You are right, as always, Comrade Gordon," I said. "I shall be pleased to report to headquarters that you and Comrade Worth are happy bedfellows."

That left them with nothing more to say, and we got back to work, preparing for my departure. It took a week to get Worth straightened out on all of the details of the operation and to acquaint him with the courier schedules and the innumerable methods of making contact with our various informers.

Also, during that week, I arranged through Bu-X for me to borrow for one night from the F.B.I. an apartment maintained on the top floor of the Sal Sagev Hotel, which was just down the street from our headquarters. I was formulating a plan and I wanted a place safe and high up, just in case it could be worked out. . . . I was thinking of Sam Gordon.

I took the 11:15 A.M. train out of Las Vegas on August 25, 1956, after a brief farewell to Worth, Gordon, and a couple of others, none of whom was sorry to see me go. I hadn't endeared myself to anyone in Las Vegas, with the possible exception of a change woman who patrolled my favorite slot-machine area at Overton's and openly admired the graceful flick I gave the handles of her machines. I had a ticket to New York, via Union Pacific to Chicago, and Pennsylvania the rest of the way. I stayed on the train to Salt Lake City, some ten hours later, and then got off, turning my ticket over to a chap who was waiting for me at the outbaggage room of the railroad station.

I went out to the airport by cab and got into a converted Mustang that was warmed up and waiting and was flown back to Las Vegas in just over an hour. It was fifteen minutes shy of midnight when I walked into the Sal Sagev Hotel by the service entrance and took the freight elevator to the top floor.

There was a young fellow in the apartment, a Joe College type with a crew cut, who looked like anyone you'd see on any

58

street in America. I wrote a brief note and I gave it to him, with explicit instructions on how it was to be delivered. The note said: "Miles not to be trusted. I can show you why. Come with bearer."

What was especially intriguing about it was that it was written in facsimile of the hand of the late Selig Abeles.

About twenty minutes later this kid came back with Sam Gordon in tow. Sam made the kid come in first, then he followed him. He had a .38 Police Positive in his right hand, and he wasn't missing a detail of that room. I told the kid to beat it, and when he had gone, I invited Sam to have a chair, by an open window. He shook his head and looked around the apartment some more, opening closet doors, peeking into the bathroom, and examining the bedroom.

"I expected to see you back," he said finally.

"The hell you did," I said.

"No," he said, "I figured there was something more you wanted here."

"You're psychic," I said.

"Maybe," he asid. He said it to himself rather than to me, and he said it in Russian, which we had never spoken together. I answered him in his native tongue and he looked at me with shocked disbelief.

What I said in Russian was: "All Russians have second sight."

"Where did you learn my language?" he demanded.

"Home," I said.

"Why, you speak like a native!"

"I am, practically," I said. "My home is not far from Odessa. That's why I'm in this business."

He sat in the chair, then, and he relaxed, a little, but just enough. He put the gun in his lap and lit a cigarette. There is this peculiar thing, which I've noted before, about suddenly speaking in the native tongue of a foreigner in America, far from his homeland, and especially if he's a Russian. It seems to disarm him—to lull him into a sense of being with a friend; no matter what murderous thoughts he was thinking a few moments before, his face lights up and he wants to exchange confidences. I don't mean to say that he ceases entirely to be alert and cagey, but he is certainly in a state of mind that psychologists call "affective," and that isn't good if you are supposed to be guarding your own life in a critical emergency.

I moved over beside Gordon and sat on the edge of the

59

window sill, beside his chair, and talked Russian with him for maybe ten minutes, until he got good and relaxed.

Then I stood up, hit him, grabbed him by the shoulders, and heaved him out the window. I caught a fleeting glimpse of his body hurtling through space as I closed the window softly, picked up his gun, which had clattered to the floor, and walked out of the apartment.

I went down by the service elevator, which was waiting for me with its door open, out the back entrance as I had come in, and climbed into a cab at the curb. I went back to the airport.

And the note with my name on it? The college-boy type had lifted that out of Gordon's pocket as they rode up in the elevator together.

All in all, it was a defenestration that any Russian could be proud of.

17 I caught up with my train again in Laramie, Wyoming, early the next morning. My replacement, who had been instructed to keep out of sight as much as possible, which couldn't have been much of a trick during the night, was waiting for me at the rear end of the platform. He slipped me the envelope with ticket stub and Pullman receipt and walked away. I checked the car and space number and got aboard. When I got to my seat, there was a girl there, dressed in a gray traveling suit and with a Greta Garbo hat tied under her chin. She gave me a very funny look when I sat down across from her, then got up and walked away.

I can't abide mysteries. I stewed for a few minutes, then got up and followed in the same direction. I found her in the dining car, sitting alone. It was around 8:00 A.M., and the train had started up by that time. I took the seat opposite her just as though we had been together and gave her a cheery good morning.

She nodded at me and went to work on half a grapefruit.

I ordered scrambled eggs and bacon and then said to her:

"I got the impression, back there, that you were expecting someone else."

"I was," she said.

"Tell me all," I said. "I've occupied that seat since Las Vegas."

60

"No you haven't," she said.

My coffee came and I poured some for myself and then filled her cup.

"Oh," I said. "I see what you mean. I was back in the observation car."

"You were?" she said.

The conversation seemed to peter out on that note. I looked out the window at an expansive display of bleak Rocky Mountain scenery, and finally my food arrived. I was hungry and I wasted none of my energy on chitchat until I had disposed of it. Then I said:

"This guy you were hunting for—was he about my size, with the same kind of suit on, only a few years younger?"

"Could be," she said.

"And he got on the train at Salt Lake City?"

"Maybe," she said.

"Won't I do?" I asked.

She looked me straight in the eyes, then. She had a smooth, tight skin and a lot of personality. She gave the impression of beauty, but her features separately were all just a little out of proportion in a most pleasant manner—nose too small, mouth and eyes too large, and chin too square. She was a blonde, but a quiet one; not frilly and flamboyant at all. Sort of between ash and gold.

"No," she said.

I sighed. It was always like that. I'd meet someone I really liked, with charm, personality, looks, clothes—even a proper shade of blond hair—and she would take a fast look at me and my homely face, and I wouldn't even get a time at bat, to say nothing of getting to first base. She'd say, "No."

"There's a lot of activity around Utah and Nevada these days?" I said.

"So?" she said. She had become ice-cold, so far as I was concerned, and her eyes, which were gray, had become studiously impersonal.

"So," I said, "what is a girl from an Indiana farm doing in Salt Lake City?"

I took a stab at that one, but it wasn't as long a shot as it would appear. Her accent was a dead giveaway, to a person with an ear for language.

"You don't know anything about me," she said. "You're just guessing."

But I had piqued her interest, and when I suggested we go back to my car, she came along like a lamb. She was still dis-

61

tant, but that was a matter of only slight concern. I wasn't on the make for her, in any way that normal people want to make love for the conventional reason. Sure, if we got cozy and smootched a little, it would make my job easier. That was all. I still had my job. And in this particular instance, there was developing an unsavory aspect to it.

Actually, I was contemplating whether or not I'd have to get rid of her. It was beginning to look as though here was one more person who knew too much.

Back in my car, we sat side by side, she next to the window. I put my feet up on the opposite seat and leaned back and relaxed. It had been a busy night and I was tired.

"Whereabouts in Indiana are you from?" I asked.

"Outside of Indianapolis—about thirty miles north," she said.

"And I suppose that now you live in New York," I said.

She thought that over, and finally she smiled at me and most of the ice melted away.

"You're very observant," she said. "Now let me guess—it was the hat, wasn't it?"

"Partly," I said. "Hat, shoes, suit—the whole look of you. Very satisfactory."

"Thank you, sir," she said.

"Now, do you want to tell me what you were doing in Salt Lake City?" I asked.

"No," she said. The ice came back.

It was getting thick. Here was a dame on a train who acted as though she were engaged in some highly secret gumshoeing, and it didn't add up at all. She just wasn't the type. Anyone can distinguish a nice girl from the bums that are engaged in my business. You just can't be wrong about that. A girl like the late Sonia, for instance. You could spot her a block away. She might as well have been carrying a sign. But this chick was all wrong for it, from her young innocent face right down to her pretty toes that peeked through the open ends of her basket-woven shoes. And yet, if it went on this way and if she refused to give, I was going to have to do something about her, innocence or no. I couldn't have any curious female walking around New York, of all places, telling people that I was not on such and such a train when it left Salt Lake City on such and such a night.

"Let's talk about something else, then," I said.

"I'd better be getting back to my compartment," she said.

62

"No, stay here, and I won't ask you any more embarrassing questions," I promised.

"Well, all right," she said doubtfully. "For a little while. I might as well talk to you as read."

"That's better," I said. "Where in New York do you live?"

"We live in Rye," she said.

"We?"

"Yes, my father and my mother and my brother and me. That's 'we.' "

"You work, or anything?"

"No, I was just out of school last year and I haven't decided what I'm going to do yet."

"Plenty of dough, eh?"

"Not plenty, but enough."

"This is nice country, out here," I said.

"Oh, yes," she said. "I like it very much. I'd love to live in the West."

"You could become a farm wife," I suggested, "with red hands, gingham dresses, and pains in your back."

"Oh, no," she laughed. She put her feet up on the opposite seat, beside mine. She had extraordinarily pretty legs.

"But more likely," I said, "you'll wind up in a plush Park Avenue penthouse with two Pekinese dogs and a daily box of chocolates so as to make your beam broad enough to become a dowager—with legs like that," I added.

She put her legs down.

"You say very mean things," she said.

"Mean!" I exclaimed. "There's nothing mean about my complimenting you on your underpinnings."

"No," she agreed.

"And as for Pekinese dogs and chocolates, what's wrong with them?"

"Nothing," she said.

"Well, that leaves only the broad beam," I said, "and I'll gladly withdraw that. . . . As a matter of fact, you don't look like the type."

"What's your name?" she asked me.

"John Harrison," I said. "What's yours?"

"Dorothy," she said.

"Dottie," I said. "Dottie what?"

"Dottie's enough for now," she said.

"You traveling alone?" I asked.

"Yes," she said.

"And you have a compartment?"

63

"Yes," she said.

"Well, I'm going to disappoint you," I said. "I'm not going to make any indecent proposals."

She put her legs up on the seat again.

"I'm not disappointed," she said. "I didn't expect you would."

"You didn't?"

"No," she said. "I can tell. You like me too much."

That stopped me. I tell you, this younger generation sometimes says the damnedest things!

"Assuming that's true," I said, "what would that have to do with it?"

"Romance," she said. "All men are incurable romantics—especially when they look like you."

"I must be getting old," I said. "I've never been accused of being a romantic before."

"That's it," she agreed. "You're getting to that age."

"That sounds like it came out of a book," I said.

"It did," she said.

"I must read it sometime," I said.

"I'll lend it to you," she offered. "I've got it with me."

"Now, look," I said, "I don't want to read a book. I'm not a romantic, and I'm not as old as I look or feel. I just didn't get any sleep last night."

"No?" she said. "What were you doing?"

"I was out killing a guy," I said.

She laughed. It was a very musical laugh. She leaned over and patted my cheek.

"You're just a little delirious now, but you'll be all right," she said.

"And," I said, "I was on this train."

"Oh, no you weren't," she said, still laughing. "I saw you walk out of the station in Salt Lake City and get into a cab, just before the train left."

That did it. Now I didn't have any choice. She did know too much. Once again it had been narrowed down to the simple, stark formula—someone else's life or mine. Oh, sure, maybe she was all right. Maybe she was what she appeared to be, and maybe if I spent a couple of weeks checking up on her I'd find that there was no menace in her. Maybe. But I didn't have a couple of weeks. And I want to stress one thing: you just don't take chances, ever, anywhere, no matter how remote or slight, if you are to do this kind of a job at all. Either you do the job

64

or you don't, and if you do it, you do it all the way no matter who gets hurt.

Consider this: Here on this train was a person who knew me by sight, who knew the one fact that would destroy an alibi that would save my assignment, and maybe my life, and who was on her way to the one city in the country where that alibi was to be used, if it became necessary. That doesn't give you very much choice, does it?

We chatted some more about things in general and then I walked her to her compartment, which was two cars back. She said she was going to take a nap, and I went on to the club car in the stern. At eight o'clock I picked her up in her room and we went up to the dining car together and had dinner at a table for two. She looked all shining and young and alive and I couldn't look at her. There weren't any tears in my eyes because I'm not the lachrymose type, but there were tears in my heart.

I guess this must be my mating season," I said to her.

"Oh?" she replied.

"Yes," I said. "The way I feel about you . . . I'm in a tizzy."

She reached over and squeezed my hand, which I'd left on the table. "Eat your soup," she said. "It'll take your mind off your troubles."

So I ate my soup and I felt my hand burn where she'd touched it.

"I like nights on trains," she said. "Speeding through the darkness like a comet out in space—passing clusters of lights that might be meteors or stars. . . . It makes me feel good."

"The Diesel engine pulling this drag generates 125,000 horsepower," I said. "It operates at a cost of about seven cents per mile for fuel, and has an efficiency rating of more than 75 per cent, as compared to the steam engine rating of——"

"All right," she interrupted. "I can take a hint. So what *do* we talk about?"

"I can't think of a single safe subject," I said, "with the possible exception of volcanology, and I don't know anything about it."

"We could just be quiet," she said softly. "I don't have to talk, or be entertained, when I'm with people I like."

So we were quiet. After dinner we went back to the club car and started drinking Scotch. Not too much; just enough. We talked now and then, but not too much of that either. The

65

car thinned out and we still sat there. Finally we were the last ones, and then I got up.

"I'll walk you home," I said.

We got up a couple of cars and I stopped in the vestibule of one. There was no one in sight. I opened the upper half of the door.

"Ah, that's nice," she said. "I need air."

I looked out and estimated that we were going at least ninety miles an hour. Nobody could live through a fall at that speed. I put my arms around her and she started to push me away. Then I could feel her change her mind. She snuggled up close. So I was going to tear my heart out and throw it in the track-side cinders. . . .

I bent down and kissed her. It wasn't like any other, ever.

She opened her eyes after a while and looked at me. She had her arms around my back, holding tight. I don't know what I expected her to say, but it wasn't what she did say. What she said was:

"What's your name, really?"

"As near as I can make out," I said, "it's John Miles." There wasn't any longer any reason why she shouldn't know that. She wasn't ever going to tell it to anyone.

"That's what I thought," she said. "I didn't think that other one was John Miles, after I got to considering it."

"That's interesting," I said. "Why not?"

"He was too pretty," she said.

"Oh, then you knew what this Miles looks like?"

"Not exactly. All I had to go on was the car and seat number."

"So?"

"So he didn't seem to be it, that's all."

"Don't talk in riddles," I said. "You haven't that much time."

She sighed and held up her mouth for another kiss. I obliged.

"I have a message from my daddy," she said. "I came out here with him, but now he's in jail, so I have to go home alone."

"That's a shame," I said.

"Well, it is!" she said. "He got arrested after an automobile accident. Down in Las Vegas."

I pushed her away from me and held her up against the bulkhead with a not too gentle hand.

"Who's your father?" I demanded.

66

"Colonel Loring Janus," she said. "You're hurting me."

"You sweet little fool!" I said as I let my hand drop. I felt weak and I sagged against the door. "I can't believe it—an ape man like that having a daughter like this!"

"Don't you dare say a thing like that," she flared. "He's not an ape man! He's the dearest, sweetest——"

"I apologize," I interrupted fast. "I guess I was thinking about somebody else—a tough New York cab driver by the name of Joe Hogan."

"What's my father got to do with such people?" she demanded, real miffed.

"Nothing," I said. "I assure you it was all a mistake. Now what was this message?"

"He said," she repeated slowly, making an effort to recall his exact words, " 'Not thine own mouth. Take care of the kid.' "

"Ah?" I said.

"I don't know what it means," she said.

"It's from the Bible," I replied. " 'Let another man praise thee, and not thine own mouth: a stranger, and not thine own lips.' The rest of it means that I'm to take care of you."

"I knew about that part," she said.

So I kissed her again, but differently, if you know what I mean.

18 The next couple of days were as difficult for me as any I encountered in all of those years—from the standpoint of my personal feelings. I know, of course, that personal feelings have no place whatsoever in a job like mine, and that I might have been jeopardizing my assignment and my life by having them, but it was the single such luxury that I allowed myself. Then I turned them off as much as I could and filed them away—for future rehabilitation.

The only person who ever penetrated the fat layer of insulation around my psyche, or whatever you want to call it, during these years was this Dottie Janus. And while we're on this subject, what an ironically appropriate name that was! Not that there was any deceit in her, but if ever there was a symbol that fitted me and my profession, it was the medallion of this two-faced Roman god Janus. I was his high priest, his *rex*

67

sacrorum, his disciple, and I might add that the only one, with the possible exception of some of the members of Bu-X, who did not taste of my double-dealing was this Miss Janus herself.

We spent most of the time en route to New York together, and as far as it was possible we kept out of sight. Her compartment solved that problem on the Union Pacific. On the Pennsy train out of Chicago, I changed our space to adjoining bedrooms.

We talked. Some of it was fairly important.

"I'm no one for you to know, and I'm certainly no one for you to have kissed," I told her the next morning after breakfast.

"I guess I'm the best judge of that," she said.

"You honor me with your faith and your trust," I said, "but you don't know a damned thing about me except how I look on the outside."

She snorted at that. "I know everything about you that's important to a woman," she said.

"Woman!" I echoed. "You're hardly out of diapers."

"I'm a lot older than you'll ever be," she said. "Any female is."

Did you ever get into an argument like that with a woman? I'll tell you one thing, you'll never win it.

"You're a babe in the woods," I said. "You're a little lost sheep—I mean ewe. You're a sitting duck for any smart operator with a line. . . ."

"And you're out of your fat mind," she said. "Are you deluding yourself with the idea that I'm not the one who picks the man I want?"

She stood up, then, and posed. She lifted her skirt to her knee and showed that gorgeous gam. Then she leaned down suddenly and kissed me, and before I knew it she was in my arms on my lap. . . . But she didn't stay there. She got up just as suddenly, and sat down very decorously beside me.

"I see what you mean," I said weakly.

"And another thing," she said, "when and if I pick you, I'll tell you what I'm going to do about it."

"Now that's a nice, maidenly attitude," I said.

"Maidenly, my foot!" she replied. "Don't sit there and tell me you don't know what's been going on in the world for the past fifty years. Why, you're worse than my daddy!"

"Won't I have anything to say about this picking and choosing?" I asked.

"No," she said, with finality.

68

"You may be right," I said.

"Of course I'm right."

"Now that we have that settled," I said, "let's get sensible for a moment. . . . What were you doing in Salt Lake City?"

"Oh, that again!" she groaned.

"Let's have it. The whole story."

"Daddy had to make a sudden trip west and I insisted I'd go with him as far as Salt Lake City, where I was going to visit my roommate from school. He refused absolutely to have any part of me or my plans, so naturally I came along with him."

"Naturally," I said. I was beginning to get some perspective on this little schemer.

"He left me at the station and went on—to Los Angeles, he said. I didn't hear from him for almost a week, then I got this message about the accident and telling me to make a certain train home and to find a certain big, rugged-looking man in a certain car and a certain seat. So I did. That's all there was to it."

"Simple," I said. "What made you notice me in the Salt Lake station?"

"You were my idea of a big, rugged-looking man," she said, "so, of course I noticed you."

"Of course," I agreed.

"And that's when I decided that you were my type, if you want to know," she added. "Just in case I ever saw you again."

"Type for what?"

"This is not the time yet," she said.

"All right," I said. "Let's get sensible again. . . ."

"I take that as a belittling remark," she said with severity.

"I apologize. What I mean is, let's get on with this discussion as it concerns the immediate situation, which has several aspects that you should know about."

"Such as?"

"Such as, whether or not I was on this train. The answer to that, in case anyone asks you, ever, is that I *was* on the train and that you did not see me in the station or getting into a cab."

"Check," she said. "But I had that all figured out. You were so upset when I told you I'd seen you get into that cab." She laughed at the recollection.

"You couldn't possibly have known that I was upset!" I declared. "Now I know you are exaggerating."

Suddenly there were tears in her eyes, and she put her head

69

down. "I felt that at that moment you hated me," she said in a low voice, "and I couldn't stand it."

I gave her my handkerchief. "You were partly right," I said. "However, we got by that crisis, and now we're approaching the Appalachians and a few facts of life. . . . Regardless of what complimentary and girlish notions you may have about me, I am engaged in an occupation that will not bear scrutiny or discussion. I will be occupied with it for several years, and during that time I must confine my female associations to a level you wouldn't know anything about— I hope. And at the end of that time, I will probably be dead. . . . I'm not being melodramatic. That's the way it is. And when I say goodbye to you in New York, it will be a last, final goodbye, for keeps."

"Well," she said with a sigh of resignation, "I guess that if I decide I want you, I'll just have to wait for you, that's all. Millions of women have done it ever since men invented war."

"You weren't listening to me," I said.

"Oh, I heard you, all right. Words. . . . That's just the way it seems to you right at this minute. You may even be right, but I think I'll take a chance. I'll wait, if I have to."

"That's silly," I said. "You don't know anything about the man you'll be waiting for."

"You're a friend of Daddy's," she replied seriously, "and that's enough for me. He's never wrong in people he likes."

"He likes me?" I asked. "What makes you think he likes me?"

"I could tell," she said. "That message of his—he didn't say a 'big, rugged-looking man.' That's what I said. What he said was, a 'big cousin to a gorilla'—so I know."

Then we were on the last leg of the trip, coming up through Jersey, and she was in my room saying that final goodbye— for keeps—when I found out that we were in love with each other. I had twenty-eight minutes to Newark, where I was getting off, to experience for the first time, and what I certainly believed would be the last time in my life, the soaring happiness of being with and talking to and kissing the one woman in the world who was only mine. For ten minutes of it we did nothing but stand there holding each other close, becoming accustomed to this most wonderful experience that is given to man. I might have whispered several words in her ear, but whatever they were they meant only one thing, "I love you."

"Eighteen minutes," I said.

70

We sat down and she took my big hand in the two of hers and held it up to her cheek. I felt a tear strike my finger.

"This isn't goodbye, then?" she asked.

"Not if I can help it," I said. "If there's any possible way that I can come back to you, I will. That I swear."

"I'll wait for you," she said, looking up and smiling into my eyes. "No matter how long it takes; no matter what happens, I'll be waiting."

"That's a big order," I said. "I'm not accepting that as a promise."

"I do promise," she insisted.

"Don't," I said. "Please don't. You'll only regret it. Put it on this basis: if that's the way it works out, then that's the way it was meant to be. Otherwise, no. The chances are a hundred to one against it, and that's nothing to promise on."

"Is there no way that I can ever hear from you?"

I shrugged. "Maybe, maybe not. If too long a time has passed, ask your father. He might know; if he doesn't, then nobody does. . . . But then, he might not tell you."

"He'll tell me," she said.

"Whatever you hear, tell no one," I said. "Whatever you see and whatever you hear, don't believe unless your father says it is so. Will you promise me that?"

"I promise," she said.

"That will probably be the most difficult promise you ever made," I said.

"I swear it," she said. "I know more than you think."

"You probably do," I said, "and it doesn't worry me a bit."

"It worries me," she said. "Oh, if only we had peace in this cockeyed, insane world! What a terrible place to live in!"

"Shh, it is not," I said. "It's a glorious world. I have never known it to be so wonderful. . . . Why, damn it, woman, you've made a Pollyanna out of me!"

"Pollyanna Candide," she said and laughed. "Everything happens for the best in this best of all possible worlds."

Then the train started to slow down. I lifted up the shade and saw we were going through Elizabeth. I got my one bag from under the seat and set it near the door. Then I held her in my arms again and I kissed her.

"*Au revoir,*" I said.

"*À bientôt,*" she said.

I picked up my bag, opened the door, and went out. As I closed it, I saw her standing straight in the middle of the room and smiling. That's the way I remembered her—Dottie Janus.

71

19 There were no happy faces (a very relative term, indeed) around Christopher House when I returned. During my trip from the West, when I'd been too occupied to read any newspapers, Congress had finally reached the belated decision that the subversive activities of the Communist Party were illegal, which is something like concluding that skunks smell like skunks. So they outlawed the C.P. and fractured diplomatic relations with the U.S.S.R. You no doubt remember well what happened after that—the Big Red Roundup and Rodeo that set the whole country on its ear and reached into enough high places of government and industry to cause a sizeable amount of consternation. The party had been expecting and waiting for this move for many years, and all the mechanics of going completely underground had been worked out and the orders issued, to become effective on O (for Outlaw) Day. What caused the longer-than-usual faces on my comrades were the violence and effectiveness of the roundup and the loss of more than half of their key men, none of which they had anticipated.

If the F.B.I. had been anathema before, you should have heard the screaming and the damning that went on during this happy crisis. I do believe that if we'd had enough M.V.D. men to turn the trick, we would have been ordered to go out and wipe from the face of the earth every man who had been within spitting distance of J. Edgar Hoover.

Christopher House itself was in the process of being disbanded and our rooms rented to legitimate tenants (so as not to arouse suspicion through any wholesale debouchment), and I was instructed to take a room in a midtown hotel. I went to a flea-bag called the Grahame, which was conveniently owned by a couple of comrades and nestled between a parking lot and a Chinese restaurant on West Forty-seventh Street. I got a musty room with a cruddy bath, which was plenty good enough for the proletariat. It had the usual collection of repulsive hotel-room furniture, topped off with a monstrosity of a stuffed chair done in pancreas red.

That evening I dropped by the Kovol-Nichols apartment and had dinner with him and his plump mistress, and saw that they had their books boxed and most of their personal belongings packed for an early getaway.

The dinner chitchat was anything but charming. This frowzy

72

dame, who called herself Mrs. Nichols, was one of these fast, wet talkers who have a bright comment on every subject from plumbing to the inner significance of Picasso's daubs. She was the kind of woman who keeps you continually off balance with verbal jabs to the ear, and never lets anyone get set for a roundhouse statement on any subject, even if the talker happens to be an alligator wrestler discussing his latest holds, and that's getting pretty specialized.

People who liked her probably called her bright, or some such. Maybe she was. My own sour attitude about her may very well have stemmed from the fact that I can't stomach Communists of any of the several sexes.

She might have been just right for Nichols, who was inclined the same bright and talkative way himself. I am one of those who holds that human beings do not seek opposites or contrasting personalities in their mates; that they hunt for familiars, for people who think and react very much as they do—hence the bickering that accompanies so many marriages. The moment you find someone who does have a constantly novel approach to the humdrum problems of daily living, you are too stimulated to bicker. It is only when these attitudes are familiar that you begin to pick them apart.

However that may be, these two were of a kind, both physically and mentally, and seemed to live in a lively disharmony, yet basically they agreed on everything. Communism itself takes care of a large measure of that agreement because most of the problems that ordinarily stimulate thought among human beings are matters of creed and dogma and are not open to reason or discussion. I am certain that that's why so many so-called and self-styled intellectuals embrace Karl Marx and his disciples. They have discovered that the intricacies of logic are beyond them, and they gulp the slogans that are substituted for reason with avid relief.

"I have so wanted to meet you," said Nichols' woman, who was introduced as Selma. "I've heard Bill speak so much about you."

Selma didn't speak Russian, so we had to use English, and that made for a stilted evening on Nichols' part.

"Now, Selma," he said, "you know that is an exaggeration."

"But you *have* mentioned Mr. Miles, many times," she insisted, turning her watery blue eyes on him.

"We should not discuss that," said Nichols severely.

"Well," said Selma, sitting down and showing a couple of

73

short, fat legs up to the knee, "I like that. You invite a guest and then you forbid me to be nice to him."

"Let us change the subject, if you don't object," Nichols said. He turned abruptly to me. "I trust you had an agreeable trip."

"Uneventful," I said, "But pleasant."

"I received very disturbing news over the weekend," he said.

"Another one of our people was killed," said Mrs. Nichols brightly. "Apparently he was thrown out of a window."

"Please, Selma,"·interrupted Nichols, "let me tell it. After all . . ."

"Oh, I must see about dinner, if you will excuse me," she said. "I'm cooking something I know you'll love. It's an old Danish recipe I got from my mother—goulash. I hope you like goulash. But this of course isn't at all like the Hungarian goulash which I suppose you're used to. It's——"

"Please, Selma," said Nichols.

"Well, I know you two have a lot to talk about, so I'll run." She did.

"Who was killed?" I asked.

"One of our most valuable people," he said solemnly. "Sam Gordon."

"Not old Sam Gordon!" I exclaimed. "Why, that is terrible. When and how?"

"Right after you left, apparently," he replied. "He was thrown out the window of a hotel in Las Vegas—some odd name. Let me get the report."

He went out and came right back with four typed pages and he read them to me. It was a fairly accurate account, and the conclusion that Gordon had been thrown out of the window, which was contrary to the coroner's finding of "jumped or fell," was logically presented.

"That is a personal loss to me," I said. "Old Sam was a fine man."

"I have some more here which I didn't read you," said Nichols. "This report says: 'I strongly urge that you check into the movements of Jan Miles at the time of Gordon's murder. Miles left on a morning train, but he could have come back. He quarreled constantly with Gordon and with me, from the time I arrived here. I do not resent his personal attitude and I know that such sentimental considerations have no place in our philosophy, but I found him unco-operative in the extreme, and I do not believe that his attitudes are good for party dis-

74

cipline. This is not an accusation against Miles, and I ask that his movements be checked only for our protection. Signed, Edgar Worth.' "

"Interesting," I said. "Do you mind if I read it and digest his flowering prose?"

He handed me the report without comment and I read and reread the last paragraph.

"There's no doubt about it," I said, "he detests me."

"You quarreled with Worth and Gordon?"

"Just with Worth," I said. "I would never quarrel with a man like Gordon—about anything."

"Worth disputes this."

"He doesn't know the full story," I said. "Gordon and I had no occasion to be friendly, for a long time and even after Worth's arrival. But right after we started speaking Russian together, we developed a deep affection for each other. It is my misfortune that this happened so shortly before I saw him for the last time."

"That sounds reasonable," said Nichols, lighting a cigarette. "And I do know this Worth is a difficult man to get along with. We have had great trouble keeping him in his jobs with the capitalists. He has many complexes."

"People with asthma always have," I said. "That sickness is only a physical manifestation of the many aberrations that beset them."

"An interesting theory," he said. "Well, we are losing too many men, and especially at a time when we need them more than ever. This imperialistic America is getting ready to attack our fatherland. Even today we are at war, defending our borders from these forces of reaction. We have important work to do."

"I am a soldier, waiting for orders," I said.

"You are a good soldier," he said. "Tonight, after dinner, I will give you your orders."

"I hope you have checked my movements since leaving Las Vegas," I said. "Those charges of Worth——"

"We have checked," he replied. "As a matter of fact, we found a girl you had been with on the train, a silly little thing by the name of Janus. . . . You do not show very good taste in your women, Miles."

"Oh, that one," I said, and laughed. "What can you expect to find on a train?"

"She was extremely stupid," he said. "It was not until we had slapped it out of her that she told us the truth."

75

I shrugged. "As long as she did tell you the truth," I said.

"Oh, we got it. We picked her up in a car. We told her you wanted to see her, and she got right in. After I slapped her," he said, looking speculatively at his right hand, "she told us you were on this train—that you had spent that first night together in her compartment."

"There are no secrets from the M.V.D.," I said.

"You will always find that to be true," he said.

Selma Nichols came in, then, and announced that dinner was ready. As we went into the dining room and sat at the table, I looked this Kovol-Nichols over speculatively and selected the spot on the right side of his chin where I would like to hit him when and if I ever got the opportunity to work him over, one of these days, for Dottie. . . .

20 My orders on that September evening of 1956, from Kovol-Nichols, were to sabotage. I was put in charge of a group of six men and one girl who were the planners and the directors of all the Communist sabotage of American industry in the East during that period. We ranged together and separately from Birmingham to Boston and as far west as Chicago, Kansas City, and Memphis, causing the ruining of irreplaceable machinery, the wrecking of trains, the time-bombing of airplanes on crucial flights, the arson of untold millions of dollars worth of buildings, the sinking of ships, and the general disruption of the American defense effort and the national economy. We were indirectly responsible for hundreds of major and minor disasters; we were the ones who told our Communist cells and our Communist union leaders what to do and when.

Do you remember the fire at the Republic plant on Long Island which destroyed nearly half the factory and burned up a score of jet planes? That was us. Do you remember the New York Central troop-train disaster at Fonda, New York, which killed 203 and injured nearly 400 soldiers, all on their way to the Far East? That was us. Do you remember the Willow Run explosion? That was us. . . . These are just a few of our more important efforts. It would take a separate book to list them all and to tell you the sordid, tragic details of those seven months and my Seven Ghosts.

76

The F.B.I. called us the Seven Ghosts, and we drove them crazy. Actually there were eight of us, counting myself, but the woman they never figured. She was the smartest of us all, a sexy, bedroomy little kitten with claws of steel, a mind like a wolf trap, and the white, soft thighs of a Venus. . . . With her along, we never had any trouble getting information, if it was a man who had what we wanted to know. And with her along, my hearties never had to bother with any other women themselves, which is a point.

This dame's name was Rita Barstow and she originated in Hollywood and learned treason in some of our best schools, which had better remain nameless. She was a natural, redhead, about five feet, three inches tall, 112 pounds, and she had spent a couple of years dancing in Broadway shows and night clubs and sharpening her wits and party-line immorality on the innumerable crackpots who infest the phony world of modern art. What broke your heart about her was the shining and rare combination of beauty and talent that she threw into the gutter for the cheap little thrills that Communism offered up as lure.

Among others, Rita seduced a couple of F.B.I. agents for us, and that's how we got to know about our appellation of Ghosts. She also seduced a Bu-X man, but she got nowhere there, except in and out of a bed, and I didn't have to tip anyone off to the trap. He was one guy who was too smart for her, which gave me the lift I needed when my own morale was pretty low. Do you think I enjoyed this kind of work against my own country?

During these operations I came in contact for the first time with Kovol-Nichols' boss, and actually the boss of all the Communists in America, including the Ambassador and chief United Nations delegate. This was a large, square, hard comrade by the name of Igor Godovisky. He was ostensibly a clerk with the U.S.S.R. delegation to the glass box at Forty-second Street and the East River and he was known in that aerie of sound, fury, and busted dreams as a taciturn, deferential type who did a minimum of work at his job and contributed practically nothing to the gaiety of nations outside of an occasional scowl. Actually, he was Major-General Igor Godovisky, the confidant of Beria, Molotov, and Stalin, and one of the most bloodthirsty of that whole crew of vampires. A conservative estimate by his own M.V.D. places Godovisky's personal corpses well up in the thousands.

You wouldn't think that a high-powered operator like that

77

could be in our country unannounced and unreviled, while using his own name, and never coming into mention by the press as a V.I.P., yet that is what happened, and I cite it here to illustrate the effectiveness of the trite Iron Curtain that divided the free world from the slave, as well as the anonymity of some of Russia's most powerful men.

We had been operating a little over six months when I was called into Godovisky's presence by Nichols. I had just returned to New York from a caper in Akron, where we had engineered the burning up of a large and critical stock of natural rubber in a fire you may remember because of the cries of anguish that went up from the banks of the Potomac. I was visited by this dumpy Mrs. Nichols in my room at the Grahame around 10:00 A.M. of a Sunday in February, 1957, and you can take my word for it she was the one female in New York I wasn't happy to see.

"Come in," I said heartily when I opened up and saw her jittering in the hall. "My, you look well."

"Thanks," she said as she entered and looked around hopefully at the mussed bed, then at my maroon silk dressing gown. "You sleep late."

"Whenever I get the chance," I agreed. "Sit down and visit." I motioned to the chair by the writing desk.

I helped her off with a black karakul coat and laid it on the bed and took the black beret she handed me. Then I sat down beside the coat as she settled into the chair, carefully crossing her legs to show me some knee.

"Bill is in the country," she began, talking fast. "He called me and said he wanted to see you—today. He is with a very important person and that's why it's very secret and why I came over here to tell you, rather than using the phone."

"Speak right up and say anything that's on your mind," I said, motioning around the room. "My walls haven't got ears."

"Oh!" she said. Then more quietly, "Oh. I didn't think. You know, I'm so used to talking right out when I have anything to say, I just can't get used to all of this. Bill gets furious at me. He says I jabber too much, but you know his sense of humor. . . . My, that's a pretty dressing gown."

"Write it," I said, indicating the desk beside her.

"About your dressing gown?"

I shook my head. I went over to her and told her softly, "Write your message. Write out what you came to tell me. When you've done that, then we can chitchat. O.K.?"

She nodded at me and turned to the desk. She wrote an

78

address in Oyster Bay and instructions how to get there and the time, 1:00 P.M. She handed it to me and, while I was reading it, she wrote on another piece of paper: "You're very nice. Do you like me?"

What a spot!

I wrote under her scrawl: "Yes."

She stood up and snuggled against me, putting her chubby arms around my waist. "I like you," she said, "but I'm afraid."

"You are?" I said. I patted her hair. It was thick and wiry.

"I'm afraid that it's not anything fine and spiritual," she said. "I'm afraid that it's just ugly sex."

I choked.

"What did you say?" she asked. Her voice was breathless. She left her mouth open. I damned Bu-X and all its works.

"Look, honey," I whispered in her ear, "if I'm going to get out to Oyster Bay by one, I've really got to rush."

"You do want me too!" she said fiercely, looking up at me with her moist eyes.

"Sure," I started to say, and there was a timid tapping on my door. Let me tell you that was the most welcome doortap I've ever heard in my life. I disengaged myself, gave a good imitation of a sigh of frustration, and opened the door a crack. It was Rita, who was temporarily sharing the bed of an explosives man down the hall.

"Well?" I said.

"Can I come in?" she asked.

I opened the door wide for her and she glided by in that floating power walk of hers that riveted your thoughts to Subject A. Then she saw Selma, and the two of them squealed and locked each other in an extravagant embrace of greeting that was as phony as a Communist promise.

"Darling!" exclaimed Selma.

"Darling!" exclaimed Rita right back.

"I haven't seen you for years!" said Selma. "Tell me all about yourself! My, you look pretty—you don't show your age the least bit!"

"You look wonderful!" said Rita. "Why, you've put on only a teeny, weeny bit more weight, haven't you?"

"Bong!" I said. "End of round one. Now if you ladies will excuse me, I'll get dressed and get on my way. I've got business."

"Looks like you've had the business all morning," said Rita sourly.

A girl like Rita is constantly on the make for every present-

79

able man she sees, and the fact that I had eluded her was an affront to the core of her womanhood. And now, finding Selma in my room, which her mind could encompass only in one light, the affront was broadened to a full-scale physiological insult.

"Selma, of all people!" she said.

"Look, Red-top," I said, "get that mind of yours off your favorite hobby, say your piece, and then blow. And that, by the way, is an order."

"I'd better go," said Selma timidly.

I helped her on with her coat, handed her the beret, and escorted her to the door. Rita was leaning against the wall in a characteristic pose, which is the way Carmen might have done it if she had had Rita's equipment. I shook Selma's hand.

"Goodbye, and thanks for coming over," I said.

"Goodbye," she said, and backed out.

"So long for now," called Rita. "I'll see you around."

I closed the door and walked over to the redhead.

"What did you have in mind?" I asked her.

She smiled at me, but behind her smile was doubt and wariness. We had tangled on our first job together, when she had sneaked into my room in Baltimore early in the morning with a passkey. That time I had said some very harsh things to her.

"I just came in to say hello—maybe to talk," she said.

"Well, thanks for dropping by," I said. "You did me a bigger favor than you suspected."

"You're not angry?"

"No," I said.

"God!" she said, "how can you stand a slob like that Selma? I'd think she would make a man sick!"

"She hasn't anything to do with me. She's Nichols' woman," I said.

"Yeah, but she's crazy for you. You'd have to be blind not to see that. . . . She could have killed me!"

I started to dress. With all of her dripping sex, this Rita Barstow had as much effect on me as fat ladies' night in a Turkish bath. She sat on the bed, leaning against the headboard with her knees up to her chin and her arms around her legs.

"You have wonderful back muscles," she said.

I shaved my face and washed. When I came out of the bathroom, she was lying full length, posed just so. I got out a clean white shirt and a black tie and put them on, then got into my one good suit, a gray pin-stripe. I was ready for the boulevards.

"You've got another woman somewhere," she said. She sat

80

up suddenly and swung a leg to the floor, which disarranged her skirt with calculated indecency. "I bet you're ashamed of her—that she's some little bourgeoise trollop. . . ." She stood up and stretched, walking toward me with her arms in the air. I used to have a dog that stretched that way while he walked.

"I've got to go," I said. "Do you want to stay here, or are you headed somewhere?"

"I'll go back to Mike's room," she said. "Maybe I'll read." She looked at me hard and her eyes smoldered. "What's the matter with me?" she demanded in a husky voice.

She grabbed me and kissed me, then bit me hard on the lip. I pushed her away and rubbed my hand over my mouth to see if it was bleeding. It was.

"Goodbye, Rita," I said. I opened the door and moved out into the hallway. As I turned down the corridor, I saw her standing holding the door open and leaning against the jamb.

"You son of a bitch," she said.

21 I went to Oyster Bay by train and took a taxi at the station to a roadhouse about a mile and a half out of town. I went in and asked for a Scotch, but the bar was not open yet. When I got outside, the taxi was gone. I walked a half-mile down a side road, skirting around puddles from the melting snow of the previous day, and came to the gates of the old Phelps estate. I had known this place as a boy, when the last of the Phelpses and my dad had been partners in a brokerage house, and it saddened me, on my walk to the familiar front door, to see how its present occupants had allowed the once-beautiful formal gardens to become a tangled mess of overgrown ugliness. Why is it that Communists so love to desecrate each beauty that they seize?

I was admitted to the house, a stately and obsolete pile of some forty rooms that only the proletariat could afford to run, by a very correct comrade in striped pants. He seemed to know who I was and he nodded indifferently when I gave him my name.

"This way, please," he said in Russian, and I followed him to the library, to the left of the main hall. Seated in a large leather chair behind a desk that faced the door, and puffing a slim panatela, was box-faced General Igor Godovisky. To the

81

left of the desk, with his back to me, was roly-poly Kovol-Nichols, and he turned his head at our entrance, then jumped to his feet.

"My General," he said in formal Russian, "this is Miles, our most effective operator. Miles, this is General Godovisky."

I bowed from the waist, then went over to the desk and took the general's proffered hand. It was hard and strong, and he shook hands with typical Russian enthusiasm.

"I am honored to be a guest in your house," I said. Then I walked around the desk and shook Nichols' hand and told him that his charming wife had given me his message.

"What? You are married?" asked the General. "Ho-ho, Kovol! I never would have thought it of you—a ladies' man!"

Nichols stood on one foot, then the other. "We are not really married," he said.

"Ah, then it is the same one," said Godovisky, his face falling. "This Selma, eh? Well, Kovol, she is safe enough."

"Thank you, my General," said Nichols. "We seem to be, ah, well suited to each other."

"Now you, Miles," said Godovisky, leaning back in his chair and examining me through slits of eyes, "I hear good reports about you."

"Thank you, my General," I said. I stood at attention before his desk. Nichols also remained standing until the general invited him to sit again.

The general then talked for a long fifteen minutes on the Communist doctrine as it had been formulated to combat the encroachments of the imperialists; on the high aims of the U.S.S.R. for the enslaved masses of the world; on the goals of the M.V.D. in America; and finally on the critical situation that had evolved from the outlawing of the C.P. and the subsequent roundup of Communists.

Then he got specific. "With a few hundred men like you as leaders, Miles, we could conquer this decadent country," he said. "But—we don't have them with your special training and knowledge."

"The general chooses to be very complimentary," I said.

"You have a thick Roumanian accent, but you speak my language well, nevertheless," he said. "Kovol tells me you are an excellent driver, and that you are an expert with guns. I need a man like you on my staff."

"I am honored," I said.

"You will become my aide-de-camp," he stated solemnly. "You shall have the temporary rank of colonel." He picked up

82

an official-looking paper from his desk, decorated with seals and stamps, and passed it to me.

It was my commission in the M.V.D. There were many signatures at the bottom of it. One of them was that of an old friend—Marshal Beria.

Then the general shook hands with me, and Kovol-Nichols also pumped my hand and congratulated me. The general took the commission back and said it would be kept in a safe place for me. Then he gave me an identification disc, like that Kovol had shown me that first day I met him. On one side, in Russian characters, was the name MILES, with my thumbprint under it. I didn't have to ask where they had got the thumbprint. On the obverse was the letter B in Russian script, a familiar mark to me.

The general invited me to sit at an escritoire in a corner and he handed me a sheaf of forms to fill out and pledges to sign. The forms took me more than an hour, and during most of that time Kovol and the general conversed in low tones. The pledges were easy—all I was pledging, for this and that, was my life.

When I was through with that detail, the general told me, "You will terminate your affairs with your present group as of tomorrow at midnight. Kovol will assign a successor for your work. You will report to me at 3:00 A.M., Tuesday. Is that understood?"

"Yes, my General," I replied.

He rang a bell on his desk, and the striped-pants type who had admitted me came in, clicked his heels, and stood at attention at the door.

"Lieutenant Rosov will show Colonel Miles to his quarters," said Godovisky. "He will also assign the colonel a vehicle and take care of any other immediate needs."

I shook hands again with Godovisky and Kovol-Nichols and followed striped-pants out.

I was assigned to a large but simply furnished room on the second floor opposite the stairway. The entrance door had been removed from its hinges. It was next to Godovisky's suite and had a connecting door, which was closed but never locked. In the opposite wall was a door to a small private bath. Two casement windows overlooked the porte-cochere and the entrance road to the estate. A large double bed with a good mattress was against the wall beside Godovisky's door, and over the bed was an idealized portrait of Stalin. To the left of the

83

entrance was a highboy and to the right an armoire. There was a large closet beside the bathroom. The parquet floor was bare and well scrubbed rather than waxed.

Rosov waited respectfully while I toured the room, then preceded me to the side entrance of the house off the dining room and out to the large garage. There were half a dozen cars in it, four of them new Chryslers and two Cadillacs. One of the latter was a snappy gray convertible with black top and the other was a custom limousine.

Rosov pointed to a black Chrysler at the far end. "That one is available for you if you wish it," he said.

"It will do," I said with just that touch of indifference that my rank required. "You have the owner's license?"

"Yes, my Colonel," he said, addressing me properly for the first time. He handed me a cellophane envelope with the license inside and I dropped it into my pocket.

"That will be all, Lieutenant," I said. "You are dismissed."

He clicked his heels for me, turned smartly, and went back to the house. I got into my car, listened for a moment to the motor, then glided comfortably back to New York.

Back at the Grahame, I passed the word that I wanted to see each member of my group separately at intervals of no less than one hour, beginning immediately. The first one, my explosives man from down the hall, came about five minutes later, and I bade him goodbye and gave him his orders. The last one, naturally, was Rita. By then it was after 1:00 A.M. and a proper time to be thinking about a bed, one way or another.

"This is goodbye," I said to her. "I have another assignment and I probably won't be seeing you again."

"Never?" she asked.

"Probably."

"Couldn't you, maybe, meet me . . . ?"

"Look," I interrupted, "why don't you play in your own league? You do all right there. I've got no time for women."

"Either you are some sort of screwball fanatic or you are the biggest phony in the world," she said.

Damn females! What makes them so astute?

"Or maybe," I said, "some bitch like you has given me a bad time and now I'm just careful."

"You know," she said brightly, "I never thought of that." She came over to me and stood close, looking up into my face. "I would never give you a bad time."

84

"No," I agreed, "you wouldn't—and you won't."

"I could be awfully nice to you," she said. "Nicer than I've ever been to anyone in my life before."

She meant it, this pretty, sad little Jezebel.

"You are very sweet and very desirable," I said. "Right now I have work to do. If I can ever arrange to meet you, I will."

"You're trying to get rid of me," she said.

I bent down and kissed her on the forehead, then led her to the door.

"Your orders are to stand by until Tuesday, when you will be contacted by your new boss," I said. "You will meet him through Nichols. That is all I have to tell you."

She backed up against the door and bit her underlip. "If you would kiss me just once as though you meant it, I'd leave quietly," she said.

So I kissed her, just once, as though I meant it. She left, but not quietly. About 2:30, while I was dozing on the bed with my clothes on, the phone rang. A voice said:

"Can I see you? I am expected."

"Sure, come up," I said. "Room 603."

A couple of minutes later there was a knock and a tall, skinny Negro was standing outside. I invited him in.

"I'm Jones," he said. He was slightly on the lavender side, which struck me as being very funny. I had trouble keeping from laughing at him, but the idea that this clown was to replace me seemed like a personal affront, and made me sore, too.

"Have a chair," I said, indicating the upholstered monstrosity beside the window. He sat carefully, as though his girdle was bothering him, and crossed his legs with great elegance.

"You *were* expecting me?" he inquired.

"I don't know," I said. "You do the talking. I'll listen."

"Let's cut out all the cops and robbers heroics," he said with a supercilious smirk. "After all, you know who I am and what I'm here for."

"I do?" I said.

"Oh, stop it!" he said petulantly. "I'll just wait here for Mr. Nichols, if you want to be such a bore."

"Do your waiting somewhere else, then," I said. "I'm tired."

I walked over to him and motioned to the door. An expression of doubt turned down the corners of his mouth and he got up slowly.

85

"I thought this was all arranged," he said.

"Not necessarily," I said. "Get out."

He did, and I lay down again and dozed for half an hour. The next knock I heard was that of Nichols. I opened up and the little man was standing out there looking angry. In back of him was Jones.

"Come in, comrade," I said cheerfully. And to Jones, "You too, if you can behave yourself."

As much as his height and paunch would allow, Nichols stalked. Jones, on the other hand, walked softly. I closed the door and turned, and Nichols was shaking a finger at me.

"Miles," he said severely, "you have gone too far. This man is your successor——"

"Just a minute," I interrupted, speaking very quietly. "You will address me properly. The correct form, as I believe you know, is Colonel."

It was a small thing, but it did give me a great deal of pleasure.

I talked to this Jones, then, for a couple of hours, with Kovol-Nichols listening in, and I told him all he needed to know about my staff, about our plans, and about my personal contacts that none of the rest knew about. Then I got some sleep, and early in the afternoon I got up, got dressed, and went out to make a Bu-X contact. I needed a lot of money, and fast. There was something that I had to do that I had been putting off, and now it began to appear as though Bu-X contacts would be fewer and farther between if I was going to do a proper job for Godovisky.

I met this guy in the post office on Lexington Avenue just above Grand Central, where I went to buy some stamps, and I wrote on a money-order application, "Get me $10,000, give it to me here in an hour." Then I walked out. I ate a leisurely breakfast at a ham-and-egg joint up a couple of blocks and went back to the post office to buy some more stamps. The stamp man shoved a package at me and I put it in my pocket and scrammed. I strolled over to Fifth Avenue and up to Cartier's, and I went in and bought a fair-sized emerald in a platinum setting—nothing gaudy—and told the clerk to ship it to Miss Dorothy Janus, at an address in Rye. I gave him all but $50 out of my package, then offered him the rest of it if he would take the ring up there himself that afternoon and deliver it in person. He said he would, and he asked me who he was to say had sent it.

86

"No name," I said. "Just describe me as a gorilla-type guy."
"That's all?"
"That's all," I said.

22 What General Godovisky wanted and got when he put me on his staff was a combination body-guard, alter-ego, valet, confidant, interpreter, and drinking companion. I was with him twenty-four hours a day, from noon rising until dawn retirement, and after retirement, in the room adjoining. In that household, we followed the schedule of the Generalissimo in the Kremlin and did the bulk of our work at night. The most popular hour for appointments was 3:00 A.M. or thereabouts, and the small amount of sleeping that went on would have vindicated Edison. We were doing big things. We were fighting a war against America, and our small, tight group in the Phelps Mansion was the Advance G.H.Q.

Our contact with the U.S.S.R. was mainly by courier—trusted travelers from overseas who came in a score of different guises, giving us our orders and taking back the reports on the enemy's dispositions and activities. Some of them traveled legitimate carriers; some of them were parachuted from planes that generally flew up from Mexico; many were landed from the six submarines assigned to our command and which put men ashore from Maine to Florida in areas which had been carefully selected and which, incidentally, were all known to the F.B.I. We used our submarines sparingly because of that, but on many occasions we had no choice and we had to chance it on picking up the men and information without detection. Since my return I have read some F.B.I. reports on this phase of the action and I was surprised to discover how seldom the M.V.D. eluded them.

About a month before I joined Godovisky's staff, word had been passed to him that he had been marked for assassination by a group of Titoists. There was some suspicion that these "Titoists" actually were American agents from some counter-intelligence branch, which might well have been true. So far as I knew, Bureau-X was the only organization ever sanctioned by the government that was permitted to jump the gun on the declaration of war and act in any manner not strictly "legal."

But it was well within the realm of possibility that, with the Communist Party outlawed and diplomatic relations broken off with Russia, the rules had been revised and open season had been declared on some of the prize pigeons of the Soviet world. And if this were true, certainly Godovisky would have been high on such a list, to anyone who knew who he was and the power he wielded in the Soviet Union.

Anyone who lives by violence alone is always a safe bet for assassination, even if some specific organization is not gunning for him. The blood of countless thousands was on the hands of this Communist executioner—a fact which he well knew—and so it was not unexpected that he should develop nerves over rumors and noises in the night. For that I was thankful, for it was directly responsible for my assignment as his body-guard and my elevation to the exalted rank of colonel in the E.K.U. section of the M.V.D. So I did my job as efficiently as I knew how, which was plenty good enough to keep him alive —for me.

I went armed at all times. I carried a .380 automatic in a shoulder holster for ordinary dress, and, in a specially built compartment under the dashboard of one of the cars I used, was a tommy-gun. This car, incidentally, carried a four-number license with no preceding letter, which was the type of plate issued to New York State cars, and beside the plates, front and rear, was a silver-and-bronze state shield, which was covered over with a leather jacket. The car was, in all outward respects, the vehicle of a state official. I had a beautiful set of papers to go with it, identifying me as a chauffeur for the Department of Taxation and Finance, Bureau of Motor Vehicles. It was used only on special occasions, when I was trailing Godovisky to give him protection on some of his more critical trips.

On other occasions I drove the general's limousine, and that, too, had a specially built compartment under the dash, which held two .38 caliber Smith and Wessons. This car, a Cadillac, had bullet-proof glass and heavy-gauge steel on doors and sides and was relatively safe. When there were no pressing matters to discuss, I would drive the general into the U.N. and on other missions in this. Otherwise I would sit beside him and we would be driven by a big ex-taxi jockey by the name of Cohen, who doubled as mechanic. On these trips we also took along the girl Greta Gombol, a smart if homely little cookie who acted as private secretary and took voluminous notes on everything you said and half the things you thought. Greta, born of Russian parents in Perth Amboy, was bilingual, bi-

88

sexual, and monominded. She was an honor graduate of Barnard and had three degrees and no sense of humor. She called me "Muscles," privately and not kindly. She didn't like me, which was fine because I detested her. She always smelled gamey, and believe me, this statement is not based on bias.

Well, came the big railroad strike in the spring of 1957 and things began to pop. This strike was the major effort of General Godovisky and his army in that period, and it had been planned and executed with thorough efficiency to coincide with the Russian-supported attack on Yugoslavia so as to cripple our supply lines to the Mediterranean. An Atlantic Coast stevedore strike had been planned to go with the rail tieup, but this fell through at the last minute, probably due to the machinations of Dingdong Kelley, who was still the Communists' No. 1 man on the waterfront and the mainstay of the F.B.I. undercover corps. I'm just guessing at all this, but I think my guesses are accurate.

So much has been written about this railroad strike that I won't bore you with any details. I'll confine this account to the Grand Central riot of May 23, 1957, wherein eighteen lost their lives and nearly a hundred were wounded.

On that day, a few minutes after noon, General Godovisky, Greta Gombol, Cohen, and I drove up to the Park Avenue entrance to the Grand Central building. The general, Greta, and I got out, and Cohen drove away. His orders were to return in two hours and pick us up at the same spot.

The three of us went into the building and up to an office on the second floor, inhabited by a certain railroad vice president who shall remain nameless here. We entered by a private door and thus avoided secretaries and other employes. Godovisky gave orders and received information—all noted by Greta—and I sat looking out a window across a court at a little blonde, typing and eating candy. Then a courier came in through the private door—he was the primary reason for this rendezvous—and gave eight large manila envelopes to the general. The three of us got up, then, and the railroad man said:

"Why don't you stroll through the station, now that you're here, and have a look at what's going on?"

"We shall do that," said the general in his thick accent.

"Turn to the left as you go out," said the railroader. "There's an elevator at the far end of the corridor that will take you down to Grand Central."

We shook hands all around and the three of us went out.

89

We found the elevator and got out on the balcony on the west side of the station and walked over to the rail and looked down. The vast floor space of the station was almost deserted. The ticket windows were closed. There was a woman at the information kiosk speaking to its sole occupant. The baggage room at the far side was open, but the attendant looked lonesome. A couple of porters were pushing lazy brooms along about Gate 26. At each of the four entrances to the station rotunda, visible from the balcony, there was a group of policemen forming rough lines. At the main entrance from the waiting room, to our right, there were a dozen cops, one captain and one inspector.

All was quiet and serene, and only rarely did the yowling of the thousands of pickets on the outside penetrate to the tomblike interior. Godovisky said, "Come," and led us down the stairs to the main floor and headed for the waiting room. I assumed that he wanted to have a personal look at the picket lines.

We were about ten feet from the doors when all hell broke loose. A screaming, fighting mob came bowling through, brushing the cops aside and knocking some of them off their feet. Two other phalanxes rushed the police at the east entrances, but these cops had seen them coming and were swinging their night sticks and beating off the attack. Only a few of them got through.

The three of us beat a hasty retreat to the balcony stairs, but we didn't go up. More pickets came through from the balcony doors and we were practically surrounded.

"This way!" I said to the general and Greta. "We can get out of the way over here!" We ran around the corner to a baggage-checking room and I helped the two of them over the counter and vaulted after them. There was an attendant there who watched our invasion, but he didn't say anything after an initial mild protest. He was goggle-eyed at the screaming, running pickets.

Why did they invade Grand Central? Who gave such an order? That question has been asked a thousand times, and the only answer given that seems to make sense is that they wanted to show their strength. . . .There were no trains running anywhere in America, nor were they likely to be for some time.

I don't know who started the shooting. We could see little of the action from our revetment. At the sound of the first shot, the girl Greta ducked behind the counter. The general was standing beside me and he looked at me with raised eyebrows.

90

"That sounds bad," I said.

"It is foolhardy," he replied. "We did not need this."

Suddenly there was a fusillade of shots and the whole place was filled with the reverberations of gunfire. A couple of squads of National Guardsmen double-timed by us in formation, each holding a carbine at ready. The tempo of gunfire increased and seemed to be moving toward us. It looked bad.

"Maybe we'd better get out of here," I suggested.

"Perhaps," said the general. "It wouldn't do to be recognized here."

"You make a run for the corridor over to your right," I said to Greta. "There's a tunnel that connects with the Roosevelt Hotel."

I helped her over the counter, and she sped off, her skinny legs fairly flying.

"I'll reconnoiter," I told the general. I jumped the counter and went around to my left and took a fast look at the main floor. I saw cops and soldiers near the information booth; a few bodies were scattered here and there. One group near the track gates was doing most of the firing, down toward Lexington Avenue, and bullets were coming back at them from behind pillars and other cover. I ducked back and was starting toward the baggage room when a tough group in sport shirts —about a dozen men, each with a pistol in his hand—came through the doors from the train-dispatching room.

Their leader was Dingdong Kelley.

A couple of them saw me but paid me no particular attention. I had no gun in my hand and I looked peaceful enough. I was walking toward them when they deployed and started shooting at the group inside the station beside the gates. I couldn't see what damage they were doing; I could just see their guns flash and jump. The general had ducked down, and every second or so he'd raise his head and take a fast look. He was just about facing Dingdong Kelley, who was crouching behind a corner and blasting away at rapid fire, then ducking back to reload.

Suddenly Kelley barked an order and his men sprang up and began a retreat through the doors by which they had entered. Most of them threw their guns away, sliding them along the floor in my direction. Kelley didn't throw his away. He turned at the door for a last look.

I guess it was then that he spotted Godovisky. The general was standing up straight. It was a made-to-order situation for an F.B.I. undercover man if there ever was one. In the flash

91

of an eye, Kelley raised his gun and pointed it at the general.

That would have been curtains for me. Without Godovisky, I was a dead duck. If I lost him while I was his bodyguard, I was through—with the M.V.D., Stalin, and my assignment.

Kelley never shot. I put a bullet in his heart. I shot for his gun hand and nicked it, but his hand was raised, and behind it was his heart. I might as well have shot myself. It is the one action of my life from which I have never recovered, and never will.

23 How many people saw me shoot Kelley? Godovisky, but only a split second after my gun blazed. Two cops who were running around the corner behind me—and so far as they were concerned, at that moment I was a hero. A couple of pickets retreated toward the shuttle subway entrance; they were unarmed, with their hands up in the air, so the cops didn't bother with them.

The cops kept on going and went out the doors after Kelley's gang. I walked quickly to Godovisky's side, helped him over the counter, and told him to follow Greta out the Hotel Roosevelt passage.

"I'll meet you at the U.N.," I said. "We can't be seen together. Someone might grab me for that." I indicated Dingdong's slumped flesh lying in the doorway, with a lifeless leg holding the door open.

Godovisky stopped for just an instant to shake my hand. "You saved my life," he said. Then he scooted.

"Just for the junior prom," I said after his departing back. "Your turn comes later." I said it in English, of course, and not very loud.

I started to ease my way to the shuttle, when three more cops and a couple of National Guardsmen came around the corner in back of me and yelled at me to halt. I turned to face them and looked down the barrels of two carbines and three .38's. I raised up my hands to show they were empty.

One of the cops walked up to me and said, "Who the hell are you? What are you doing here?"

"I was hiding in there," I said, pointing to the baggage room. "I was caught in this thing. I've had no part in it."

"Who are you?"

92

"Name's John Miles," I said. I pulled out a new and properly visaed Roumanian passport, made out in that name, which Godovisky had supplied.

The cop looked at it, turned the pages slowly. "A foreigner," he said finally. "You better come with us."

"Look, mister, I've had nothing to do with this," I pleaded. "I'll get canned from my job if I get involved."

The cop hesitated. After all, there *was* no reason why I should have been held. Another cop and one of the soldiers came up, and this second cop looked at the passport. I stood there with my face hanging open.

"I guess he's all right," said the first cop. "He don't look like he was in any fight." He patted my hip pockets, but not my chest, and said I could go.

I breathed a sigh of relief. But too soon. The two policemen who had run by just as I dropped Kelley came back through the doors, with their guns in their hands, and walked over to us.

"This is the guy!" said one. "He shot that son of a bitch over there." He pointed to Kelley's last remains.

Then another cop came up. "Do you know who that is?" he demanded, thumbing over his shoulder. "That's ex-Councilman Kelley!"

Boing! Into the callaboose!

They took me to the East Fifty-first Street Station and kept me under guard in a back room for nearly eight hours while they worked over some of their more important prisoners from the riot. They gave me coffee and ham sandwiches a couple of times and didn't bother me when I went to sleep in a chair for an hour. Then my turn came. I was taken to the detectives' room on the second floor and I was turned over to four very impatient and short-tempered gents whose interest in my replies to their questions was purely academic. What they really wanted to find out was whether I was as hard as I looked.

Along about the time that my belly began to hurt from the more or less constant drubbing, they got tired of it, and I was never unappreciative of the welcome fact that they were enervated themselves by their long and arduous duty.

"We've got enough on him to burn him," said one who was addressed as Steve. "Let's send him downtown."

"O.K.," said a couple of the others. Then the fourth, known as Joe, a wiry little bantam of a man who had hit hardest by far, walked over to me and said, "I never saw a big bohunk like you I couldn't take with one hand."

93

"So you can lick me," I said "What's the point?"

"Stand up, you son of a bitch," he said. "I want to take one good swing at you."

"Sure," I said. I stood up. He swung and I stepped out of his way. He tried it again and I got my shoulder up and blocked it. He was getting exasperated.

"Listen," I said, "I'll make it a sporting proposition. I'll hold still for three cracks in the jaw if you'll let me hit back once. And we'll match to see who goes first."

That interested him, but this Steve broke in and called it off. "Nothing doing," he said. "You think I want to get my partner murdered too?"

"What do you mean, murdered?" demanded Joe. "You trying to belittle me? I'll lay him out as cold as a turkey!"

"No," said Steve firmly. "Lay off. You're away out of order. He's been a good guy. He's told us all we want to know and he hasn't squawked. Let well enough alone."

"Nuts," said Joe with real disappointment. "He's just my size."

They argued some more about it, then sent me down to the City Prison on Centre Street and gave me a comfortable cell and let me sleep. The next morning I was in Homicide Court with the detective Steve and the two cops who had seen me shoot, and after waiting around for three hours, I was formally held without bail for the Grand Jury and sent back to the lockup. I was indicted a couple of days later, on one charge of murder and another of Sullivan Law violation for the .380 automatic they had taken from my shoulder holster.

The trial wasn't anything much—just routine. You may remember how it was quickly crowded off the front pages of the newspapers by the revolt in China. Only when one of my Communist lawyers would act up and get himself cited for contempt did it get any sort of play. The order went out, probably from Godovisky, not to hippodrome it, and so these lawyers were relatively quiet and well behaved. Dingdong Kelley's association with the F.B.I. was never brought out, so the one potential sensation remained undeveloped.

It was an airtight case, despite the fact that all of the testimony came from eyewitnesses. That's a paradox of murder trials—usually the eyewitness case is the weakest and the circumstantial evidence one of the strongest. Usually a smart lawyer can make a monkey out of an eyewitness and prove to a jury that this guy who saw it all has astigmatism, cataracts, dizzy spells, is a congenital liar, beats his wife, and probably

94

wasn't there at all but in Weehawken when the shooting took place. Usually, but not in the case of these two cops. They were of the new breed of police, both ex-G.I.'s and college men, and they were as smart as a couple of Central Park squirrels.

Despite my lawyers, it was all over in two weeks and then I was sitting there at the counsel table and watching the jury file out, along with the handful of spectators. I looked at these ghouls who had come to see me killed and then my heart suddenly skipped around and bounced against my Adam's apple. There in a back row, sitting with her head bowed, was Dottie Janus! I don't remember clearly what I did when that realization suddenly hit me, but I must have looked silly. One of the lawyers turned to me like a surprised owl and said, "I don't know what the hell you have to grin about. It don't look that good."

"Oh, yes, it does," I said with a happy leer.

"You're off your rocker," he said.

I got my face together and noticed, for the first time, with whom I had been exchanging civilities.

"Go chase an ambulance and leave me in peace," I said.

The bailiff and a couple of sheriffs took me to the prison cage, and I had just got a container of coffee about a half-hour later when they were back.

"Come on, sonny," the bailiff said, "this is where you get your bad news."

I gulped about half the coffee, burning my throat, and then went back in. I looked for Dottie and she was still there, all by herself in a corner. I sat down, not much interested in anything else in that courtroom. Then the judge came in and the jury came in and there was the usual mumbo-jumbo and someone said, "guilty," and then it was repeated a dozen times and then I was on my way back to the cage. There wasn't too much light in the back of the courtroom and I couldn't see Dottie's face, but I got the impression, from the way she held her left hand over her eyes, that she was crying. . . . But anyway, there was a ring on her left hand that I recognized, even in that dim light.

95

24 I mentioned earlier in this report that my course of action on this assignment had been worked out with Bureau-X only very general lines and that everything specific was left up to me, to improvise as conditions demanded. No such eventuality as trial and conviction for murder had been foreseen. And yet, so far as Bu-X was concerned, this was all considered normal operating procedure, and if that's the way I wanted it, no questions would be asked. If I found it necessary to kill an F.B.I. man before witnesses, then accept arrest, trial, and conviction for it, the only possible conclusion that Bu-X could reach was that I had done it to further my own ends. Also, that my judgment was not to be the subject of inquiry. As proof of this latter, they made no attempt during this critical period to communicate with me or to offer me any assistance, and, of course, I asked for none. There was going to be no compromising of my situation by any worried paternal organization. They trusted me.

It was hardly a proper time for me to turn to Bu-X. A colonel in the M.V.D. would expect his own to look after him, especially after he had saved the life of his commanding officer. So I waited to see what would happen next. The only thing of any importance that happened in the next three months was a note from Godovisky in his own hand, which translated itself into: "Be of good cheer." The minor occurrences were that I was sentenced to be executed in the electric chair and that two appeals were turned down by the higher courts.

During the time the appeals were on file, I resided in the City Prison on Centre Street, but after the final turndown, I was put in a prison van, handcuffed to a stanchion by my seat, and started on my journey to the death house at Sing Sing Prison, Ossining, N. Y.

I was taken by prison van, rather than by train, because of the strike. There were still no trains running in the East. The Army by then was successfully operating a couple of the western roads but they had had to abandon eastern operations temporarily because of the number of train wrecks and other sabotage.

There was one other prisoner in the van with me, a young punk who was shaking himself to pieces for lack of a shot of dope. He had been convicted only the day before of a holdup

96

killing in a liquor store. What he needed was medical attention.

We left Centre Street around noon and drove up what I guessed to be East Side Drive. There were several whistles and horns besides our own that accompanied us, so I figured we had a police escort. I couldn't see out. After we started running faster on what might have been a main highway, I noticed that this escorting noise left us.

We rode about an hour, slowing down occasionally and making no more than two full stops, and then we came to a third stop. I heard voices outside, a couple of them yelling angrily. Then there was a fast burst of machine-gun fire and half a dozen separate shots. The machine gun suddenly went off again at the back of the van, and then the door was swung open. A guy in a state police uniform came inside, carrying a portable acetylene torch with a tiny blue flame at the tip. He turned the flame up to a loud hiss and burned through the chain that anchored me to the stanchion.

While he was burning, I said, Hello, to him in Russian, and he grinned at me.

He helped me out of the van and into the Chrysler with the official state tags, which was parked just ahead of the van. We got into the back seat, where my liberator gave me a top coat and a hat. The driver was Cohen and he threw me a broad scowl of welcome. Two others were in the front seat with him, both dressed as state police troopers.

We went north about half a mile, and I recognized the outskirts of Ossining and knew where we were. This caper had been staged on Highway 9, just north of Scarborough, and this is one of the busiest highways in the East, carrying a large percentage of the truck traffic into New York City. There was certainly no lack of boldness in these Communist maneuvers.

We came to a cross street with a traffic light and there was a large sign in the middle of the highway announcing that this section of Route 9 was temporarily closed for repairs. Behind the sign there was a long line of trucks and cars, and the front end was turning into the side street, following a huge red arrow on the sign.

Cohen indicated the sign with his thumb and said to me, "That's how we got privacy. We planted two of 'em; this one first, and the second right after the van had passed a couple of miles south. . . . It was too easy."

We went on into Ossining, taking a salute from a traffic

97

cop at a main intersection, and we made a right turn on Route 133. About a mile on we passed under the parkway and continued on 133 just west of Millwood and the Taconic State Parkway, where we made a sudden left turn into a private road. We were in an estate with a big two-story stone house back and out of sight of the road. Cohen stopped at the back door of this mansion, which was in a state of gloomy disrepair, and the troopers and I got out and went into a large hall and pantry that gave off the kitchen. Cohen drove the car into the garage farther back and closed the garage doors.

The troopers led me to a bedroom on the upper floor, where one of them produced a bunch of keys and got me out of my handcuffs. Four suits, shirts, and underclothing were laid out on the bed and we got into these as quickly as possible. The troopers put the uniforms and my jail attire in a bag, closed it, and one of them took it and motioned me to follow him. He took me to a door at the rear of the hallway and opened it, disclosing a narrow stairway going up. We ascended it to a large attic room, with a low ceiling and dormer windows on two sides. It was filled with trunks, old furniture, boxes, and junk. We went toward the front of the house, and in a wall there was a door. It led to a large closet. My guide turned on a ceiling light in the closet, then pushed a panel in the rear wall, and this opened to a small space, about eight by eight feet and too low for me to stand upright. It had a chair in it and a box mattress on the floor. He put the bag of uniforms on the chair and invited me to enter.

"We just fixed up this place for you," he said to me in Russian. "It'll keep you safe while the police search the house, as they undoubtedly will. After that, maybe you can have more freedom."

"At that," I said, "it looks more comfortable than the death cell in Sing Sing."

"We'll be back, to bid you goodbye," he said. "We've got to wait until the car is fixed up before we leave."

He went on out, and pretty soon he returned with the other two, and one of them was carrying a bottle of vodka and four glasses. They were all Russians, and they seemed to be very happy over their feat.

They poured drinks·out of the bottle and they stood around in the closet, talking about their adventure at length. They described the killing of the prison-van driver and guard with clinical detail. Then we toasted the bottle down to Stalin, the U.S.S.R., the coming war, General Godovisky, and any others

98

they could think of. The three also drank one toast to me. It went something like: "To the most deadly slayer of capitalists of us all," and it was a pretty compliment from that crew.

Eventually they got around to telling me their orders and General Godovisky's plans for me. One of them, a type named Chenkov, appeared to be the spokesman and leader.

"This place will be safe for a couple of weeks," he said, "so the general wants you to remain here. Only you must not go out or show yourself under any circumstances."

"Naturally," I agreed.

"We will take the car and go back to New York. Cohen is changing the license plates, and we should have no trouble. This house is occupied by one who calls himself Morgan, who is now away. He will return in about two hours. He knows that you are here, in this room, and he will look after your needs. No one else in the house is to see you."

"There are others?" I asked.

"Morgan's wife," he said. "They have a couple of children but they are away for the summer. Other comrades may be in and out, but it is General Godovisky's express wish that you remain hidden."

"I shall comply with the general's orders," I said. "What happens after the two weeks?"

"Why, you shall be taken out of this accursed country," said Chenkov.

"Good," I said. "Home to Russia, I hope."

"Home to Russia," he said. A faraway look came into his eyes and we squeezed a last toast out of the bottle.

"Home to Russia," we said in unison.

"But you know, comrades," said one of the others seriously, "this America is not such a bad place."

"You're joking," I said. "How can you think that?"

"Well," he replied dubiously, "you can buy anything you want here. Everybody seems to be well dressed and well fed, and they all have automobiles—even the poor farmers and the factory slaves."

"That is true," said Chenkov, "but it is only the outward appearance that you see. You do not see their misery and their hopelessness under the crushing heel of capitalism. You do not see the Negroes being lynched in the South, and the Jews being driven from their homes in the ghettos by the Ku Klux Klan. These things you are ignorant of, my comrade."

"I have been in the South," said the other one. "I was landed there, in what is called South Carolina, from a submarine."

99

"We know that, comrade," said Chenkov. "And you have seen that about which I speak."

"Well, not exactly," he hedged. "I saw many Negroes and I saw many whites, and in all truth they seemed to get along together very well. Even the Negroes there drove in automobiles."

"That is just the outward appearance," said Chenkov. "Come, little brother, our car must be ready."

We had a warm shaking of hands all around and I bade them adieu. I turned out the closet light, closed up the wall of my cell, and lay down on the mattress. I might have dozed off. What brought me suddenly to consciousness was the noise outside of the arrival of several cars. Car doors were slammed and then there was the sound of a bell ringing below. This was followed by a loud banging, front and rear. Then I heard the tires of another car crunching up the drive, and the mumble of voices, entering the house, reached me.

There was undoubtedly a search going on. I heard feet tramping around on the floor below, then several pairs mounted the attic stairs. They came toward me.

One voice said, "If he's here at all, he'll be up in this attic."

"What's that door there?" asked another voice.

"It's a closet," someone replied. "It's empty."

I could hear the closet door being opened.

"This is preposterous, searching my house this way," complained the one who had replied. "It will just upset my wife and she'll have another breakdown."

"We're after a murderer," was the deep-voiced reply. "If he's here, your wife will have a lot more than a breakdown; she'll be dead."

"What makes you think he's in my house?" asked the first.

"A car was seen coming in here with a lot of men in it," he said. "Like I told you, that's the car we have been searching for. It's the getaway car of these killers."

I could see the beams of a flashlight through a couple of small cracks in the closet wall. Then someone pounded on the wall with a fist and said, "It's hollow back there."

"What's back there?" said another voice.

"How should I know?" was the answer. "I didn't build this house. I only rent it."

I had practically stopped breathing long ago. I lay there without moving a muscle, and I repeated a short prayer over and over to myself. It seemed like hours before there was any further conversation. I was certain someone had gone to get an

100

ax and break down my wall. Then the deep voice spoke up again.

"Maybe he took to the woods," he said. "I certainly don't see any evidence that there was anyone in the house."

"How about those four glasses and that empty vodka bottle in the kitchen?" said another.

"I told you," was the complaining answer, "I had some friends in before I went to town, and we finished off that bottle. Ask my wife. She'll tell you too."

"She already told us," said deep-voice. "She told us right in front of you, so you'd both have the same story."

"O.K.," said the first with an exasperated note, "just arrest us, then, and charge us with harboring this criminal of yours. See what that gets you."

"Don't be so touchy," said deep-voice. "Nobody's accusing you of anything."

With that, the footsteps started away from my closet and went on downstairs. I began to breathe again.

A couple of hours passed. Then there were the steps of a single person on the stairs, and they came up and to the closet. The closet light was turned on and then the door to my cell slid open. I was greeted by mine host.

He was a bald, spare little man with gold-rimmed glasses and the look of one well hen-pecked. "How do you do," he said. "My name is Julius Morgan."

I got up off the mattress and shook his hand. "Thank you for your hospitality," I said.

"Oh, it's nothing," he said, waving vaguely. "Anything you want?"

"I could stand some dinner," I suggested.

"Clarabell will have it ready within an hour," he said. "I'll bring it up to you. Anything else?"

"Nothing," I said. "Thanks."

He went out, closing the wall door after himself, and he was back within the promised hour with a tray loaded down with hamburger steak, fresh corn, bread, coffee, and cherry pie.

And that's the way it was for two weeks, without any variation in our conversation. Every time I tried to get him to talk, he would say that same, "Oh, it's nothing," and wave vaguely. Then he would ask, "Anything you want?" That sort of thing can make you awfully lonesome for human companionship.

101

25 The two weeks took a long time to pass. Morgan brought me the *Times* and the *Mirror* daily, and I was interested at first in the colorful accounts of the prison-van break and the manhunt going on for me over some seventeen states. Most of the stories called the case baffling and none, after the first day, mentioned again the state car and its occupants, which were seen by a policeman in Ossining coming from the direction of the "massacre" a few minutes later. Maybe somebody told someone to lay off. The *Times,* on the third day, carried a very brief account of an interview with one Igor Godovisky, described as a clerk attached to the U.S.S.R. delegation to the United Nations, who admitted that he had once employed a John Miles as chauffeur, but knew nothing about him beyond the fact that he was a Roumanian national who had a proper passport. As the days passed, the stories got less informative, shorter, and further back in the papers. It was little more than a three-day sensation.

My waiting time enabled me to change my appearance somewhat by putting on a little more weight, which always shows up first in my face, and by growing a full beard. This came out mostly black, with spots of gray here and there, and I got Morgan to buy me a Homburg hat to go with it. I looked like one of those guys right off the boat on his way to Washington to pick up his handout. Along about the middle of July, on a hot, windless night, the black Chrysler that was once my personal vehicle drove up the road to the farm and brought Chenkov and action.

He came right up to my hideaway and told me we were on our way, at last.

"We have a rendezvous with your boat at 3:30 A.M. out on Long Island," he said. "We have a long way to go and not much time."

"Where on Long Island?" I asked.

"Just a little this side of Montauk. We have a man there to signal, and he will leave a sign which will tell us where we are to meet him."

That set me to thinking. Of all of the really stupid activities of the Russians, their carelessness with their submarines was outstanding. Bringing one in close enough to Long Island to land or take off a man was asking for it. Already, within the year, they had lost two submarines to our Navy off our East

102.

Coast, and now they were about to risk another. And yet, I had to get away on that one; I had to live long enough to get to Russia and get on with my job.

"I'll have to stop and make one phone call before I leave this country," I said.

Chenkov looked dubious. "Is that advisable?" he asked.

"I think so."

"There is no one we can trust," he warned.

"This is not a matter of trust," I said. "It is a comrade—a countryman who is close to me. You listen to the call and you will see what I mean."

"Not a woman?"

"No."

"I don't like it," he said. "General Godovisky was most emphatic about this one point—that you were to see or contact no one. Already he has been compromised because some of these stupid people at the U.N. have told the police that you were his chauffeur. It would finish him in America if there were any further slips."

We walked downstairs together and got into the car. Neither Morgan nor his wife were visible, so there were no farewells. Chenkov asked me to drive and handed me his license, made out in the name of Charles Miller, and some other papers. I swung the Chrysler around in the courtyard and headed down the lane, and he began briefing me on my submarine contact and its personnel, chief of which was the political commissar named Slotkin. He read off the route we were to take to Long Island from a slip of paper, naming the road numbers and the turns. We were headed back to New York and over the Whitestone Bridge. We took the Taconic Parkway and turned off through White Plains, and I stopped at a chain drugstore on a corner beside a parking meter.

"The phone call," I said. "You come with me and listen."

He sat there and looked at me. It was a touchy moment. I had to move fast if I was going to move at all.

"I'm afraid of it," he said.

I let out a deep sigh and shifted the subject. "I wish you were going home with me," I said. "This is a beautiful time of the year in Moscow."

A faraway look came into his eyes. "Some people have all the luck," he said. "I have my woman and my two children there, waiting for me. Will you do me a favor? Will you call on them and tell them that you saw me and that I am well?"

103

"Of course I will," I said. "It's the least I can do for a comrade and a friend."

He pulled a fountain pen and a notebook from his pocket and started to write the address. I opened the car door.

"I'll be right back," I said.

I hurried into the drugstore and found an empty phone booth. I dialed a Rector number, and a man's voice answered. I thanked God there was no delay. "Miles," I said. "Texas," he said (Code for "All Clear, Talk.") "Keep the Navy off the Atlantic near Long Island tonight," I said. "I'm riding a shark." "Done," he said. Chenkov came up to the booth door at that point and opened it. There was a mild look of annoyance on his face. I said into the phone in Russian, "I'll see you in a week. Goodbye, comrade," I hung up and came out of the booth.

"You see," I said to him, "nothing incriminating. I had to throw him off the track. He would be expecting me."

"Who?" he asked.

"This comrade," I said. "It is no secret. He is from my home town in Roumania and we fought the Germans together," I said.

"Maybe it is all right," he said. "Now we must hurry. We are very late."

It took us until 1:00 A.M. to get to Patchogue, but from there on the road was fairly empty and we made better time. Between Amagansett and Montauk, and west of the State Park, there is a long deserted stretch, with no houses and only brush-topped dunes and a few stunted trees as scenery. After a couple of miles of this we slowed down and came to a sign on a pole. The sign said, "No Hunting, Fishing, or Trespassing." Chenkov told me to stop there and we both got out. He went around to the trunk and opened it, taking out a large leather sack, with a padlock on the top, that contained courier mail. He handed the bag to me, then got into the car and drove away, to hide it in a previously selected spot. I ducked behind a dune and waited for him. He joined me in about a half-hour, carrying the sign on its pole, and we moved together toward the ocean.

It was a moonless night, with a few wisps of clouds passing between us and the stars. There was a fresh, cool breeze blowing in from the ocean, which was welcome after the hot ride. Nothing stirred in those barren acres except us.

It seemed like at least a mile to the water's edge. We came first to a low cliff, and on the top of this Chenkov planted the sign. He attached three small electric torches in a row to the top

104

of it with wire, and then he turned them on. They were so shaded that they were visible only to seaward and within a limited area. Then we slid down the cliff to the beach and we sat down to wait. Presently we saw the dark form of our signalman sliding down the cliff, and he came up to us and said in Russian:

"They're late."

"They're always late," said Chenkov sourly. "If we operated on their schedules, we'd never get anything done."

"This is not a good place to stay too long," said the other. "We have less than an hour before a patrol will be by."

Chenkov pulled out a pack of cigarettes, thought better of it and put them back.

"You will be sure to see my woman?" he said to me.

"Of course I will," I said. "I will do that first, after I have reported in."

"That makes me very happy," he said.

A half-hour passed in silence. The vast expanse of blackness that was the ocean remained unbroken.

"Damn their souls," said Chenkov, using an idiom that was seldom heard in Communist Russia. "In a few minutes we will have to go back and do this all over again another night."

"That is true, comrade," said the other.

Five minutes more. Ten. Then a faint red light flashed briefly, far to our left. Chenkov spotted it first. "That may be it," he said, pointing. "Look out there. Follow my finger." We all stood up and looked.

There was a second brief flash. Then there were three in a row, very fast. Our signalman had taken a flashlight from his pocket. It had a green lens on it. He flashed back two short, then three short. The red light flashed twice in reply.

We sat down again. Five minutes passed. Ten. Fifteen.

"Those pigs!" exclaimed Chenkov. "Now we are in the danger period." He turned to me. "Do you want to take a chance, or shall we tell them to go away?"

"I'll take a chance," I said. "Let them come in."

"It's your neck," he said. "Maybe it's ours too. Well, this is no time to be timid."

"There is an old Russian saying," said the signalman. "He who hesitates is lost."

"They have that in English too," I said. "Probably stole it from us."

"Very likely," said the signalman.

We heard the faint sound of oars slapping the water, still off

105

to our left, and we got up and walked up the beach. Chenkov carried the courier pouch. About fifty yards up, we made out a rubber boat with one rower in it. The water was as calm as a lake, with only small ripples breaking on the shore. He stopped just off the shore and called:

"Hello, comrades, give the password."

"Stalin is great," said Chenkov.

"That is no lie," said the rower. He came on in, and I stepped into his craft. Chenkov and the signalman came to the water's edge with me and handed me the bag, then shook my hand.

"Good luck," said Chenkov. "And don't forget my woman."

"I won't," I said. "Good luck to you both."

My oarsman was barefooted and he jumped out and pushed us off the beach. Then he hopped back in and picked up his oars.

"Welcome to the Soviet navy," he said to me.

"Thanks," I replied. "I hope you have more of it than this boat."

"We have the greatest navy in the world," he said. "But confidentially, our submarine stinks like a sewer. You will not enjoy it."

"I am sorry to hear that," I said. "But it is worth much discomfort to get away from this accursed country."

He stopped rowing and leaned toward me. "You don't have to use propaganda on me," he said. "I was ashore once, for a week in Florida."

"What you saw," I said severely, "was just the outward appearance. You did not see what was underneath."

He rowed in silence until we picked up the silhouette of the submarine. Then he said, "You may be right, but on the other hand, you may be wrong."

"That sounds logical," I agreed.

We came alongside the starboard deck of the submersible just forward of the conning tower, and several hands reached for mine. I handed up the pouch first and then was helped aboard. I took off my Homburg and bowed to the quarterdeck. One of those who had helped me up put his arm around my shoulder and said urgently:

"We must hurry, comrade. Come this way and climb this ladder."

He led me to the bridge ladder and I scrambled up. There were a couple of officers on the bridge and one of them pointed to a hatch at my feet and said, "Hurry down. We've got to dive immediately."

106

We were already under way and I could feel the throbbing of the powerful diesels as I slid down to the main control room. All those topside came tumbling after me, the skipper last, and the hatch was banged shut and secured. I stood aft in the control room watching them and listening to the orders of the skipper, and noticing, for the first time, the thick, ripe stench that came billowing up from the hatch forward of the periscope which led to the vessel's innards. My oarsman certainly could not have been accused of exaggerating. It was so thick you could feel it.

"Rig for diving!" the skipper ordered. "Rudder fifteen degrees left. All diesels full ahead." He scanned the sea with the periscope as gongs sounded throughout the ship. Gradually the deck began tilting forward. We started down.

"Level off at snorkle depth," the skipper called. "Rudder amidships. Steady as she goes. Scan with radar for one minute and give me a report."

A big Russian, with boots and pea jacket and the familiar red-star insignia on his cap, but without any braid or other mark of rank, had moved beside me, and when I looked at him I saw that he was regarding me speculatively.

"Colonel Miles?" he said, sticking out his hand. "I am Slotkin, political commissar of this vessel of the People's Navy. Welcome aboard the *A. I. Mikoyan.*"

I shook hands with him with accustomed Slavic vigor. "Glad to meet you, comrade," I said. "I was told to report to you by Comrade Chenkov."

"And how is my dear friend Chenkov?" he asked.

"Lonesome for Moscow," I replied. "He misses his fatherland and his wife and his babies."

"We all do," said Slotkin. "But those accursed Americans won't let us live in peace in this world, so we must defend ourselves."

"It is a sad state of affairs for all of us," I sympathized. "I have just spent six miserable years in their country."

"You have an accent that I don't place," he said.

"I am a native of Roumania," I said.

The radar man, who was on the port side of the control room and forward, suddenly called, "Vessel bearing 340. It is approaching us at high speed."

"Take her down!" commanded the skipper. "Stop all diesels! Electric motors ahead two thirds! Down snorkle! Give me a depth reading!"

"Thirty-two fathoms!" called the sound man.

107

"Stop all motors!" ordered the skipper, his eyes on the depth gauge. "Fill all tanks and let her settle to the bottom!"

We leveled off and seemed to be suspended in space for a long ten minutes. Then there was a bump forward and another aft as the deck settled into a slope to stern.

"Cut all generators and pumps!" ordered the skipper. "Man the sound stack and all detectors. Members of the ship's company will remain where they are and will make no sounds nor move about."

"Propellers approaching off the port bow," reported the sound man.

We all waited, holding our breaths.

"They're using asdic," reported the sound man. "Now they are scanning us. They are right on us, from bow to stern!"

The skipper was standing with one hand on the engine-room telegraph, his face tense, and sweat rolling down his temples. Commissar Slotkin was staring straight ahead with unseeing eyes. He was bracing himself with a hand on the bulkhead behind him. The four others in the control room were frozen in attitudes of fearful waiting.

I had a lot of faith in Bureau-X, but not enough to keep the chill out of my spine. Through no fault of theirs and with the best intentions, they might have failed to make the proper contacts in time, or this single vessel now stalking us could have been out of communication with its command through error or intent. For no particular reason. I began counting. I suppose I was curious to see just what number my life would stop on, if it were going to stop.

"They are twin screws," the sound man reported. "Estimated speed now 12 knots. Range about 1500 yards."

"Just give me the range readings," said the skipper.

"Note any changes in course and speed," said Slotkin. It was not said in the tone of an order—rather as a suggestion.

"Of course, comrade," said the skipper, turning and nodding at him. "Note course and speed."

"Range 1200 yards. Course and speed unchanged."

"Right," said the skipper.

"Range 1000 yards, course unchanged. Speed diminished. About 10 knots."

"That is not good," said the skipper, turning to Slotkin. "Have you any suggestions?"

Slotkin shrugged. "It is not a good prospect," he said. "No, I have no suggestions."

"Range 750 yards," reported the sound man.

108

"Now come the hedgehogs," said Slotkin, turning to me. "You know them—their rocket bombs?"

"I've heard of them," I said. "But I never expected to meet any of them on this end."

"Range 600 yards. Course unchanged. Speed 10 knots," said the sound man.

I stopped my silly counting and said the Lord's Prayer silently. Then I looked at each man and I wondered what he was thinking at this moment when he was facing death. What does an atheist think of when he is meeting what to him must be the end of all things? Does he find in his innermost being a consolation in his worship of Stalin and Lenin? Is this sufficient as a *raison d'être*? Or does he just ignore metaphysics and dwell on his own commanding fear, driving all other thoughts from his mind? It was an interesting speculation—but quite fruitless.

"Range 300 yards. Course and speed unchanged," said the sound man.

"Maybe we should make a run for it," said the skipper to Slotkin. "It would appear that they're not going to use their hedgehog but will depth-bomb us. We might get away from that."

"Stay where you are," said Slotkin. "I'm gambling that they didn't pick us up after all."

It seemed like a month before the next report.

"Vessel passing overhead. Speed unchanged," said the sound man.

I guess we all braced ourselves then. I know I wondered just what it would be like on the receiving end of a depth charge. The only thing I was sure of was that it would not be pleasant.

Then we heard a faint explosion, as from a great distance. It was too mild to shake us, and we would not have heard it at all if we had not been so quiet. This was followed by another, and then another. I counted them—eight. They were spaced two, and four, and two. They were probably made by a deck gun.

I relaxed and leaned against the bulkhead. That two and four and two meant only one thing, and had been used for years by my Naval Intelligence unit to signal those within hearing.

It meant, "All Clear."

109

26 It took us twenty-seven unbelievable days to reach the Soviet Union. Our original objective had been the Baltic Sea submarine base at Tallin, in Estonia, but we had so many difficulties with our vessel, including three major breakdowns, that it was decided not to risk the crowded waters through the narrow Kattegat, since we had no guarantee of being able to stay submerged. As a result, we headed for the naval base at Murmansk, and it was fortunate that we did, because, among our other troubles, we lost all the fuel oil out of our starboard tanks during one of our breakdowns, when a crewman opened the wrong valves, and we had to break radio silence and call for a tanker.

My joy and relief at finally getting out of that pigboat even overshadowed the triumph of landing, finally, in the Soviet Union. I had lost at least fifteen pounds on the trip through inability to stomach the appalling stuff served up as food, and I was closer to complete depression than I remember ever having been. And that state of mind is a dangerous one for a person whose life depends upon the correctness of every move, every word, and every thought.

Well, I lived through it. And I was certain that Magellan's tour around the world was a joy ride compared to our Atlantic crossing. This submarine of ours was one of the German-built boats the Russians had latched onto after World War II, and I had heard from our Navy back in the forties that we had been forced to give up on them, after long tests, because they were of faulty design and construction and would not stand up. Nearly every piece of machinery on our boat failed at one time or another, and this was helped no little by the typically moujik attitude of the crewmen toward all things mechanical, which is generally one of contempt salted with ignorance. The officers knew their business well enough to get by, but the kind of discipline one encounters under Communism will hardly produce the nicely balanced teamwork that is so necessary to operate to full efficiency such a complicated piece of machinery as a submersible. And after all, what good would it have done to shoot or imprison the men for carelessness or other acts of omission? Then you wouldn't have had anyone to run your boat; but under Communism no other way has been discovered to enforce discipline, either.

When we lost our fuel oil, we set a rendezvous with a tanker

110

in the western vicinity of the Barents Sea, off North Cape, and as though this wasn't bad enough, sitting on the surface where British and Norwegian planes could spot us, a crewman lit a cigarette on deck while we were refueling and started a fire that very nearly did for us. Fortunately the tanker had foam sprayers rigged, and the blaze was put under control with only minor damage, the death of one of our men and the burning of two others.

So I had sufficient reason to enjoy leaving the *A. I. Mikoyan*, and by the time I reached the M.V.D. headquarters with Slotkin, lugging the courier pouch, I was almost jaunty. This headquarters was in a building on Murmansk's main street, and we reached there quickly from the naval dockyard in a police car driven by a friend of the commissar. Slotkin took me to the office of the commandant, a major by the name of Gussik, on the ground floor, and I noted that the layout of the building coincided in every detail with the briefing I had received on it from Bureau-X.

But I had had no briefing on Major Gussik, and he was a different kettle of *kasha*. He was one of these Mongolian types so common in Russia. He had black, straight hair that grew so low on his forehead that it almost met his eyebrows, and he had a thin mouth and hostile eyes.

Slotkin introduced me, but the major did not get up or offer me his hand. He just sat there looking nasty.

"Comrade Miles is to receive transportation to Moscow so that he may report to M.V.D. headquarters there," said Slotkin.

"By whose orders?" said Gussik.

"These are the orders of General Godovisky," said Slotkin.

"I know nothing about that," replied Gussik tartly. "Why have I not been informed?"

"We were in no position to send messages," said Slotkin.

"And I am in no position to comply with such a request," said Gussik. "Inform General Godovisky that I await formal orders from him."

"General Godovisky is not available to receive messages," explained the commissar. "He is in America. We cannot communicate with him for many weeks."

"I am in no hurry," replied Gussik, settling back in his chair.

This was getting thick. It was obvious that Gussik did not know who Godovisky was—which would not be an unusual situation in Russia at all. Very few of the underlings knew the top men, even in their own divisions. But it was making my "homecoming" a battle with red tape, rather than a wide-open

111

welcome for a "hero"—and in the Russian code, with the public murder of an assassin and the private killings of countless "enemies" during my sabotage operations on the credit side of my ledger, I was an authentic hero.

"I am Colonel Miles, attached to the Ekonomicheskoe Upravlenie," I butted in. "I am on an important mission."

"Important for you," said Gussik, turning a baleful eye on me and examining me from my Homburg to my American brogues. "Let me see your papers."

I tossed him my Roumanian passport, some papers Shenkov had given me, and a temporary identification card which Slotkin had made out. He looked at the card first, with studied disdain. Then he read with a great show of deliberation the Chenkov papers, which included a copy of my commission and an E.K.U. identification signed by Godovisky. Then he thumbed through the passport.

"This is not even your photograph," he said. "This is not the photograph of a man with a beard. There is no proper visa or entry permit for the Soviet Union. These papers are not at all in order, and so I must assume that you have entered my country illegally."

"The Major is very astute," I said. "Will he please explain to me how a member of the M.V.D. can enter the Soviet Union illegally."

"You have the accent of a foreigner," he replied, as though that explained everything.

I tossed my M.V.D. medallion on his desk in front of him and I made a speech. "I am acting as an official courier," I said, "and I do not intend to be delayed by your red tape or your refusal to accept my identification, which is clear enough for any officer in the secret police. My orders are very specific and they are that I report to Moscow as soon as possible. I am one who believes in carrying out orders, and that is exactly what I intend to do right now."

He picked up my medallion and studied it. He tossed it speculatively in a big, hairy hand, then rang a bell on his desk. A bulky character in the M.V.D. uniform of blue trimmed with red piping, and wearing a Sam Browne belt and pistol, came in from an anteroom, marched up to the desk, and stood beside me.

Gussik said to me, "All that you say may be true, but my orders, too, are specific, and I, too, am a man who believes in carrying out his orders. My orders are to admit no persons into this port without prior notification, under any circumstances.

112

That is plain enough. So I ask you, why was I not notified of your coming? And you do not give me a satisfactory answer. Therefore, I shall have to place you under arrest until I can communicate with Moscow and determine your status."

He handed me back my medallion and motioned to the guard. "Take him away," he said.

That really burned me, but I doubt that I would have done anything about it right then and there if this big, stupid guard had not pulled out his pistol and put it on me. That was too much. I turned to him as though I were going to follow him out, then disarmed him with one of those misdirecting waves of one hand, while the other does the work. He pulled the trigger, but the shot went wide, as it was calculated to do, and I had the gun in my hand. For good measure, then, I cracked him on the neck with the side of my palm, just at the right spot, and he went out cold.

I turned to Gussik, who was sitting there as motionless as a Buddha, with a scowl on his face, and I slid the gun across the desk to him.

"I do not mind your having this because I trust your judgment," I said. "But one thing I will not stand for is to have any of your subordinates threaten me with firearms. If you wish to place me in custody, please indicate to me where I shall spend this custody, and I will go there without escort. Is that understood?"

It was, perhaps, a strong statement under the circumstances, but it was calculated to appeal to one such as Gussik. I know these Mongol types and their appreciation of forceful methods.

Gussik glanced at the gun but he did not touch it. He seemed to be lost in thought. I saw Slotkin, out of the corner of my eye, standing with a look of surprise and disbelief on his face. He was fidgeting from one foot to the other. Finally Gussik looked me in the eye and his scowl deepened.

"That beard of yours is misleading," he said. "I have never seen one move so fast. That is an excellent trick."

"It comes in handy," I agreed.

His face relaxed and he shoved the guard's gun aside and picked up my papers again.

"I suppose I could telephone Moscow about you," he said. "That would be the quickest way. Whom shall I call?"

"Commanding officer of the E.K.U. section," I said. "Or, if he's not in, I presume his aide will know."

"And where is this section located?" he asked. "These peo-

113

ple move around so much, it is hard to keep track of some of them."

"Furkasovsky Alley," I said. "This is one of the oldest sections in the M.V.D. I am surprised that you do not know it."

"I have enough trouble keeping track of my own," he said. Then he turned to Slotkin.

"Have you no duties?" he asked him.

"Not at present," replied Slotkin.

"This is no place for a political commissar," he said. "You have reported in. Now I say goodbye."

Slotkin shook my hand and left. Then Gussik rang his bell again and he ordered the answering guard to remove his fallen companion. "Get him a drink," he said. Then he turned back to me.

"We should have a drink too," he suggested. "I must see that you are properly welcomed to the Soviet Union. We can do all of this telephoning later."

"I'm with you, Major," I said. "I can use one, at this point, after that pigboat."

He put on his cap and we went out together to his car, a large Zis, parked at the curb below, and he drove me to an establishment in the old residential quarter of the city, which was a combined restaurant, bar, and bordello for the high-ranking Communists of the area. It was a three-story stone building on a courtyard and it was run by a man and woman who obviously disliked each other and their jobs. They treated us well enough, however, for we were, from the standpoint of Russia under Communism, visiting royalty. There is none of higher estate in any Russian city than the commandant of the secret police; such is the caste system in this Utopia of the proletariat.

We were presented with their finest distillations, their most succulent dishes, and their youngest and most accomplished girls; it was not only a duty but an honor. Gussik wasted no time getting into a room with a companion, and I determined, after a couple of drinks, that this establishment had a bathroom with plenty of hot water. I picked a big, strong country girl by the name of Gasha and appointed her my bath maid. I sent . her off to fill my tub, had a final vodka, then went in and soaked off the traces of the submarine. A man can pick up plenty of such traces in four weeks.

After my bath, I ordered dinner, and this was served by the *patronne* in her own dining room. She informed me with tact and hesitation that it was very unlikely I would get Major

114

Gussik sobered up and out of there that night, and she suggested that I take one of the rooms. This did not appeal to me because of the mounting din of revelry overhead, and when I demurred, she mentioned the Arctic Hotel and said her associate would take me there.

It was around midnight, but still daylight in this far northern latitude, when we left the house and drove in the major's car to the hotel. My guide took me in and introduced me to the clerk as a friend of Major Gussik, and so I had no difficulty getting a room. I was able to relax completely for the first time in a month, and I slept until noon. Upon awakening, I found an M.V.D. man stationed outside my door, and he ordered a good breakfast of fresh herring and tea for me. After eating, he escorted me to the M.V.D. headquarters, and I was greeted with pleasing deference by the guards on duty and taken to Gussik's office.

The major looked none the worse for his night out and shook my hand with a show of friendship.

"But why did you leave?" he asked. "Were the girls not to your taste?"

"They were fine," I said, "but I was too tired, after four weeks on that submarine. I couldn't have stayed awake for Catherine the Great."

He commiserated with me, then he said, "I have heard from Moscow. I telephoned them the first thing this morning, and they want to see you. They have ordered you to fly."

"Fine," I said, "when do I leave?"

"We will have a plane for you in an hour," he said. "Our regular air-liner does not leave until tomorrow, and I have received permission to send you in an army plane."

He gave me a sheaf of forms which included travel permit, entry permit to the Central Airport at Moscow, a permit to leave Murmansk, a special form designating me as a courier on official duty, and a form countersigned by the army commandant in the area assigning an airplane to my use. The only thing lacking was a baptismal certificate. . . . He didn't forget a box lunch.

Gussik himself drove me to the airport, which was a couple of miles south of the city, and he regaled me during the ride with a complete rundown of his night's victories, which were several, to hear him tell it. We checked in at Operations without any hitch and walked out together to a twin-engined cabin job on the apron, modeled after our Beechcraft. It had red stars on wings and fuselage, and the squadron designation on the nose. The pilot was waiting for us at the foot of the ramp, and he shook my hand and called me comrade. A half-dozen secret police were around the apron, and they watched us narrowly as I bade Gussik farewell and boarded the plane.

There were a couple of Red Air Force pilots in one of the seats and they nodded to me as I sat opposite them. Our pilot took his place, started the engines, and taxied very fast to the end of a runway. He swung the craft around and opened up his engines for the takeoff without any of the warming up and checking of instruments that one becomes accustomed to in America. None of that folderol for the Russians! And if one should be foolish enough to bring up the subject, they'll look at you with astonishment and reply that if you want to be safe, then don't fly. There's no answer to that. . . .

For a thousand miles and five hours we flew south, over the forests of the Kola Peninsula, across the edge of the White Sea, over Lake Onega, and then over the endless steppes north of the Red Capital. No facts about this workers' paradise can be gleaned from the air, beyond the vast extent of this Soviet land. It is only on the ground, among the people in the cities and on their farms, that you see the grim, ruthless, unsmiling nature of it all. For this is truly a land of toil and poverty and hopelessness, and it is today as it has been for hundreds of years. Communism has changed it little, and nothing for the better for the average Russian. The only change perhaps has been to increase his burden. You do not have to be in Russia long to learn this. . . . Naturally I had not observed Russia under the tsars, but I have heard about it and I have read about it all my life, and I know from those who have seen it that the revolution has altered nothing, from the slave labor camps of Siberia to the regular famines of the Ukraine; from the brutality of the masters in the Kremlin in Moscow to the humorless, joyless lot of the moujiks seeking to scrape their bread out of an unfriendly land. To find out how Russia is today, read about how Russia was a hundred years ago, and then you will have it.

I landed at the Central Airport in Moscow on August 5, 1957, carrying my courier pouch and feeling a deep sense of gratification at having arrived, at last, at one of my major goals. My spirits were high because now I would begin to reap the benefits of all those years of work and planning and discipline. I swung through the gate into the huge waiting room of the airport and stopped off to one side of the doors, looking at the faces of the passing throng and trying to spot one that would be looking for me. Finally I found two of them, belonging to

116

a couple of gents in well-cut dark civilian clothes, which appeared ostentatious amid the uniforms, and they were standing beside an information counter in the center of the room, giving a close scrutiny to all who passed. I walked over to them, unnoticed, and slid the courier pouch down to my feet.

"I'm Miles," I said. "Were you hunting for me?"

They both turned toward me and gave me hard-eyed stares of disapproval, probably because they had failed to spot me first.

"Yes," said one finally. "Where did you come from?"

I motioned with my arm. "That way," I said.

"Well, comrade," said the other, "you have caused us no little trouble. We have been waiting here two hours."

"I got on a slow plane," I said. "So, welcome to Moscow, eh, comrades?"

They both loosened up a little and stuck out their hands and gave me their names. I greeted them with my usual vigor, picked up the pouch, and said, "You lead the way, I'll follow. I've had a rough trip and I want to settle as soon as possible."

We went out to a parking space and climbed into a Zis, one driving and the other sitting in the rear with me. They didn't want to talk, so I babbled on about this and that, confining my questions to those that could be answered by grunts. Inside of an hour we pulled up in front of that famed and dread yellow brick building on Furkasovsky Alley, which is the headquarters of the M.V.D. The two got out first and I followed. As I turned to them on the sidewalk I saw a man coming out of the glass doors of the headquarters. He stopped an instant before turning north and walking away, and he looked me full in the face, but without recognition.

He was the guy from back in New York—from the brawl at the South Street pier and the Third Precinct Police Station whom I had hunted for so long—the unfriendly character who had called himself Alexis Ivanovich Bodine.

27 M.V.D. headquarters in Moscow accepted me for what I appeared to be, which is saying little enough. Such acceptance in no wise relieved me from the responsibility of proving myself all over again, nor did it ever discourage the ceaseless investigation that went on into my life, my thoughts, my actions, and my attitudes. Being an officer in

117

the M.V.D. merely invited a more concentrated and thorough search of my antecedents, my past and my present, and there was never a moment of any day or night that relaxation or a careless word or thought were permitted. Necessary for mere survival in that company of superhuman robots was a kind of self-discipline that has taken generations of selective breeding to perfect, and it is as completely foreign to the free world as the omnipresent fear under which it exists.

Friendship is unknown. Love is unknown. Pleasant emotion is unknown. Any human impulse by which we in America are taught to live is, in this Russia of the M.V.D., an aberrative weakness that will surely and certainly lead to destruction. The only safe emotional reaction, just in case one ever felt an overwhelming need to identify himself with the human race, was hate. . . .

It was safe to assume that the courier pouch I had brought with me contained a complete dossier on Jan Miles, and after some four hours of waiting in an anteroom on the third floor of the Furkasovsky Alley building, under the scrutiny of two granite-faced agents, I was ordered into the office of a Brigadier General Igor Zurakov, who had only recently returned to favor from exile in Siberia for some technical deviation which Bureau-X had analyzed for me as jealousy. Zurakov was a gaunt, jaundice-skinned Georgian with a nervous tic in his left eye that often gave his severe face a momentary look of zany humor. He was both impatient and garrulous, and a most difficult man to spend any time with; he never permitted a subordinate to relax in his presence and he seldom permitted anyone talking to him to finish a sentence.

"Miles—that is not a Roumanian name," he said to me.

"No, sir," I agreed.

"What is it, then?"

I shrugged. "English, maybe. I never knew much about my ——"

"Never mind. We will find out. I suppose you are all soft and sentimental after those years in America?"

"No, sir," I said.

"Don't contradict me," he stated. "How was Godovisky when you saw him last?"

"In good health," I said. "However, he lives in constant ——"

"I know," he interrupted. "I know how he lives. Did he give you any message for me?"

"No, sir."

118

"Good. I want no personal messages from him. So you saved his life?" There was a distinct note of bitterness in his voice.

"Yes, sir," I said.

"And he saved yours. A very nice, friendly gesture. I hope you appreciate it."

"I will appreciate it if I can be of some use to the M.V.D.," I said hurriedly, to get it all in.

"That will remain to be seen," he said. "Sometimes we can use men with your training, although you would be a lot more valuable to us in America than here. It was a great mistake and very shortsighted of General Godovisky to permit you to become involved in those American courts. I am sure that affair could have been handled differently."

I had no answer to that.

"Well, don't you agree?" he demanded.

"No," I said. "I do not."

"What! Do you propose to tell me that you and General Godovisky were not clever enough to have avoided capture and trial?"

"Not under the circumstances," I said.

"And what were these so important circumstances? What is of more importance to an M.V.D. officer than to outwit our enemies and emerge victorious?"

"In this case, the life of General Godovisky," I said.

"Humpf," he said. "That is your version of it."

"It is," I agreed. "My choice in that instance was to kill the general's assassin or to——"

"Enough!" he said. "This is not a debate! I am impressed by several things in your record, and so I have decided to continue temporarily your commission as a colonel. If you can prove that you speak German as well as you have claimed, we can use you in the West. . . . But you will have to go to school first, to show that you deserve such rank. There is no place in our organization for those who are not thoroughly familiar with all the latest methods of our organization—the science of the secret police. This you will have to learn. You will report to Colonel Malinkov in room 254 and you will take orders from him until further notice. And shave off that beard. Dismissed."

I saluted, executed a proper about-face, and marched out. I went to the office of this Colonel Malinkov on the floor below, and after an hour's wait under the suspicious eyes of half a dozen clerks and a bang-haired secretary with extraordinarily large breasts and fair gams, I was taken into his presence. He

119

was another gaunt type, with a Lincolnesque ugliness and big, hard-knuckled hands that hung on bony wrists. He was about my age and height, but thirty pounds lighter, and his uniform, of an excellent light-weight worsted, hung loosely on his frame. He smoked cigarettes constantly, lighting one from the other, and seldom took them from his mouth, so that he blew ashes and sparks as he talked. His lapels and the desk in front of him were full of this debris. Malinkov came from the Valdai Hills region, the son of a farmer, and had been educated as a schoolmaster, a profession which he followed but briefly. Outside of a normal lack of humor and an inclination to view all things literally, he was not a bad type.

He shook hands with me and he offered me a chair, which was a good indication that he had found nothing in me, as yet, to be afraid of.

"So you have just come from America?" was his opening gambit. "Tell me, comrade, what do you think of that country?"

"I don't like it," I said. "It is not for us. It is a soft country, undisciplined, decadent. They are altogether concerned in America with money and the pleasures of the flesh, and one yearns for an ordered life and the work for great things."

"That is what I have heard," he said. "You confirm what most visitors to the West say, and yet . . ."

He sighed and blew ashes and sparks at me.

"The outward appearance is misleading," I said. "I have heard many of our own people who have been there talk of their cities and their railroads and their industries and their automobiles—but when you look beneath this surface sham, then you see all of the bad things; the enslaved masses being ground under the heel of capitalism."

The familiar cliché brought a knowing light to his eyes. "It is our duty to liberate these slaves," he said with solemn conviction. "Mother Russia will give birth to the new freedom for these downtrodden masses."

All of that sounds ludicrous to an American, but it is what these Russians actually believe and parrot. Here was one of the enforcers of the most vicious police state the modern world has known—one of the masters of the 190,000,000 abject slaves—whose entire thinking had been so warped by the propaganda of the Big Lie that he was ready to stake his life on it. I don't expect American readers to understand the peculiar and senseless psychology that produces such an attitude. Only a Russian, born in despair, nurtured on hate, and given a monomaniacal dic-

120

tator to worship as a god, could encompass such a notion, and that is the one important point about Russians that one must always bear in mind. They do not think as Americans, in any way, ever. One must never forget that the hundreds of years of Western civilization that are the background of American thought are no part of the Russian inheritance. What misleads so many of us, I know, is that, dressed up in Western clothes and seen in the setting of a civilized exterior, Russians look just like other human beings. But you've got to remember that they're not.

"I suppose you have many others here in the M.V.D. who have been in America and who know the injustices of American life," I said.

"Yes," he replied, "we do have many. America has always been the principal enemy of the Communist democracy."

"I should like to meet some of them and compare notes," I suggested.

"You will have that opportunity because you will work with our American section for the time being," he said. "I am the chief of that section and that is why you are reporting to me."

"I saw one man when I was coming into the building at noon that I once met in New York," I said. I described him—the one who had posed as Alexis Bodine.

Colonel Malinkov became thoughtful. "Very likely you saw Captain Petsky," he said. "He was in New York for several years on a most unusual assignment. We use Captain Petsky for bait."

That was nothing I did not know.

"He called himself Alexis Bodine when I met him then," I said.

"You have a good memory," said Malinkov. "That is the name and the identity that he uses."

"Then I take it," I said, "that he is the bait to catch this same Alexis Bodine?"

Malinkov's sober face set into lines of grim determination. He pointed a bony finger at me and emphasized each phrase with a downward swing. "We have been hunting for this brutal killer for almost fifteen years, and I am sick at the sound of his name," he said. "He is a vicious and ruthless enemy of the people and he must be eliminated from this earth. He has killed eleven of our agents that we know of, and one of them was the younger brother of the deputy commandant of the M.V.D.—General Godovisky!"

"I heard of this Bodine during the War," I said, digesting to

121

myself this startling news about Godovisky's brother. "He was in my native Roumania in 1944 as an agent for the Americans, and I was surprised when I met one who called himself Bodine in New York."

"Why were you surprised?" he demanded.

"Because," I said, "I have also heard that this Bodine was killed in Italy."

"Don't you believe it!" he exclaimed. "Bodine is not dead; that we are sure of. The Americans are hiding him; they are making it appear that he was killed in the war, but we know better."

"Ah, then I take it the M.V.D. has seen him since?"

"No," said Malinkov, relaxing to a slight degree, "no one, so far as we know, has seen him since he was in Italy. We have an excellent description of him, along with his finger prints and photographs, which we obtain from his American Navy file in Washington, so we know what he looks like. He has never turned up anywhere that we have been able to determine."

I looked at my fingertips and made a print with my thumb on the glass top of his desk. Those fingerprints that he had I knew about very well. They were not mine.

"If no one has ever seen him, then maybe he *was* killed in Italy," I said.

"No," said Malinkov, "we know better. If he had been killed, then his estate would have been distributed to his heirs, according to the laws of America. That was never done. We happen to know that Bodine had a considerable fortune, and in America when a rich person dies his estate does not just vanish. But all of it has vanished, and that is one of our deepest mysteries. What did Bodine do with it—and what did he do with himself?"

"That is a most interesting problem," I said. "I should like to join the hunt for this criminal."

"Perhaps you will have the opportunity," he said. "Within the past few months we have abandoned our search in America and soon we hope to institute it in Europe. He spoke many languages well, and he is familiar with the Balkans and with Germany, so we may try there."

"Why," I said, "he even may be right here in Russia!"

"I could wish for nothing more than that!" he exclaimed.

"I hope you will call on me if I can be of any assistance," I said. "I have had good training in tracking down people."

"We know about that," he agreed, "but I think our use of Captain Petsky will eventually prove effective. Sooner or later

122

this Bodine will hear that another man is posing as himself, and when he hears of it, then Bodine will try to kill him—that we are sure of. We know our man. He will not hesitate to kill."

"Might you not sacrifice Petsky's life?" I asked.

"It is the chance we all take," he said, reverting to typical Russian fatalism. "What is to be will be. We take what precautions we can. Petsky is at all times under the observation of a bodyguard who will shoot without hesitation. More than that we cannot do."

"I must say this Bodine sounds like a fabulous person," I said.

"He is a cat with nine lives," said Malinkov, baring his teeth. "He is the cleverest agent, by far, ever developed in America. This is not the first trap the M.V.D. has set for this vile, ruthless murderer!"

Now there was a nice compliment, considering its source. And I regretted exceedingly that I was in no position to stand up and take a bow.

28 I spent my next eight or ten hours in the endless process of filling out forms and otherwise being registered, identified and inducted into the Moscow headquarters of the M.V.D. There was a brief break around 1:00 A.M. when a sudden headache reminded me that I had not eaten since the afternoon, when I had cracked Gussik's box lunch on the plane. When I communicated my hunger to Malinkov, he summoned a mess sergeant, who escorted me to a senior officers' mess on the top floor, where a huge buffet was set up with a dozen varieties of hot and cold meats, fowl, pounds of caviar, smörgåsbord, steaming tureens of borscht, and, for the less fastidious, boiled cabbage and black bread. Also, there were beer, wines, the inevitable vodka, Scotch, liqueurs, and tea. It was a layout that one might have envisioned at Maxim's or the Colony, but never in Communist Moscow. I was very happy that some of my new comrades had Western tastes and I ate my fill, drank a couple of Scotches, and then returned to Malinkov's suite to complete my work. I had been assigned to an office adjoining his, with a male secretary to help me, and along about 4:00 A.M., when I had reached the bottom of the

123

pile of forms, a barber came in and announced that he would shave off my beard.

Malinkov arrived at the same time and explained that it was necessary so that I could be properly photographed. When the barbering was completed and the photographs taken, in a special studio in the basement rigged with scores of lights, Malinkov picked me up and we walked out together, into the early morning air of Moscow. Dawn was just breaking—the most beautiful time of day in any city.

"We have arranged for you to stay at the Hotel Mossoviet," he told me. "It is just a few squares from here and we can walk, if you wish."

"Suits me fine," I said. "I don't know your city and I shall have to do a great deal of walking in it to learn my way around."

He chatted amiably enough, pointing out landmarks and commenting on them, and when we reached the main entrance of the hotel, he pointed south and said:

"There before you is Red Square. At the south end is St. Basil's, and that wall to your right is the Kremlin. This is the heart and the soul of our city and of the Soviet Union. There is no more historic spot on earth."

I arranged my face into a proper attitude of enraptured attention and looked upon this square that had witnessed the pomp and bloodshed of eight hundred years of barbarian rulers. On every side were the monuments and the relics that spoke of violence and death—from onion-domed St. Basil's, whose architect was imprisoned and blinded so that this cathedral would never be duplicated, to the crenelated walls of the Kremlin, which contain the ashes of bolshevism's executioners. This Red Square is indeed red—with blood. A fit site for the heart of the Communist dictatorship. And I thought without regret that, within a matter of months, all of this would be destroyed by an atom bomb.

"It is overwhelming," I said solemnly.

Malinkov was pleased and he took my arm as we mounted the steps to the hotel lobby. Inside, at the desk, we were informed that my room was ready, and Malinkov accompanied me to it. We went to a comfortably furnished mahogany-and-old-lace chamber on the top floor, facing the square, and he explained that only M.V.D. officers and the most trusted party members were permitted to occupy such rooms.

"There is always the danger," he explained, "that an important party official could be ambushed from one of these

124

windows. That is your first lesson in the duties of the M.V.D. in Moscow."

"A sensible precaution," I agreed.

"At all times while you are here you must be particularly alert," he continued. "Spend much of your time by this window and learn to observe every person within eyesight and every movement that may in any way be suspicious."

He took me to the window and pointed below. "Watch how the people move and where they go. Miss nothing. Get in the habit of doing this, and do it always. Remember what you see, and write frequent reports of all that you have observed. You will find it is excellent practice."

I thanked him and assured him that I would comply with his orders.

"And at night, when you turn your light on or off, give the light switch an extra flick, so that the light will flash once. This will signal those watching below that your room is properly occupied. If you do not do this, you may have visitors."

"That shall be done," I said. "All of these matters are very well thought out."

"You will find that we are careful," he said. "Now you get some sleep, and report back to me at 1:00 P.M. You may order your breakfast in your room, or you may go to the dining room, whichever you prefer. I would suggest that you eat it here—and look out your window."

We shook hands and he departed, and I went over to the window and sat in a comfortable chair and looked across at the graceful tower of the Saviour rising from the Kremlin wall, and noted that the golden hands of its clock pointed to 6:18. What I thought about was the M.V.D.

The Russian police system is so completely foreign to anything within American and Western experience that a proper understanding of it is not easily achieved. This system, which has not changed from the days of the tsars, is based primarily upon the notion that the people must be directed through personal contact, as one drives a donkey, and that the seat of this direction—the ruler—must be protected from the people, who are always a threat. The police, then, are simply the enforcers of this rule and the protectors of the ruler. There has never been any question of rule by law in Russia in any Western sense, and so the police are not concerned with protecting the people or their "rights." The people have no rights. Only those in authority have rights. Lawlessness, as we know it, is of minor concern in the Soviet Union, principally because the morality

125

of Western law is unknown and unappreciated. The primary basis of all police action is political, and the one great crime is what is today called deviation—which is so loosely defined and so subject to the whims of the definer that anyone who falls out of favor is automatically a criminal. In Russia, the only recognized immorality is that of disagreeing with Stalin. You will recognize a typically Oriental viewpoint in all of this, and that is chiefly why the logical Westerner has such difficulty understanding it.

In a general way, these facts were not new to me, but their specific application so that this viewpoint would become a part of my normal thinking and my life was the most important lesson I learned in the three-months course at the M.V.D. Academy. All the rest of it I knew well, for it had been a principal part of my training by Bureau-X. No one had to teach me that Joseph Stalin was the most carefully and completely guarded human being in all the world, and that the members of the Politburo, in order of favoritism, ranked next. Nor were the methods of guarding them in any way novel or unrehearsed by my Bu-X teachers. We spent hours, days, and weeks going over this same ground in the Moscow Academy, and it was no surprise to me that I received quick recognition as the brightest pupil of my class of some dozen secret police agents. The irony of this, in view of my objective to do Stalin in, helped to prevent it all from becoming too dull.

During these three months I lived a retired life at the Mossoviet, taking part in none of the social activities of Moscow or of the secret police, outside of several dinners with Malinkov at the senior officers' mess. I paid a brief visit early one evening to Mme. Chenkov, as I had promised my companion of the Long Island beach and the submarine departure, and gave her an intimate sketch of her husband's appearance and homesickness.

The M.V.D. Academy was in a former office building just around the corner from the Furkasovsky Alley headquarters, but I stayed away from there unless I was specifically invited or ordered to appear. I had no contact with Captain Petsky during this period. Actually I gave him little thought and was not anxious to renew our acquaintance. I could not see that it would serve any useful purpose just then.

My term in the M.V.D. Academy passed without incident and I was ordered to report back to Malinkov, who gave me my first assignment. Along with half a dozen others, I was placed on patrol on the Moskvoretsky Bridge over the Moskva

126

River, at the southeast corner of the Kremlin. This bridge, in case anyone is interested, is 2,351 feet and 6 inches long and 130 feet and 2 inches wide. This assignment was in the nature of a probationary post, to test my application of the lessons learned at the Academy. In time, it would lead to the elite position of personal bodyguard for one of the greats of the Third International. It was even well within the realm of probability that, with my rank, I might be appointed to that envied company that guarded the sacred person of Joseph Stalin himself.

It was on this bridge patrol that I made my first contact with the Russian underground. This was a farmer who was driving an ancient horse and a rickety cart that broke down near the center of the span and snarled the traffic.

I never did find out how I had been spotted by the underground, but while I was hauling the culprit off to be questioned at the secret police post (a farmer whose cart breaks down in sight of the Kremlin is an obvious criminal) he uttered a couple of phrases during his protests that very few people would have used.

"The river is deep," he said.

I agreed. "Also, it is wide," I added.

"It is twenty-three feet deep," he said.

"What river?" I asked.

"Kizil·Irmak," he said.

He didn't pronounce it very well, but he unmistakably said the Kizil Irmak, which, if you're curious, is in Turkey.

"Have you a date yet?" I asked.

"Not yet," he said. "Our present guess is next August. We will let you know."

"What is the purpose of this, then?" I demanded.

"Captain Petsky," he said. "He is a danger. He suspects."

"Why don't you people take care of him?" I asked.

"If we kill him, it will be worse," he said. "Then none of us would be safe and we could not get the date for you."

We got to the police post, at the south end of the bridge, and the officer in charge and I slapped the farmer around and accused him of various crimes. He was an old man, past sixty, and he didn't give us much trouble. There were tears in his eyes when we stopped hitting him. He denied every charge that we threw at him—sabotage, deviation, neglect of duty, counter-revolution, being an enemy of the people, and a few others. He kept on insisting that his cart was old and that the axle had given away from age and not through any fault of his or as a

127   .

result of any plot to disrupt the orderly progress of the U.S.S.R.

"He is undoubtedly a member of the underground, intent upon assassination," I said to the officer in charge. "He belongs in the dungeons of Lubyanka."

The old man pleaded with me to have mercy on him, falling to his knees and reaching a leathery hand to my trousers. One of the uniformed policemen who had directed the removal of the cart from the bridge came in and reported that the bridge was clear.

"What caused this breakdown?" demanded the officer in charge.

The policeman shrugged. "The cart is very old," he said. "It might have broken down anywhere."

"Get this old bag of bones out of here," ordered the officer in charge. "I have had enough of him. If I ever see him again, I will lock him up for the rest of his worthless life."

That ended the incident, except for the numerous reports to be made out and filed. I went back to my post in deep thought. I was well aware that I would not have been warned about Petsky unless the situation were serious.

But what to do about him? How could he be disposed of so that his killing would remain undetected as murder? Mere appearance of an accident would not be enough. The inquiry that would follow would be the most thorough police investigation that could be mounted.

One sure way to avoid suspicion on such a project is to make the killing one of many that occur simultaneously. You make it a disaster of wide enough proportions, then the death of any individual loses its significance.

What I had to hunt around for was a good, hot holocaust that was about to happen.

29 One aspect of the Petsky problem that proved not too difficult to solve was satisfying my own curiosity regarding the nature of the danger he presented. This was facilitated by the fact that Petsky, late in October of 1957, got married, which was not a common practice among M.V.D. officers. Generally they took properly investigated and trusted females to live with them on a temporary basis, discarding

128

them when the novelty wore off. But Petsky had evidently persuaded Malinkov and General Zurakov, at least, to approve his setting up a formal household, and the one he took for a bride was this large-busted secretary of Malinkov. Well, this removed the girl from her "club," for one thing, and set the two of them hunting for quarters. And in the meantime, they occupied a room right under mine in the Mossoviet.

It was no trick for me to arrange to bump into Petsky in the hotel lobby. I brushed by his shoulder one evening as he was on his way to the elevator, excused myself, then gave him a big hello.

"Why, Bodine!" I exclaimed. "Imagine meeting you here!"

He looked at me narrowly, with that same mean, dour expression that I remembered from New York.

"Your face is familiar," he said. "I do not know your name."

"Miles," I said. "Jan Miles. I met you in New York back in 1954. We were in a police station together after a fight on a pier."

A light of recognition came into his eyes, but his expression didn't change otherwise.

"I have heard of you from Malinkov," he said, "but I wasn't sure you were this one I had already met." He took a long, hard look at my face, cataloguing all of its features, then he stuck out his hand. "I am glad to see you in Moscow, comrade," he said.

I shook hands with him and told him that Malinkov had discussed his assignment with me and that I had been informed he was Captain Petsky.

That seemed to surprise him. "Come up to my room where we can talk," he said. "I do not want to mention these things here."

We went up together and he explained that his bride was away for the evening attending a lecture. His room was furnished exactly as mine was, and we sat opposite each other by the window, with a small table between us. It was getting dusk, but he did not turn on the light.

"I would be interested in knowing how much Colonel Malinkov told you about me," he said.

"That would hardly be discreet on my part," I replied. "I will discuss this matter with you in front of Colonel Malinkov, but not with you here alone."

He thought that over. Then he asked, "Why did you call me Bodine instead of Captain Petsky if you knew who I was?"

129

"No important reason," I said. "I merely knew you first as Bodine, and I had you so associated in my mind."

"It is an easy name for you to remember?" he asked.

"Which?" I countered, "Bodine or Petsky?"

"Bodine," he said.

"Yes, I can remember it," I said. "I had heard of this Bodine before, as I believe I told you in New York."

"How had you heard of him?" he asked.

"When I was home in Roumania—in Galati," I said. "He was spoken of there as an agent for the Americans. Why I remembered the name, too, was because there was an Old Bolshevik by the name of Bodine, and I had heard of him, also."

"This is all very interesting to me," he said, "and I hope you will excuse all of these questions, but this assignment of mine has become my lifework and I seldom can think of anything else."

"I'll be happy to answer any questions you ask, it if will help you, comrade," I said.

"Was this Bodine ever in Galati?" he asked.

"I believe so," I said. "Those who spoke of him seemed to think he had been."

"I have found no record of that," he said.

"There hardly would have been a record, would there?" I asked.

"Perhaps not. I have been wondering if I should not go to Roumania and continue my inquiries there."

"It may be a cold trail by this time," I suggested.

"It may be that this Bodine has returned to the Balkans," he said. "That would always be a possibility."

"Yes," I agreed, "it would."

"Or he may be in Germany," he suggested.

"True."

"Or he may be right here in Russia."

"Again, possible," I said.

"Excuse me," he said. He got up and crossed the room to the light switch and turned on the overhead light, first giving it the characteristic flash. Then he went to the bureau beside the bed and he returned with two photographs in his hand. He placed them on the table in front of me.

One was the U.S. Navy file photo of Alexis Ivanovich Bodine. The other was a very recent M.V.D. identification photo of Jan Miles.

I looked at them a brief moment, then exclaimed, "Why, that is my picture! Where did you get it?"

130

"M.V.D. files," he said. "I see every picture that comes into our files, from whatever source. Do you know why I picked out that one?"

"No," I said. "It isn't a particularly good likeness."

"Look at the two of them together," he said. "Do you know the man in that other picture?"

"No," I said.

"That is Alexis Bodine," he replied. "Now, compare those pictures. Do you see any likeness?"

"Why, yes," I admitted candidly, "there is a definite likeness. . . . The nose is different, and the scar on the forehead is in a different place. The hairline in this Bodine picture is a bit lower—but yes, you are right. There is something about the expression that is very close in the two."

"That's what I thought," he said.

"It is a shame that this trail has led up a blind alley," I said.

"Who knows about blind alleys?" he said, getting up and moving again toward the door.

I expected him to douse the lights, but he didn't. He just stood there, and it dawned on me that he was waiting for me to leave. I took my time getting up and walked over to him slowly.

"It has been pleasant visiting you, comrade," I said. "I wish you luck in your quest."

"Oh, I expect to have luck," he replied, "when I go to Roumania with my photographs. . . . I have quite a collection."

We shook hands and I left. Outside of his door there was an M.V.D. man standing with his back to the wall. He gave me a cold, fishy eye as I passed him on my way upstairs. He was a good symbol for the newly discovered peril that was threatening to wreck my plans and destroy me.

30 There was no moving fast enough on this Petsky-Bodine matter, for every hour that I let pass without doing something about it multiplied the menace and brought me that much closer to disaster. It was potentially the most critical situation that could develop in my assignment, even including the final assassination of Stalin himself. For in the case of Captain Petsky, there was no such thing as a quick killing and to hell with the consequences. It was a lot more than merely getting the man in the sights of a gun. It had to be done with maximum finesse; it had to be done quickly; it had to be done in a manner that would not throw the slightest suspicion my way, even to the point of a single question being asked as to my whereabouts or my intentions. And, just to foul it all up and add that much more to my difficulties, safety demanded that the bride Luba Petsky perish with her husband, because no one can be sure exactly how much any husband has or has not told his wife in the confidence of the nuptial bed.

I have always been most successful in my more vicious activities when I have confined them to the immediate framework of occurring events. Opportunities always present themselves; all that is necessary is to have the astuteness to recognize them. Or, another way of putting it is that, given the necessary determination, one can usually make the opportunity.

While I was on the Moskvoretsky Bridge patrol and under the eye of Furkasovsky Alley, and while Petsky was occupied with his Moscow routine, opportunity was out of the question because there were no events in our lives that involved the two of us. That is why I had to wait and that is why I worried off some ten pounds of fat that I acquired with the good living of a secret police officer.

Five perilous weeks crawled by with maddening slowness. At the beginning of November it started to snow, and by the middle of December the drifts were piled high on all open spaces and many of the streets were impassable for vehicles. Even for Moscow, it was a record snowfall. Stalin and most of his Politburo, including Marshal Beria and a secret police guard of several hundred men, were in the Crimea. A new summer palace—or rather, summer fortress—had just been completed that fall for the Generalissimo between Simeiz and Alupka, and it was reliably reported through the M.V.D. grapevine that the dictator was in residence there amidst his private army and his closer associates of the Politburo. Moscow was virtually isolated from the rest of the country, except by air. Hundreds of machines and thousands of men and women had kept the runways of the Central Airport open, for these were dire times. I don't have to remind you that the armies of Hungary, Roumania, and Bulgaria were battling furiously for their lives along most of the border of Yugoslavia during that winter of 1957-58, and that the Yugoslavs, with the help of America and the other Atlantic Pact nations, were showing disastrous strength.

132

As a result of Russia's withdrawal from the United Nations, early that winter, after the long rows over the Balkan War, we had a great influx of expatriates, and it was inevitable that these would include General Godovisky.

The general came back to Moscow on December 23, 1957, and it is a date I will always remember, for it brought several subtle but important changes in my own status that bridged much protocol and red tape.

Although personalities very seldom enter into the activities of the secret police, there are occasions when an assignment is the chief interest of a certain commander, and while he is in close touch with his command it is pursued to the utmost. This was the situation regarding the search for Alexis Bodine and General Godovisky's interest was quite understandable in view of Malinkov's revelation that I had killed the general's younger brother. When he descended upon Furkasovsky Alley this bleak December day and pushed out General Zurakov, all the way to Berlin, one of his first orders to Colonel Malinkov was to get cracking on the Bodine case.

Malinkov was given carte blanche, and Captain Petsky was given detached orders to go seeking this enemy through Europe. He was further given permission to take his wife with him in the early stages of the search, to act as his assistant. All of this I learned through the M.V.D. grapevine. And my gamble in this was that Petsky had not dared yet to communicate his suspicions about the photographs of Bodine and Miles to his superiors. But that was only a minor gamble; it would have been an unheard of breach of discipline and protocol for Petsky to hint at any suspicions against a higher officer of the secret police without something substantial in the way of proof. Actually, by M.V.D. tradition, it would have given me the right to challenge him to mortal combat. Such proof naturally would not have been required for any charges against a civilian, no matter how high his station in the Communist world, but senior M.V.D. officers were in a position of sacred trust and were beyond the flimsy and vicious rumors that hounded the ordinary Russian. This, too, was a tradition handed down from the days of the tsars.

At the first opportunity, which was at 4:00 A.M. of the second morning after his arrival, I went to Godovisky's office to pay my respects. It was Christmas morning in America, but I didn't allow myself to think of that. I had been informed the day before by his aide that that would be a propitious time and that I could expect a friendly welcome. That is what I got.

133

"It is very good to see you again," he said, shaking my hand firmly. "I'm glad we didn't lose you."

"It was a narrow thing, my General," I said. "Just a few more miles and I would have been in the death house."

"Oh, we would have got you out of there," he said. "As a matter of fact, I hardly expected such complete success of our operation on that highway. Our major plan was a prison break, for we have many comrades inside that dungeon, but I'm happy that we didn't have to put it into effect. It might have cost the lives of many of our people."

"It has worked out very well for me," I said. "There is no place I would rather be than here."

"You may find it dull. We don't have the excitement of our work in America."

"I can stand a little less of that," I said.

We talked about the Grand Central riot and some of our more successful sabotage efforts, and then he inquired into my present duties. He seemed disappointed that I had not advanced further in all these months than to the position of a lowly bridge guard.

"I may have a place for you on my personal staff," he said. "You will be notified within the week."

"I shall get around to that, my General," I said. "Since Cap-said.

"You have comfortable quarters?" he asked.

"Very comfortable—at the Mossoviet."

"Alone?"

"Yes, sir."

"We have many attractive girls in Moscow, and the secret police have their pick."

I shall get around to that, my General," I said. "Since Captain Petsky has got married, I have been thinking about it."

"Ah, yes, Captain Petsky. He is a favorite of mine."

"He has told me about his assignment—about this Alexis Bodine. I had hoped that I might be assigned to aid him."

"You? Why?"

"It is a case that piques my curiosity. I have never considered it possible that a person actually could vanish and remain hidden if a search for him was determined enough."

"Exactly my view," he agreed. "Yet, if this Bodine is still in America, you could not return there."

"No, my General, but I might be of some use in Europe. In the Balkans, for instance. I know them well. I am a native of Roumania and I have traveled through all of those countries."

134

"I had not heard of a proposal to search the Balkans," he said.

"Captain Petsky has some photographs, and he wants to try to get them identified there," I said. "It may be a valuable lead. He seems to have one man in mind—although he didn't tell me who."

General Godovisky thought that over, then got Malinkov on the telephone. He asked for a report on Captain Petsky's assignment, to date, and listened without expression or comment for five minutes. Then he said, "Fine. Issue the same orders for Colonel Miles and instruct Miles as to his duties. I want no confusion over rank in this. Miles and Petsky are to work together, but the only orders are to come from you. Naturally Colonel Miles will remain senior in all matters of protocol. Detach Colonel Miles from his present duties as of today."

There was some more conversation from the other end, then the general hung up.

"You will report to Colonel Malinkov at 2:00 P.M.," he said. He stuck out his hand and I shook it. "Good luck," he said.

I bade him adieu and went upstairs to the mess and had a couple of Scotches. I had a lot of figuring to do before I saw Malinkov that afternoon. This was going to call for sabotage with at least one very novel aspect—a disaster from which I would be the only one to escape. That would take some working out.

31 Not all of my activities on this assignment of death were completely joyless. Put it down to perversion or aberration or complexes, or whatever you wish, but the prospect of catching up with this Petsky was not unpleasant. Of all the Communists I had dealt with, he was the only one who had injected the personal equation into my normally academic dislikes. I traced this back to New York and the Third Precinct Police Station, when I had heard him claim the identity of Alexis Ivanovich Bodine. That name and identity were my most sacred as well as secret possessions, and to have them desecrated by such a hateful specimen of humanity as this Petsky was beyond acceptance. . . . I'll hand

135

it to the Communists. Their psychology in baiting such a trap was sound. They had used the single method of flushing me into the open that had any chance of success, and they never knew how close they came to pulling it off. My refusal to heed the orders of Bureau-X and my search for Petsky along West Fifty-fourth Street were the two really stupid actions on my part in all of this period. I was not unappreciative that a Greater Power had prevented my achievement of a personal disaster.

Petsky and I received our orders together from Malinkov. A twin-engined Red Army transport, modeled after the American DC-3, was assigned to me, as the senior officer, and along with it a pilot and a co-pilot, both young M.V.D. types who had come out of the air force. Our flight, to Bucharest, originally was scheduled for January 3, but we were delayed two days until it stopped snowing and the runways of Central Airport could be cleared.

During this wait I was informed by Malinkov that we would have a couple of extra passengers, that a certain Kovol and his wife would go with us to Bucharest on their way to Austria.

"Not the one who called himself William Nichols in America?" I asked hopefully.

"The same," said Malinkov. "He and this woman of his had to leave America several months ago, and they have only recently arrived in Moscow. Do you know them?"

"Know them!" I exclaimed. "Nichols was my superior for more than a year during all of my sabotage activities. We worked very closely together."

"I had not remembered from your dossier," he said. "Well, you will then renew an old friendship. We want them to travel on your plane rather than by any regular air line so that they will remain protected. It is a nuisance for him to travel always with this woman. It makes it most difficult to keep him under cover."

It gave me a real lift to know that I might, at last, be able to close the score on this brutal sadist. I told myself about all of the hundreds of people he had sent to their deaths and I reviewed what I knew of his career as chief of saboteurs in eastern America—but what I actually was concerned with, if I must be frank, was the slapping around he had given Dottie Janus.

Then thoughts of her tossed me right down into the depths, because they led inevitably to longing and loneliness for the only girl that I had ever loved, and I wondered what she was

136

doing and if she remembered me. And even if she did, I was almost certain that the promise she had made on that train coming into Newark was now long forgotten. It seemed a thin thing, at that distance, upon which to hang any hopes. And yet, against all reason, I did. That is something I needed to keep me going—hope.

It was, then, in an unfriendly mood that I boarded our plane on January 5, 1958, but no one expects a Communist, least of all a secret police Communist, to be pleasant company, so this went unremarked by my traveling companions. A good thing.

Petsky, naturally, had shown chagrin and confusion when he had been informed that we were to work together on the Bodine assignment. He made little effort to hide his feelings, and they were plainly mirrored in the attitude of his bride, Luba. I must concede, however, that the two of them were normally so disagreeable that it was not too noticeable.

He and his Luba took a seat up forward and ignored me. Behind them sat his M.V.D. guard, a sergeant by the name of Dumbrov, who carried his gun with an ostentatious breast bulge and prided himself on being quick on the draw. He was from the Cossack country and probably was a handy shot, but he never got a chance to try it defending his captain.

The Kovols sat across the aisle and a couple of seats back, over the wing. They both greeted me at the airport like a long-lost cousin, and Selma was as gushy as Old Faithful and sixty times as often. I must say, in her defense, that she was in some ways the least unpleasant of the Communists I had disposed of in one way or another. I sat across the aisle from them and talked to them both, or rather, listened to her. They told me about their hopes for Austria. They loved Russia. They were so happy to get out of imperialistic America into the free air of the Soviet Union. They loved the snow. They loved the people. It went on like that, with endless detail, until all of the droning, including that of the engines, put me to sleep.

Our first scheduled stop was Odessa, some 700 miles south by west, where we were to refuel. In a plane such as ours, with a ground speed of little more than 150 miles per hour, we figured four and a half hours for the flight. Our E.T.A. at Odessa was 1:30 P.M. We expected to stop there at least an hour, have luncheon at the airport, then fly the 260 miles to Bucharest well before dark. This last leg of the trip was to be made with fighter escort. The Yugoslavs, using American and

137

British jets, had a nasty habit of shooting down anything that flew, and especially unescorted Russian transports.

I woke up in the vicinity of Orel an hour and a half south and went up to the greenroom and had a talk with the pilot and co-pilot. As commander of the flight, this was a normal procedure. I talked to them about flying and engines. They were not any more friendly than any Russians in the secret police, but they didn't seem to mind talking to me.

"That engine of yours looks like an American Wasp," I said to the pilot.

"Same general design, only this is better," he said.

"More horsepower?" I asked.

"Couple of hundred more," he said.

"What's that city down below?" I asked.

"Orel," he said. "We get more hours out of them without overhaul, but sometimes they burn up."

"Well, keep 'em cool this trip," I said. "We can't afford to crack up this cargo."

"That's bad luck to say that," he said.

"Oh, I suppose we could all jump, if anything happened," I said. "I see a lot of chutes in the stern."

"Not us," said the pilot. "We stay with the ship. That's orders."

"Too bad for you," I said.

While this chitchat was going on, I took a gander at the instrument panel and noted the altimeter and air-speed readings. We were flying at only 5,000 feet, which was less than the minimum for my own safety if I were going to ditch this plane according to the plan I had worked out. I had quite a few things to do before I could jump out of it, and at the calculated rate we would start losing altitude, 5,000 feet would not give me much margin of safety or any time to waste on unnecessary movements. However, this was my opportunity— the one I was making suit my ends—and both my nature and my training left me no other choice than to seize it and force it into the mold of my necessity.

I went on back out of the pilots' compartment and collected a couple of dirty looks on the way from the Petskys. I also got one from the sergeant behind him. Selma started to gush at me, but I kept going. I went back to the toilet in the tail and I examined the plexiglas window in the fuselage. As I had anticipated from my study of the plans of this plane, I found the window was set in with metal screws and would be no trick to remove.

138

On my way forward again, I made a quick examination of the top parachute on the pile. It looked good enough from the outside. But what can you tell from the outside of a parachute? I moved over to the door and gave the locking mechanism a flip. It unlocked. I left it that way and walked back to my seat.

I dozed again, for nearly an hour, then woke up and read Stalin's first-page proclamation in *Pravda* declaring America the aggressor in the Yugoslav war and calling upon the Soviet Union to unite for common defense. It didn't give me any hints; it was still short of a declaration of war or of intent to commit war. It was tough, but not any more than normal for the Red Tsar.

I was waiting for the Dnieper and Kremenchug. We were due over there about noon. That's the heart of the Ukraine grain belt, and that's where I figured my accident would have to happen. I couldn't afford to get too close to the Roumanian border and the hundreds of fighter planes operating in that area.

It was 12:08 when I spotted the river. I picked up my brief case, which was all the baggage I was carrying, and went back to the toilet again. I looked over our passengers before I closed the door, and all were peaceful. Kovol and Selma were dozing. Luba seemed to be reading, and Petsky had his head back and might have been asleep. The sergeant was awake, but not his usual alert self.

I closed the door, set my brief case down on the deck and opened it. I took out a screw driver and went to work on the window. I had it off in a couple of minutes and was hit by the sudden rush of air from the slipstream. With the door closed, it did not make too much disturbance.

I took my .380 Colt, which I had loaded with incendiary bullets, from my brief case and tried holding it out of the window and aiming it. There was a hell of a breeze, but not too much to get a steady aim, which was in line with previous tests I had made. I withdrew my arm and took a can out of my briefcase which could have been nothing else in the world but Portuguese sardines. This was not sardines, however. It was standard M.V.D. sabotage equipment much used in America. I opened the can with a regular opener and very carefully removed a small ring from its nest amid a tarry substance. This ring was attached to a wire, and I let it hang free so that it could be pulled.

I stuck my arm out of the window again, with the gun in my hand, and I fired seven shots at rapid fire into the main

139

gas tank and into the starboard motor. Then I dropped the gun out the window, grabbed the sardine tin, and pulled the ring. I counted three, opened the door of the toilet, and slid the can into the aisle just beyond the last seat. It made a small pop and started to give off tremendous billows of acrid black smoke, which completely curtained the forward part of the plane.

So many things happened in such a short space of time that it was impossible for me to register them all. There was a hell of an explosion from the starboard motor just as I opened the plane door, and by the time my smoke bomb popped, the interior of the plane was glowing red from the flames. One of the women—Luba, I think—was screaming, and the sergeant came bucketing back to the stern through the beginning of my smoke. I reached him beside the plane door and cracked his chin with a hard, short right. He went down. I grabbed the top parachute, got into it, pulled the buckles with one motion, and swung the plane door in. The chute harness was very loose, and the thought flashed through my mind that I was in for a rough trip.

The plane had started to heel over into a spin to starboard, and I had to grab the edge of the door, which was on the port side, to keep from being thrown back and away. I edged myself up against a tremendous pull of gravity, and finally the slipstream caught me and I was out and falling. I said the shortest prayer of my life and pulled the ripcord. The ground looked no more than fifty feet away and coming fast. Actually I had about a thousand feet, which proved to be only a few feet over the minimum for the type of parachute I was using.

The jerk of the chute opening, in that loose harness, nearly did for me. It was like being walloped with half a dozen hockey sticks by a berserk team of giants. I caught one fast glimpse of the plane, spinning in flames, just before I hit hard on the edge of a wheat field, in a fence row of briars. My left ankle collapsed on a boulder and I lay there and looked up at the pale summer sky. Off down the fence row, an angry black crow was scolding me in purple Russian from the branch of an apple tree. And Russian, in case you don't know it, is a language of vituperation.

140

32 For the next month or more I had a bad time with my ankle and a worse time with the M.V.D. The principle involved in the secret police irritation was that, as commanding officer of an airplane as well as senior officer of a special mission, I had lost not only the plane but all the other members of the mission. You just can't do worse than that and stay alive in the Soviet Union. Normally, it would take a great deal less to earn a ticket to a Siberian slave camp or a firing squad. There was no such thing as condoning an accident or excusing mechanical failure; all such occurrences came under the general classification of sabotage, and any individual involved, no matter how remotely, was automatically a saboteur. That is the way the Russian Communist mind works; that's the way it is, and I can't help it if it doesn't make sense. I could cite thousands of instances of such insane conclusions, as can anyone who has ever dealt with Russian Communists. Perhaps the classic such incident concerns the plane, a four-motored bomber, which lost a propeller over Moscow during a review of troops in Red Square in the late thirties. The propeller fell into a crowd on a side street, killing no one but injuring several. Stalin was nowhere in the vicinity at the time, but it was a day when he was to have reviewed the troops. The chief mechanic of the air squadron and the pilot were both arrested and were never heard of again. There could never be any question, in a Russian mind, of their "guilt." Guilty of what? You'll have to figure that out.

That unquestionably would have been my fate too if it had not been for two factors. The first was that I had proved myself many times over as an efficient man of all work, as long as the work was dirty enough. The second was Godovisky's personal confidence in me and my motives, coupled with the fact that he could still use me. Those were the factors I gambled on when I laid my plot to crash the plane. Naturally I expected it all to work out favorably or I wouldn't have done it.

The inquiry into the crash was exhaustive to the point of the metaphysical absolute. The holocaust had been so complete that there was no question of evidence of human fault, failure, or ferity. The bits and pieces of the transport and its human cargo that were gathered together and examined revealed nothing damaging to any man; there was nothing to

141

dispute my account of the sudden exploding of the starboard engine while I was in the toilet, and my almost impossible escape from the burning, spinning plane. I went over that story so often that even now I am not at all convinced which is the true version.

The hearing at Kremenchug was conducted by the local M.V.D. commandant, who was a young, bright product of the New Russia which has so perverted all knowledge and thinking that her children are made to appear as intellectual clowns.

Certainly this Major Osspenkayo was one of the most completely illogical young men it has ever been my duty to meet. He ignored all evidence of common sense and placed the full responsibility and blame for the crash upon me, frankly admitting that my survival was the sole basis for his conclusion. He damned me and anyone else who sought to dissuade him by logic or reason. The mental contortions by which he supported this conclusion were imposed upon most of his witnesses, who were technicians, plane designers, and such. It would have made an interesting study of thought processes in modern Russia, were it not for the fact that I was on the receiving end. And also, guilty as hell.

This hearing dragged on for an interminable five weeks, and at the end of it, with no final decision reached, I was ordered back to Moscow. I was given travel orders to report to my court-martial at M.V.D. headquarters and a bitter, reluctant farewell by Osspenkayo on February 8. I arrived in Moscow two days later after a voyage on some of the slowest and most uncomfortable trains in the world. We went from Kremenchug to Kharkov, to Kursk, to Orel, to Tula, and finally to Moscow, and at each one of those intermediate cities I changed trains and waited anywhere from a half-hour to four hours.

As our train pulled out of the station at Kharkov, I was aware that a young fellow with the look of a minor bureaucrat was discussing me with his companion, a very pretty girl. There was nothing obvious about it, but with my highly developed sensitivity to my surroundings, I could not miss it.

Right outside of the city, the train entered on a bridge and crossed a river. The girl got up suddenly and came to my seat. I was sitting on the aisle, beside an ancient dame with a caged chicken in her lap, and the girl bent down and whispered in my ear, "The river is wide."

I nodded.

"It is deep, too," she said.

142

"How deep?" I asked.

"Twenty-three feet," she said.

I looked out the window, as though to confirm her statement, then turned back to her.

"What river?" I asked.

She laughed and she walked back to her seat.

I got up and sauntered to the end of the car, and the boy with her followed me to the vestibule. I turned to him and he smiled at me. That was a rare sight—a smile.

"What river?" I asked him.

"Kizil Irmak."

"What date?" I asked him.

"August," he said. "We think the eighteenth."

"You will let me know if there's a change?"

"Yes."

He walked back to his seat, and I walked back to mine. So I had a date, at last! On August 18, 1958, Russia would launch her attack against America and Joseph Stalin would be, I hoped, "executed" as the first war criminal of World War III. It counted just a little over seven months. And all I had to do for those seven months was to keep out of trouble. That didn't appear to be too difficult, now that Petsky was in his Valhalla. However, I must concede that my own genius for getting involved in unpleasant situations removed any joy from the contemplation of that period.

I reported to Furkasovsky Alley on February 11, late in the afternoon, and after a normal wait of an hour and a half, while General Godovisky was being barbered and fed, I was admitted to the Russian version of a military court, which consisted in this case of a five-hour rehearsal of charges and accusations against me which had no remote connection with any known facts or human experiences. No provision was made for any defense nor for any answering statement by me. The trial was conducted by the general. An M.V.D. legal eagle by the name of Rumin acted as prosecutor and did most of the talking. I won't bore you with any of his account because there was nothing in it either interesting or pertinent. After his monologue, Godovisky himself made a short speech of an hour or so, and then I was asked to sign a "confession," which I readily agreed to do.

"Honored judge of all men," I said, standing at stiff attention, "I acknowledge and bewail my manifold sins and wickedness which I, from time to time, most grievously have committed by thought, word, and deed against thy People's Gov-

143

ernment, provoking most justly thy wrath and indignation against me. I do earnestly repent, and am heartily sorry for these my misdoings; the remembrance of them is grievous unto me; the burden of them is intolerable. Have mercy upon me; forgive all that is past, and grant that I may ever hereafter serve and please thee. . . ."

I doubt that the general confession has ever been so misused, but I hope I will be forgiven by my church, for certainly no disrespect was intended. It was something that I knew and it seemed to apply most aptly to the situation; I know of nothing else in literature that does. However that may be, it had a very satisfactory effect upon the court and won me a compliment upon my attitude from Godovisky.

Then I signed the "confession"—a document of some twenty thousand words—and all those present witnessed it. Godovisky and the others shook my hand, and Rumin, who had been quite bitter about me a short time before, complimented me on the majesty of my statement to the court.

"That had a fine Russian literary flavor," he said. "Was it your own?"

"No," I admitted, "it is a thing I picked up from the British."

"One would hardly expect them to have such good taste," was his clincher.

And now, you may well ask, what was the outcome of all this legal hokus-pokus? Had I been found "guilty" or "not guilty"; and what had I "confessed" to? Unfortunately, there are no simple answers to those questions. The fine Oriental mind of the Russian is far too devious to explain here, and you would have to understand it thoroughly, along with all the modifications made by Communist ideology, to arrive at the bottom of all this. Even then, I fear that Western logic would be your undoing, and you would end up making no sense out of it at all. The final result, if there was any result at all, was that routine was satisfied and that, with a "confession" in my dossier, I was subject to summary execution if such a course ever should become convenient to my superiors. The fact that no such document would be needed if my execution ever were decided upon is just a capitalistic quibble.

For the rest of February and up to the end of March I was back on the Kremlin patrol, but this time at the Spasskaya, or Saviour, Gate. Since Stalin was not in residence, I was not attached to his personal guards. I was for a brief period in command of the guards at this Kremlin entrance, and then one early morning as I was coming off duty, I was informed by a messenger that I was to report to Godovisky.

It was close to 5:00 A.M. when I got to Furkasovsky Alley, and I was admitted to the general's office without delay. There was an air of urgency throughout the entire building that dawn, and it was communicated to me in many different ways, by the grimness of the guards, the hurrying of secretaries, and the tenseness of the agents. Something big was popping.

Godovisky wore a determined expression on his broad face, and his eyes were closed down to slits when he leaned back in his chair and examined me as I stood at attention before him. He did not speak for some moments. Then he said, "I am placing you in command of a picked group, and henceforth you and your organization are to take orders from no one but myself or Marshal Beria. Is that understood?"

"Yes, sir," I replied.

"You and your group will execute all orders with dispatch, and will never, under any circumstance, discuss them with anyone, either in Furkasovsky Alley or anywhere else. Is that understood?"

"Yes, sir," I said.

"You will under no circumstances ever make any written reports to anyone but Marshal Beria or myself nor will any of you keep any diaries or other records of your activities. Is that understood?"

"Yes, sir."

He handed me a slip of paper upon which was written an address on Arbat Avenue and he said, "You will go to that address and assume command of the forces that are there. You will find secretaries and other assistants. You will use the password Arbat and you will be known as Arbat. Only those who use the name Arbat will be admitted to that headquarters. Is that understood?"

"Yes, sir." I memorized the number on the slip, then placed it in his ash tray. He lit a match to it.

"There is one other password," he said. "Your principal force is composed of five men, and only these five will ever use it as a means of identification. They will use it this morning when they report to you. That is the word 'Dynamo.' If this word ever is used by any other person who reports to your headquarters, you are to dispose of that person. Understood?"

"Yes, sir."

"Your people are now waiting for you." He handed me a requisition filled out and signed. "Draw an automobile with

145

this for your personal use and meet your new staff within the hour. Good luck."

We shook hands and I left. I went to the supply officer, handed him the requisition, and he turned over to me the keys and papers and told me my car was waiting for me in the street. It was a late-model Cadillac, with a red searchlight on the top, official red stars front and rear, and a siren. That was about as far up in the Soviet Union as anyone ever got—driving a Cadillac with those gadgets on it. Unfortunately for others, the only direction from that eminence was down. Whoever had used this car before me certainly had descended fast. The front seat was badly stained, and as an expert, I can attest that the stains were blood.

I drove first to Red Square and down it to the highway between the Kremlin Wall and the river, trying out the car. It didn't run too well. The gasoline in Russia was a very poor quality for such a motor. I got it up to about seventy on this highway without much trouble, however, and decided that was good enough. I turned around and drove to Arbat Square, then out Arbat Avenue to 568. It was a large granite-faced mansion of the long-forgotten Russian nobility. I turned into a paved driveway alongside the house which led to the old carriage house in the rear, now converted to a garage. I stopped the car under the porte-cochere and rang the bell at the side door. It was opened by a shapely blonde with an angel face and an ink smudge on her nose.

"Arbat," I said.

"Come in," she said. She examined me closely, with dead-serious concentration, as I entered.

"Your name?" I asked.

"Arbat," she said.

"Arbat what?"

"Catherine," she said.

"Very well, Arbat Catherine, where is my office?"

She looked startled.

"You may smile, just in case that was humorous," I said.

She smiled slightly. "This way, comrade," she said. She led me to what had once been the drawing room. Gone were all the splendors of its gracious past. Forgotten were the long-dead ladies and gentlemen who had trod its waxed parquet and breathed its atmosphere. Dusty black drapes now covered its graceful windows, shutting out all light. A couple of shabby divans were side by side against a wall. In the center was a desk and a chair and, in a corner, another desk and chair for a sec-

146

retary. Overhead was a bare, glaring bulb. This New Order was never handsome. I went to the desk and sat. "Tell the others to come in, one by one," I said.

"Yes, comrade," she said.

She went out, closing the door. I opened the top drawer of the desk. It was empty. She was back in a moment, followed by a stubby, solid type with the usual flat Slavic face and misleading soft brown eyes. It was, all in all, a repulsive face, cruel and ruthless. He was neatly dressed in a well-cut dark suit and he walked with confidence. I told Catherine to leave and close the door, and I stood up and shook his hand.

We both said "Arbat," which sounded a bit silly, and then he said, "Dynamo." "I have been known as Arbat No. 1," he said. "We have found it less confusing if the commandant is the only plain Arbat."

He gave me a quick résumé of his M.V.D. service and admitted modestly that he held a Brown Belt in Judo. "I have been the aide to the commander of this headquarters," he said.

"You will continue as my aide, then," I said. "There are no orders for the present. How do I reach you?"

"I am in the office adjoining and I sleep in the room next to your apartment," he said. "I am always available. This red button on your desk, and a similar red button in your bedroom, will call me."

I dismissed him, and next greeted a roly-poly character whose face betrayed a happy nature despite its expression of studied severity. He likewise gave me his M.V.D. history, but I was unimpressed by his physical appearance. I had got in the habit of looking for muscle.

"You may have more than meets the eye," I said. "You are hardly the athletic type."

"No," he agreed. "I have other abilities." He lifted his hands to his chest and clapped them lightly. Then he put out his right hand toward me, and there was suddenly a gun in it. It was as neatly presented as Houdini could have done it.

"How about rabbits?" I asked.

He didn't understand that. "How?" he asked.

"Out of a hat," I said.

"Oh," he said, "I can do that too. But first I must catch the rabbits."

"And I suppose you also do imitations," I said.

"Yes," he agreed seriously, "I do. I can imitate the voice of any man I hear, and some women."

I dismissed him, designating him as No. 2, and at the door

147

he turned. "I must warn you," he said, "that I have a twin brother. He will be the next you will see; it will not be myself returning."

His twin proved as adept as No. 2 and was as alike to him as a second olive, outside of a few very minor differences. A couple of these were a small mole on the left side of his neck and a crooked little finger on his right hand, which were plenty for me to go on. Nos. 2 and 3 became my favorites in that setup, besides Arbat Catherine, of course. They were no more efficient or able than the rest, but they did everything with a verve which was an unexpected pleasure in grim, somber Russia.

No. 4 was a Mongol or Tartar type, and I guessed he originated in Siberia. He had a smooth, dark skin and a completely expressionless face. He was lean, lithe, and dangerous-looking; a good man to have on your side.

No. 5 was a tall, husky, and colorless Transcaucasian and he liked knives. He showed me one of his throwing knives and tossed it at a designated spot on the door with deadly accuracy and easy grace. When he left, Catherine came back.

"I will show you to your quarters if you wish," she said.

I followed her up the broad mahogany stairway from the main hall and into what had once been the master bedroom. There was a large dressing room and a bath, and the furnishings were not too much different from the original. My predecessor evidently had been a man of taste—which could have been a dangerous deviation.

Catherine showed me over the rooms and seemed completely familiar with them.

"And where do you sleep, my pretty maid?" I asked.

"Upstairs, on the top floor—now," she said.

"It used to be here?" I asked her.

"No, never," she said with Communist candor. "I hadn't got around to it, by the time he left. . . . Good night—or rather, good morning, comrade."

I let her go. There was something funny about this. It was too obvious that a girl like Catherine didn't belong in this nest of killers. She just wasn't the type. It was something I'd have to get to the bottom of; another one of these damned mysteries.

33 Arbat 568 was the charnel house of the secret police, and I was the overlord of the cremating ovens and director of the mortuary. In addition to my five Arbats, whose chief duties were to round up the victims and escort them to our death house, I had a staff of four lesser thugs, presided over by a chief executioner. They toiled in the depths of the cellar, doing all of the dirty work of killing and disposal, keeping the fires of the ovens hot, shoveling out the ashes, and, during the slack periods, policing the grounds. To provide a poetic note, my chief executioner had elected himself head gardener, and woe unto him who trampled on a flower that he had nursed with his loving, bloody hands.

Of all the highly secret operations of the M.V.D. in Russia, I suppose that Arbat was the most closely guarded and the least discussed. No member of its staff had ever been detached from its command alive to talk about any of its details or activities. Only General Godovisky and Beria himself, of all of the thousands around the Furkasovsky Alley headquarters, knew of its exact location and gave the orders. For all others, from the highest brass to the meanest laborer, its existence was only a dark rumor. Such secrecy added to the terror its name struck into the hearts of all Russians. I had heard of and read references to such an institution during my training period with Bureau-X, but it was all pure conjecture, based upon the supposition that such a disposal plant for excess Communists was in line with their policies and their thinking and would have been a good idea. That was the single large operation of the M.V.D. in Russia that I had not been thoroughly briefed upon beforehand. And now I was head of it, with a second-hand power of death over an almost limitless number of human beings. Believe me, it was nothing to be proud of.

I entered into my revolting duties at a critical period in the history of Russian communism. It was the beginning of the Great Purge of 1958, which was the immediate prelude to the Russian attack upon America and the launching of World War III.

So much has already been written about this 1958 purge that I will not dwell upon it here. What I should like to do is to point out the connection between it and the war that followed, which is a fact overlooked by most of the commentators I have read on the subject.

149

Communism, as a form of government, was never more widely accepted by the people of Russia than was the Tsarist regime. The Communist Party itself never embraced more than five percent of the population, so it has always been in every respect a minority government.

The historical manner by which this minority Russian rule has been maintained over the masses, whether in the name of a Genghis Khan, a Romanoff, or a Stalin, has been by utilization of secret police, by use of a large standing army with garrisons in every hamlet throughout the land, and by the maintenance of a continued threat of war, or actual state of war with some outside country. Even in times of so-called peace, this war potential has always been kept alive, if only by border incidents or minor territorial conquests.

The single factor which determines Russian foreign policy is the degree of internal peace—the degree of acceptance by the Russian masses of the restraints of their overlords. When Russia begins to act tough with her neighbors, and provokes bloodletting such as in Korea, and later in Yugoslavia, it means only one thing. It means that the forces of counterrevolution are rising again; that the Kremlin is beginning to shake.

Thus, the purge precedes the war as winter precedes the spring. If Russia had not attacked America with her atom-carrying bombers on August 18, 1958, then, before another spring had rolled over the land, the great Communist Experiment would have been wiped off the face of the earth by its own most abject victims—the Russian people.

And so, in my small way, I helped these igniters of world conflagration to lay their fires. Between early April and the end of July, I and my men did for seventeen generals, five admirals, two members of the Supreme Soviet, more than a hundred "elected" Representatives of the People from various areas and of varied importance, and countless scores of citizens, male and female. The spice was a list of twenty-three M.V.D. agents, and this rota, from the viewpoint of my personal interest, was topped by Colonel Vladimir Malinkov. What happened with Malinkov gave the whole business an unusual twist which started me out on my final chase ending in the assassination of the Generalissimo.

We seldom knew beforehand who our victims were to be. Many of them were merely brought or sent to our house on one pretext or another, supplied with the fatal password of "Dynamo." They would come ringing our bell in the early hours of the morning—anywhere between 2:00 and 5:00 A.M., which

150

were our reception hours, and they would be taken into the office of Arbat 1, the former library of the mansion. If ever there was a question of a last statement or "confession," and the victim was important enough, then I would be called in; otherwise the details were handled by Arbat 1 and the gentlemen from below-stairs.

In the matter of Malinkov, which occurred on August 5, there was a surprise in store for me which gave me no more rest until my final bullet was fired. For Malinkov turned out to be a member of the Russian underground!

And out of his condemnation came the even more startling discovery that the twins, Arbats 2 and 3, were likewise organized counterrevolutionaries, as well as the girl Catherine. I would have believed it impossible that these Arbats, of all people in Russia, could be a part of the underground. At first glance it appears to be the most fantastic of developments, and yet, on sober reconsideration, what more natural course could have been taken by these foredoomed, hopeless humans who lived always with the cold hand of death upon their shoulders than to make this one last gesture of rebellion?

Malinkov was admitted to our establishment by Arbat 4, then on guard duty, at 2:30 A.M. He came by himself. He gave the correct Arbat password and then followed it with the fatal word. He was taken to the office of Arbat 1 and he was quickly disarmed as he was lowering himself into a proffered chair. He was informed by Arbat 1 that he had fifteen minutes to live, and he was asked if he wished to make any final confession. He shook his head in the negative and asked to see the commanding officer. Arbat 1 knew Malinkov well, and so he rang for Catherine and told her of the request.

I was not particularly surprised to hear that Malinkov was sitting in our "death seat," beside No. 1's desk. I was beyond any surprise after four months of the charnel house.

"You?" Malinkov said when I walked in. "I had wondered what had happened to you. I never suspected this!"

"Comrade Malinkov is an old friend," said Arbat 1, looking at me with his melting brown eyes. "I took the liberty of granting his last request, to see my commanding officer."

"What possible purpose will it serve?" I asked.

"None, I can see that," declared Malinkov. His Adam's apple was working up and down, as it always did when he was under strain. But there was no other outward sign. "However," he added in a barely audible voice, "can I speak to you alone?"

151

I told him he could. I dismissed Arbat 1 and sat at his desk. I waited until the door was closed, then told Malinkov to speak his piece.

"You have twins attached to your command," he said. "I have a message to them from their father, whom I saw in the Ukraine within the past week. I should like permission to give this message to either one of them. Naturally I expect you to refuse. . . . That is my last request."

"How did you know that there are twins attached to this command?" I demanded.

He shrugged. "Am I not being executed for that knowledge?" he countered.

"This is not a debate!" I declared, borrowing a phrase from General Zurakov. "Answer my question!"

"I prefer not to answer," he said in a quiet voice.

I summoned Catherine with the call bell, and the door was opened for her by Arbat 1, who had planted himself outside as guard. She stood by the door and did not look at Malinkov. But he looked at her with an expression that startled me. It had been over a year since I had seen adoration shining from the eyes of a man.

"Order Arbats 2 and 3 to report to me here," I told her. "Number 1 is to occupy my office and handle all routine from there until further notice."

She left. A couple of minutes passed in silence. Malinkov bowed his head and held his hands tightly clasped together. Nos. 2 and 3 came in after rapping lightly and marched up to my desk side by side.

"This is Malinkov, from Furkasovsky Alley," I said to them. "He has a message for you from your father."

"Our father is dead," said Arbat 2 with a blank face. "The comrade must be mistaken."

"How about that, Malinkov?" I asked him.

He raised his head slowly and looked me full in the eyes. "It may well be that I am mistaken," he said. "However, the message is not important now. . . . I am much too confused to think straight or I never would have mentioned it in the first place. I know neither of these men. I have never seen them before in my life, nor have I ever heard of them."

"You are lying," I told him. "Do you know about the river?"

"No," he said.

I turned to the twins. "Tell me about the river," I said to them.

152

They both sneered at me. It was a very odd thing to happen, at that juncture. I didn't know how to interpret it.

"The river is wide," said No. 3 without any hesitation.

I agreed that it was.

"And it is deep," said No. 2.

"How deep?" I asked.

"Twenty-three feet," replied No. 2.

I turned to Malinkov. "What river?" I asked him.

He made a hopeless gesture with his hand. "Kizil-Irmak," he said.

"What is the date?" I demanded.

That was too much for him. "Stop it!" he yelled at me.

"Don't be a fool," I growled at him. "Keep your voice down. What date?"

"August 18," he said finally.

"Who is Catherine?" I demanded.

He just sat there. He still was unconvinced.

"She's one of us," said No. 2.

"Oh, no!" groaned Malinkov.

I rang the call bell on my desk and the girl opened the door and stood there, with her head up proudly. "Come in," I said, "and close the door."

She came over to my desk and stood between No. 3 and Malinkov.

"Who is outside?" I asked her.

"Just No. 4, on the main door," she said.

"Is the door to my office closed?"

"Yes, comrade," she said.

"Get rid of No. 4," I said. "Send him below to get the day's figures. Then take Malinkov up to my room and hide him. Tell him to stay there quietly until I get there. Maybe he will listen to you—he won't to me."

She left and I turned to the twins. "I've been wondering when I'd get confirmation of that August 18th date," I said. "But it gives me thirteen days and that is too much time. My whole world can blow apart in less than thirteen days."

They shrugged together.

"It won't," said No. 2. "You won't let it. And much will happen to keep you occupied. It always has."

"What do you know about me?" I demanded.

"We know a great deal," said No. 3. "We have watched you closely for many months, waiting for you to arrive here. We were expecting you, but not as our commanding officer. We were expecting you to be invited to occupy our ovens."

153

Catherine came in, then, and reported that it was all clear outside. I poked Malinkov in the shoulder and told him to get going. He got up slowly, like a sleepwalker, then suddenly seemed to gain control of himself and walked briskly to Catherine.

"When you get her upstairs," I said, "you can kiss her, if you still remember how."

34 Arbat No. 1 made no comment on my terse account of having sent Malinkov to his death myself. I believed he assumed that I had wished to spare his feelings— or whatever he used for feelings—for a friend. He informed me, when I summoned him, that Godovisky had called on my private phone and had told him he would expect me to report to him at 4:30 A.M. It was then after 3:00 and I told No. 1 that I would nap for half an hour before reporting. I went up to my apartment and found Malinkov hiding in a closet off my dressing room.

"You will reside, for the time being, in this closet," I said. "In due course you'll come out and help me with my work. After that, you and Catherine can try getting out of the country. If you make it, I'll be more surprised than you. Meanwhile, you might pray, if you know how. Your prospects aren't worth much more than a lead kopeck."

"I know how to pray," he said. "Also, I want to say that I have misjudged you." He offered me his hand and I shook it, with warmth.

"My business is to make people misjudge me," I told him. "You might mention that in your prayers—and ask that I continue successful in it. If I don't, we'll all be in our own ovens."

"I think now that I know who you are," he said to me.

"Perhaps," I said. "What difference would that make?"

"None," he agreed, "except to Godovisky."

"You're on the right track," I told him.

"Why, of course I am," he said, with a return of his old M.V.D. spirit. "Only one person in all the world would have gone to so much trouble and taken such chances to kill Captain Ivan Petsky."

"Right," I said.

154

I washed, shaved, and changed my clothes, then went below to my office. I told Catherine to sit beside my desk and I talked to her in low tones.

"Let no one enter my apartment under any circumstances," I told her. "To make it look good, when I leave here in a few minutes, come to the door with me and kiss me goodbye. Make it authentic. Then go up to my apartment and get into my bed. Keep out of the dressing room."

"Yes, comrade," she said.

"Act like my mistress, if you know how," I told her.

"Any woman knows how," she said with mock scorn. "Some of them just don't know when."

I got up then and walked out. Catherine followed me, and at the door, with No. 4 missing nothing, although his head appeared averted, I kissed her. It wasn't bad at all, but it made me think of Dottie for an instant, and that wasn't good.

I went out, got into my Cadillac, and drove to Furkasovsky Alley. I parked right outside the door, which was forbidden to any lesser vehicle, and went up to Godovisky's office. I was told to go in without waiting, and suddenly found myself face to face with no less a personage than the great Marshal Beria.

Godovisky introduced us, and the marshal shook my hand with vigor.

"I have heard much about you, Miles," he boomed at me. "Fine work, all of it."

"Thank you, Marshal," I said. "This is indeed an honor."

"It is the custom," explained Godovisky, "for Marshal Beria to meet personally the Arbat commander, so that he will know his face."

"This one has a sufficiently forbidding visage," the marshal said with what might have been a smile. He turned to me. "I understand that you have disposed of my friend Malinkov."

"Only two hours ago," I said.

"Any messages or confessions?" asked the marshal.

"None," I reported. "He refused to talk. I believe he was too surprised to talk."

"That should be the end of the counterrevolutionaries in Moscow," said General Godovisky. "With their leader gone, they will quickly fade away and die."

"Malinkov?" I exclaimed. "It is difficult to believe he was a counterrevolutionist."

"It is always difficult to believe, my son," said Beria. "We can never be sure of anyone except our own selves."

"Then I, too, am suspect," I said.

155

"You are indeed," said the marshal happily. "And so is my friend Godovisky."

The general had a samovar going and he poured tea for the two of us. For himself he took vodka.

"On rare occasions," said Godovisky negligently as he sipped his drink, "we require evidence of the disposal of one of our enemies. I shall ask you for such evidence in the case of Malinkov."

"Certainly, my General," I said. "Anything you wish. Physical evidence or affidavits?"

"In this case," said Beria to Godovisky, "we should have both. I am leaving for the South in a day or so and I shall expect you to forward the material to me."

I finished my tea on that note, and I was dismissed by Godovisky after a hint by Beria that I might expect, after the present difficulties were over, to receive the Order of the Red Star. I hope I looked properly impressed as I departed. I went below and got into my car, but I didn't go right back to Arbat 568. I took a leisurely drive along the Moskva River and watched another sunrise over the mosque towers and modern spires of this ancient capital, where grandeur and misery have dwelt so closely together for eight centuries.

The time had arrived to do careful and more detailed planning than any I had yet done. No more slam-bang methods with an eye only to the long-range result. This long range had narrowed down to countable hours, and it was vital to make each one effective in some way toward that tomorrow for which I had waited and worked so long.

I was certain of one thing, if nothing else: that, despite minor handicaps and imminent perils, I was in an almost ideal position to carry out my final assignment. Up to that hour, I was in the confidence of the one man in all Russia who could lead me to Joseph Stalin and place me in a position to assassinate him.

The facts I listed were these:

The date for my attempt was August 18, 1958.

The place was unquestionably the Black Sea fortress of the Generalissimo, for that is where Beria had told me he was going. (Not in so many words, of course. He had merely said the "South"—but that could mean only one place.) On such a momentous occasion as the outbreak of war between the Soviet Union and America it was unlikely that Stalin would not be surrounded by his most trusted followers.

The method would yet have to be determined. I would arm

156

myself with a rifle and a pistol. One or the other should suffice.

For assistants, if I needed them, I had Arbats 2 and 3, and possibly Catherine.

So I drove back to the death house, was admitted by Arbat 5 and went directly to my apartment. Catherine was in my bed, but she wasn't asleep. She was in an old-fashioned nightgown of plain white cotton that buttoned up around her neck, but even in that she managed to look enticing. I sat on the bed and whispered to her while she lay back on the pillow.

"We will have to sleep in the same bed," I said. "Someone most certainly will take a peek in here and it has not been my habit to lock the door. You'll have to put up with it for only a few hours, then it'll be safe for me to move over to the divan."

"That's what I figured out too," she said.

"Have you talked with M.?" I asked.

"Just for a few minutes while I was getting undressed," she said. "He told me that you are the only man in Russia who can be trusted."

"That's nice," I said, smelling the freshness of her as I bent close. "I hope he's right."

It was broad daylight, and I drew the drapes over the wall-length window to shut out the sun. Then I got undressed and climbed in beside her. I lay there for maybe half an hour, trying to concentrate on anything except this woman, when my ear caught the sound of a door knob rattling. She must have heard it too, because she quickly snuggled up against me. I put an arm under her and drew her close.

I felt the door being opened. I had my back to it, so I didn't see who it was. Catherine raised her head briefly, exclaimed, "Oh!" in surprise, then snuggled back down on my shoulder. I didn't hear the door close. I waited for maybe ten minutes. Then I gently withdrew my arm and looked at her. She was asleep.

The following afternoon, when I got down to my office, I told Catherine that affidavits were to be prepared on the execution of Malinkov; also that physical evidence would be required as well. I told her this in front of Arbat 1 and mentioned off-hand that he could sign one of the affidavits.

"I will sign a paper that Malinkov came in here," said Arbat 1. "Beyond that, I do not know."

"That is all that will be expected of you, comrade," I said

157

with asperity. "I am not unmindful of your knowledge, or lack of it, in this affair. Dismissed."

When he had gone, Catherine gave me a frightened look. I returned a reassuring nod, then said I would go out and asked her to have Arbat 2 or 3, whichever was available, report to me at the garage.

I left by the front door, walking around the house and looking at my executioner's flowers. When I got to my car, Arbat 2 was in it. I drove out north and into the suburbs. I told him about the order for the Malinkov evidence and I assigned him to keep a watch over Arbat 1.

"Hunt particularly for anything that he may write, such as a report," I said. "I have reason to suspect that he will shortly prepare a most damaging accusation."

"I have long known that he is Godovisky's informer," said Arbat 2.

"Who is his confidant?" I asked.

"Arbat 4," he said. "But Arbat 5 cannot be trusted either, for that matter."

I followed devious back roads indicated by Arbat 2 and finally arrived at the Central Airport. I parked in the space reserved for visiting dignitaries and told Arbat 2 to go into the main building and bring out the airport manager. "We need him for our ovens," I said. I gave him a name and a description.

He returned in about ten minutes with a very much frightened little man in an unseasonable wool suit and got in the back seat with him. I returned to my headquarters and ordered Arbat 1 to take care of our visitor.

I took some of the affidavits that Catherine had prepared, went to the cellar, and had them signed by the executioner and his assistants.

"Just routine," I told them. "We had an important roast on the fire last night." '

I got no discussion from them. I returned to my office and signed the final paper myself. It stated that Colonel Vladimir Malinkov had been questioned by me and then had been escorted by me to the crematorium and turned over to the executioner, whose sworn statement of action was herewith appended.

When I got back I gave all the papers to Catherine and told her to gather up Malinkov's personal effects and make them into a package. I had picked up a few odd teeth while I was below, and I added these. It all looked about as authentic as

158

such evidence should. But I wasn't concerned with any of that, actually. What I was waiting for was the move of Arbat 1.

It took him eight days. Where he had written his report I never did ask. I got a fair copy of some seventy-five or eighty words of it, taken from a blotter, the impression of writing on a second piece of paper that had been discarded, and burned scraps.

This copy was handed to me in my office around noon on August 14 by Arbat 3. He stood by the door to insure privacy while I read it. It was a sure ticket to my own incinerators, for Arbat 1, or an accomplice, had actually obtained access to my apartment and to my dressing room and had seen Malinkov hiding in my closet.

I suspected a secret stairway or wall passage of some sort suitable for spying on the master suite.

I burned the paper in the grate, crunched the ashes with my foot, then motioned Arbat 3 to my desk.

"When will this report be delivered?" I asked.

"I will not know beforehand," he said. "The minute it arrives at Furkasovsky Alley I will be informed. All I know is that it has not yet arrived. I was unable to discover who will be the messenger, but I suspect Arbat 4."

"Can you have it delayed at headquarters?" I asked.

"Just for a little while," he said. "That is most difficult."

"If it were to be delivered tonight, could you have it delayed until tomorrow, around noon?"

He looked dubious. "Only if I were there myself and remained in the message office," he said.

"Well, go there, then," I said. "And hold it up until noon tomorrow. Report back here to me when you have it arranged."

He said the Russian equivalent of Roger and was off. A most engaging and efficient little man.

I called Catherine in and determined that Arbats 4 and 5 were out on assignments. I told her to remain in my office and I went below to the cellar.

I spoke to my chief executioner as follows:

"I have a most peculiar fowl for you, and I want you to listen carefully. He is one who has given you orders for two years now, but you are to ignore his orders and his protestations to you, if he makes any. Remember that I am your commanding officer. Ask no questions. Do your duty. Do you understand that?"

"Yes, Colonel," he said, with a bow. "Your will is my law, as we say in Georgia."

159

"Stand here by the door, and make it quick and merciful," I said, "with a gun. He will be down in three minutes."

I went back up to my office and I summoned Arbat 1.

"Go below to the executioner and tell him that I wish to see him," I said.

"Were you not just there?" he inquired, his soft eyes looking worried.

"Obey my orders," I said shortly. "Do not ask questions. I have an important matter to discuss with you both."

"Yes, Colonel," he said, and departed.

I opened my door a crack and saw him start down the stairs at the far end of the great hall. Then, in about six seconds, I heard a muffled shot.

That was an unlucky day and an unlucky report for Arbat 1.

35 I had seventy-two hours and one human menace left between me and my final shot, at the Black Sea fortress of Generalissimo Stalin, which was to rid the world of its prime criminal by the only justice that he himself had ever recognized—the justice of the gun.

It was noon of August 15, a sultry, muggy day in Moscow, with the humidity high under a brassy sky. I had allowed myself only a few hours' sleep. It was not a time for retirement or relaxation. I got rid of Arbats 4 and 5 by sending them to do an execution in Kiev. I ordered them to fly and gave them "A" priorities, but Russian airlines being what they were, I had no expectation of seeing them again in Moscow prior to my departure.

I brought Malinkov out of his hiding place and I put him in charge of Arbat 568.

"You are Arbat 1," I told him. "You will conduct all activities of this unsavory place from now on, and I warn you that you must show no compassion for our visitors nor relax this bloody business in any way until the afternoon of August 18. By that time I will have carried out my assignment or I will be dead, but in either case it will then be time for you to attempt your escape—with Catherine, of course. I suggest the Central Airport. I suggest you obtain a plane there, by whatever means you find necessary or possible, and fly east. Don't, under any circumstances, fly west or south. You will be quickly shot down."

160

He shook my hand and said nothing. I was glad he didn't.

"You will have one assistant, in addition to your staff in the cellar," I continued. "Arbat 2 will return when I am finished with my present activities. He will tell you what he had to do for me. Don't interfere with him."

"Yes, Colonel," he said.

"I don't have to tell you about Arbats 4 and 5 when they get back. Keep a watch for them."

Earlier that morning I had sent Arbat 3 to the vicinity of General Godovisky's country estate, with orders to disrupt all telephone service to his villa at 11:30 A.M. and to make sure it was a good job. When he got through with that, he was to attempt to immobilize the general's car if an opportunity offered. I didn't have high hopes about the car, but it was not too important a detail. I felt confident I could handle this affair without it.

At noon I was shaved and dressed and ready to depart. In my pocket was a note in a passable likeness of Marshal Beria's handwriting which said:

Dear G.:
   Unable to reach you by phone. Please come with Arbat. Important developments.

                                                                        B.

Arbat 2 was waiting for me in the garage and he directed me to the suburb south of Moscow where Godovisky maintained his household. It was a graceful two-story stone structure that gleamed white in the summer sun. It was set on a high hill overlooking a peaceful countryside of large estates and attractive, cool woods. We arrived before the gates shortly after 1:00 P.M., and they were opened without question to my Cadillac and its Red Star insignia on the front. The gatekeeper, an M.V.D. man I had seen around Furkasovsky Alley, recognized me and told me to proceed to the house, up a winding drive that tunneled through chestnut trees. I halted the car at the front door and ran up the steps. Another M.V.D. man whom I knew opened the door to my ring and invited me into the baronial hall to await the general. He went off to fetch him, and Godovisky came hurrying toward me in a couple of minutes with a concerned look on his face.

"What is it, Arbat?" he demanded.

"Marshal Beria has been trying to get you. He sent me out here with this note. It is urgent." I handed him the letter.

161

"Nonsense!" exclaimed the general. "Why didn't he phone?"

"Your phone seems to be out of order, my General," I said.

He went to an instrument standing on a taboret near the entrance and lifted it up. He tapped the cradle switch several times, then put it back.

"It's dead," he said.

He opened the note slowly and read it for several minutes. He crumpled it and put it in his side pocket and looked at me with searching eyes.

"Why did Marshal Beria call you?" he demanded.

I shrugged. "I do not know, my General," I said in a soothing voice. "I attached no significance to it."

"Where does he want me to meet him?"

"At the Mossoviet," I said. "I will be happy to drive you there, my General."

"I prefer my own car," he said.

"Very well, my General," I said. "I will follow you or lead the way, whichever you wish."

"This is a nuisance," he said. "My driver is not due back for an hour. I will ride with you, then. Where are you?"

"Just in front," I said.

He picked up a cap from a table and I opened the door and held it for him.

When we got to the car, he saw Arbat 2 and he said, "Have him drive and you sit in the back with me."

Thus we started out, driving fast as only a high Russian official in a hurry drives. I engaged the general in animated conversation about a variety of topics, so that Arbat 2 could study his voice and prepare himself to imitate its every inflection and turn of phrase.

As we approached the Moskva River, in the midst of the industrial section, where many large trucks were operating, I shot him twice. He slumped forward, dead instantly. I pushed his body to the bottom of the car and covered it with a robe.

"Back to Arbat 568," I said.

"That was very neat," said Arbat 2. "No one that I could see noticed it. It must have sounded like a backfire."

"That's the Chicago method," I said. "Also New York, Los Angeles, and Detroit."

"I don't understand," he said. "Is that English you speak?"

"Why, yes," I said, "come to think of it, it is."

Back at mortuary mansion, we had our cellar crew dispose of the general's body, then Arbat 2 and I went to my office.

162

He put in a call for General Godovisky's secretary, imitating the general's voice so well that I would not have believed it if I had not been sitting there watching him.

"I will not be in today," he told the secretary. "I have important duties elsewhere. There is a letter on my desk which I want to see, and I shall send Colonel Miles to pick it up. Please admit him to my office. He knows which one it is."

There was no trouble about that. Arbat 2 hung up with a smile.

"From now on you are General Godovisky," I told him. "You will sit at this phone and you will be the general until about 3:00 P.M. of August 18. After that, see what you can do about saving your own skin. Commander Malinkov is now Arbat 1 and he will conduct all business here until that date."

I took a Mauser 8 mm. rifle with a twelve-power scope sight and a Maxim silencer on it, and a couple of extra pistols out of the Arbat arsenal, which was kept under lock in my office, and I loaded them. Then I carried them out to my car. Arbat 3 was in the garage under the car, and I handed the guns to him. This rifle had a detachable stock and could be packed into a small space. He placed the arms in a traveling case which had been fitted to a rack attached to the frame, up by the motor. The case could be easily removed and would appear to be an overnight bag.

My time was down to sixty-seven hours, and that was cutting it close. I left Arbat 568 for good, saying no farewells and taking Arbat 3 with me as driver, at around 5:00 P.M. I went first to Furkasovsky Alley, where I picked up Arbat 1's report. Then we started south.

Arbat 3 took the main highway southeast, which joined the Moskva River Drive on the outskirts, so that we would avoid Kiev and any chance meeting with Arbats 4 and 5. This is no travelogue, so I won't regale you with any descriptive paragraphs on the Russian countryside, people, or customs. Arbat 3 knew where he was going and he went fast, and most of the time I just watched the other traffic or dozed. I didn't feel nervous or under any tension. It was no time to get myself wound up that way, yet.

We reached Voronezh on the Don around midnight and Arbat 3 suggested we stop over at the home of a friend of his —another "Kizil Irmak."

"We'll go to the best hotel and check in openly," I said. "We're not taking any chances with your friends. Life, at this point, is short enough."

163

We drove up to an imposing structure of recent construction, ostentatiously named the Generalissimo Joseph Stalin, and got the best suite in the house. My Arbat papers, all signed by Marshal Beria, were as imposing as any internal passports in Russia, and backed up with the Cadillac and its Red Star, they got us the A-treatment with embroidery and bells. Even the local M.V.D. commandant called to pay his respects, but I got rid of him fast.

"We are on a highly confidential mission," I told him. "No conversation and no visitors."

He bowed himself out and we got about five hours' sleep. I woke up first and had a shower in the only such device I had seen in Russia. We ate a good breakfast together in our living room and were under way again by 7:30 A.M. That was, I figured, about fifty-three hours from my goal.

36 We continued to drive fast, and arrived at Armyansk, on the Karkinit Bay at the top of Crimea, in the late evening of August 16. We stopped for supper there and had all the *écrevisse* and *langouste* we could eat. My car attracted a couple of strolling M.V.D. types who wanted to be helpful. We told them to scram. We went on to Sevastopol for the night, stopping again at the best hotel and being received with all deference due the elite. I slept very well and didn't wake up until after eight o'clock. This was 8:00 A.M. of August 17, 1958—with one day to go. I bathed and shaved carefully and had breakfast.

We were under way again by 9:30, driving along the historic coast highway to Balaklava and Yalta. We continued through Yalta and Simeiz and shortly before noon we arrived at the huge new airport beyond Simeiz, which had been built principally to accommodate Generalissimo Stalin's and the Politburo's private planes, along with those of the M.V.D. I don't mean to say that Stalin ever flew. He didn't. There was no pilot on earth whom he would trust with his life. However, he maintained a couple of air-liners for the members of his household and personal staff.

Arbat 3 knew this airport. He also knew the civilian manager of it, who was from his native town in the Ukraine, and the plan which we had hatched on our drive was designed to

164

provide me with a means of escape if I should ever get out of Stalin's fortress.

We drove up to the main building of the airport, just as I had done with his twin, several days before, at Central Airport. We parked in the space reserved for dignitaries and we went to the restaurant and had lunch. On the way I noticed with a sinking feeling that the airdrome was surrounded with anti-aircraft emplacements, all manned. After lunch we strolled up to the manager's office and placed him under arrest. I sat down at his desk while Arbat 3 kept him occupied, and I wrote out, in Beria's hand, an order placing Arbat 3, under his own name, of course, in command of the airport temporarily until his relief arrived. I signed it with the usual "B." Then I took the manager to my car, drove back to Simeiz, and turned him over to M.V.D. headquarters there. That was no trick. My identification was such that I could give orders to any routine M.V.D. post or commander. The fact that I had a civilian under arrest was *ipso facto* proof to the M.V.D. that I was on a legitimate assignment and that I was carrying out my legal duties. The secret police are organized on those lines.

After signing a sheaf of commitment papers and affidavits of accusation, I continued on my way, passing the airport again on the road to Alupka. About five miles along I came to a turn-off, a large sign, and an M.V.D. post. The sign warned that the coast road was closed and that all travelers to Alupka were to take the detour. An M.V.D. man flagged me down with a submachine gun when it looked as though I were going to ignore the sign and continue straight ahead. He came up to my car with the gun at ready and asked to see my papers.

He became properly respectful and saluted me when he had read my identification and orders, and he explained patiently that I needed a special pass to continue on that road, despite my high estate in the M.V.D.

"And who signs such a pass, little brother?" I asked.

"Marshal Beria or General Vissarion," he replied.

"It is Marshal Beria that I am on my way to see," I said. "My orders, signed by the marshal, say that I am on a highly secret and important mission, and I have no time to be delayed for your passes."

He shrugged. "Those are my orders, Colonel," he said.

"Then I shall give you orders countermanding them," I said. "Stand aside or you'll wind up in Arbat 568."

His face paled. He snapped to attention. "Nevertheless——" he started to say.

165

"Stand aside!" I cut in. "I will see that you are not reprimanded."

I stepped on the gas and was away fast. I didn't expect a following shot, and none came. When I got out of sight, I stopped the car and wrote myself out a pass signed with a "B." Then I drove on.

After about a mile, the terrain suddenly became reminiscent of Gibraltar. There were gun emplacements every hundred yards on both sides of the road, on the beach, and back in the hills. Most of the guns looked to me like the new 152 mm. radar-controlled anti-aircraft guns, which were supposed to have a range of over 60,000 feet up. Each emplacement was manned, but not by Red Army troops. They were M.V.D. men.

There were some eight miles of these guns and then I came to a high barbed-wire fence, twenty feet high and at least six feet thick, that ran from the sea on back and disappeared over a hill. Every fifty yards or so there was a light tower with floodlights on it. There was a big double gate that was closed. Behind it there was a small guard post, built of thick concrete, and standing in front were two guards with submachine guns. Others, similarly armed, were visible out along the fence.

I stopped my car on the near side of the gate and handed my papers through a small opening beside the shelter. The guard took them inside the shelter with him and I could hear him phoning. After a ten-minute wait one of the gates was swung back a couple of feet and I was invited inside. As I reached the door to the shelter, the other guard suddenly patted my chest and ordered me to turn over my pistol to him. I gave him no argument.

Inside the guard post, I was told to pick up the phone and talk. I did. I talked to General Vissarion, commandant of Stalin's guard, and told him I had an important message for Marshal Beria.

"The marshal cannot be disturbed under any circumstances," he said. "By whose orders are you here?"

"My own," I replied. "Also, indirectly, by Marshal Beria's."

"That is not good enough," he said. "I do not know you. I have no instructions about you. Colonel Miles means nothing to me."

"I am known only to Marshal Beria," I said. "I am here on a highly confidential mission that concerns your own command

166

and the security of Generalissimo Stalin. It is a matter that Marshal Beria alone can deal with. It concerns Arbat 568."

That stopped him. Anyone who can bandy such names about with nonchalance will always get a listener.

"Where can I verify your identity?" he asked.

"General Godovisky, in Moscow," I replied. "He will be at this number (I gave him the private phone being guarded by Arbat 2) and he will also verify my mission."

"You should have told me that in the first place, Colonel," he said. "Wait at the gate and I will call back as soon as I have contacted General Godovisky. Please let me speak to the guard."

I turned over the phone and waited outside while the call was completed. The guard came to me when he had finished talking and addressed me with respect.

"If the Colonel will please wait in his car, we will have this matter settled very shortly," he said. "I hope you will forgive us for this inconvenience. Our orders are very strict."

"I understand," I said. I went out to my car and sat in it. Not more than ten minutes had passed when the gates were thrown open and I was signaled through. Official phone calls on Stalin's business were efficiently handled. I stopped beyond the gate, and a guard came up to me and said:

"You will go to the residence of General Vissarion. You follow this road about five miles and you will come to a fork. Take the left-hand road for a mile and there you will see a sign with the general's name on it pointing to the beach. Under no circumstances take the right fork. That road is forbidden and you would surely be shot. You will encounter a sign there which will warn you."

I thanked him and started off. About a mile farther on there was a second fence, identical to the first, but with fewer guards. The gates to this were opened to me as I approached, and as I drove through, the guard on duty saluted. A small armored car was parked beside the shelter there, with two machine guns sticking out of its turret, and a short-wave radio aerial, and it followed me at a distance of about fifty yards. When I came to the fork, there was no mistaking which road to take. A large sign there, rigged with floodlights, announced that the occupants of any unauthorized vehicles who entered the right-hand road without proper escorting vehicles would be summarily shot.

My trailing car followed me no farther than that turn-off. In

167

my rear-view mirror I saw it swing around and head back to the gate.

General Vissarion's residence and headquarters was one of the old prerevolutionary castles reminiscent of French châteaux that dotted this coast. It had a high tower at each of its four corners and was built around a courtyard, with a huge marble fountain in the center topped by a couple of plump, sassy cherubim. It sat on a bluff overlooking a small bay and the sea, which could be seen through an archway leading to marble steps, giving onto the private beach.

I drove into the courtyard, following the signals of various M.V.D. guards who evidently had been alerted at my coming. I parked between a couple of markers set up for that purpose, and the car door was opened by a black-suited, poker-faced agent who told me to follow him. He led me through a side entrance into a huge conservatory with glass walls, overlooking the sea, which was General Vissarion's office. Then he withdrew and we two were left alone.

It was then 5:30 P.M. of August 17, 1958. I figured I had less than twenty-four hours—to death.

Also the question did not escape me that now that I was in this place—my goal of four years—how was I going to get out?

General Vissarion was related to Stalin by marriage—through the Red Tsar's second wife Nayda, or Nadezhda, if you prefer—and was the last of the few Old Revolutionaries who had survived the countless purges since 1917. He was a young sixty or thereabouts, with iron-gray hair and a lined, pock-marked face. He smoked a pipe, like his master, and he always appeared at confident ease, which was a rare thing in the Communist Party anywhere.

"So," he said, with an easy smile, as he shook my hand, "you threaten me with Arbat 568?"

"Not at all, my General," I said. "It is merely that I had to gain admittance."

"Who are you?" he demanded severely. "I do not know any Miles."

"Colonel Arbat," I said.

He sat there dumbfounded. To identify myself thusly to anyone was equivalent to a sentence of death. Only those who were condemned ever met Colonel Arbat.

"Why do you tell me this?" he demanded. "It is not anything I desire to know."

"So that you will understand the urgency of my mission," I said.

168

"Sit down," he invited, motioning to a leather chair beside his desk. "The Generalissimo himself has told me about Arbat 568 and so I feel free to discuss it with you. What is your mission?"

"That I cannot tell you, my General," I said. "I can speak only to Marshal Beria. If he is unavailable, then I shall have to wait. I still have a few hours."

"How many hours?" he asked.

I looked at my watch and counted them up. "Tomorrow at around 1:00 or 1:30," I said. "About twenty hours."

"This is the most critical period in the history of the Soviet Union," he said solemnly. "I cannot even hint to you what important decisions are being made—decisions that will affect every life in our country. My duty is explicit. No one at the Generalissimo's residence is to be disturbed, under any circumstances. I cannot communicate with Marshal Beria, nor with anyone else there, until late tomorrow afternoon. Those are my orders, from Stalin's own lips."

I thought that over. It forced me to make a very sudden and unanticipated change in my plans. From now on I would have to improvise and I didn't like it. It was not yet failure, but it was the next thing to it.

"All right," I said finally, "then I will tell you this much. I will tell you that I must arrest at least one member of the Generalissimo's guard."

"Impossible!" he exclaimed.

"It is for the safety of Generalissimo Stalin," I said.

37 If I couldn't get near Marshal Beria, then I couldn't get near Joseph Stalin. It still did not mean that I couldn't get within sight or gun range of the Red dictator, and that was the one chance in a thousand that I now had to take—or to make. What made it such a remote chance was that I would probably have limited opportunity to explore the lay of the land and to pick a vantage point. If I found none, then I was a cooked goose. My anticipated meeting with the marshal had been primarily for that vital purpose. Now it had gone up the flue.

I stalled off General Vissarion by telling him that I had no

169

name for my suspect, only a pseudonym, but that I would recognize his face if I saw it.

"I have examined a recent photograph of him," I explained, "and it is a face that I would not forget."

"Where is this photograph?" he demanded. "Let me have it."

"It is in the hands of General Godovisky," I said. "He keeps it."

"It could be flown here in a few hours," he said. "I will telephone the general."

"That may be too late," I said. "Perhaps it would be more efficient if General Vissarion permitted me to examine his guards."

"That would take a week, to see them all!" he exclaimed. "No, that is impossible!"

"The only guards that would be of immediate concern are those who are near the Generalissimo," I suggested. "The others we could save for a later day."

He thought that over. It seemed to make sense—even to me.

"I will permit you to do this," he said reluctantly. "We will start after dinner. But we can see only those guards around this headquarters. I can accompany you on some of your rounds, but I must retire early. I have urgent duties for the morning."

"Thank you, my General," I said. "I am most appreciative of your co-operation."

"You must make no arrest," he warned me. "Tell me whom you suspect and I will take care of the rest. I will permit no interference with my men from any outside command."

He got up then, a slightly stooped figure, probably from arthritis, and he led the way to the dining room. The table was set for some fourteen, and I was invited to sit on the general's right, as his honored guest.

The condemned man (me) ate a hearty meal. It was, in many ways, an unforgettable dinner, amid this high echelon of Stalin's most personal servants—those who guarded his life. The food was excellently prepared and well served. The talk was polite but restrained. Bad news travels fast. Everyone in that place knew that I was connected in some way with Arbat 568. My phone mention had probably done it. Amid this tough, relentless crew of killers I was the most feared. Well, that wasn't much consolation when I thought of the morrow, when I'd be trying to get away from them—if I lived long enough.

General Vissarion and I started a tour of the guard posts

170

after coffee. When we walked out of his castle, at around 9:00 P.M., it was like going into the sunlight. Every part of the surrounding area was bathed by powerful floodlights. There was no darkness at night around Stalin's Black Sea fortress.

When we got to the top of the marble stairway to the beach, I could see, off to our right, a high wall, crenelated as was the Kremlin wall, which cut the small cove in two. The wall extended about seventy-five yards out into the water and back up the bluff, where it was lost to view behind trees. There were high ridges sheltering the cove on both sides, and on top of both of these were floodlights, antiaircraft guns, and machine guns, with their crews all on station. Out to sea, from the blackness, shone the running lights of a half-dozen vessels which seemed to be moving almost imperceptibly east and west.

As we moved down the stairs I looked back and to my right and saw the top two stories of the Generalissimo's palace or, if it will make the proletariat any happier, hovel. It was faced with what appeared to be pink marble in that light; it was of three stories and of the square-box, utilitarian school of palace architecture which, I suspect, evolves from the lack of imagination of its designers. We moved on down the beach and talked to half a dozen guards stationed beside the wall and near the water. Then we moved back toward the stairs and I looked up at two of the four tall turrets on the general's residence that commanded the surrounding country. I drew an imaginary line from the turret tops to the Generalissimo's wall and decided that the forward tower commanded practically all of Stalin's beach and portico. Also I noticed that there were guards on the top of them.

The general and I took a path along the wall and stopped and spoke to guards every twenty or thirty feet. The wall extended back a quarter of a mile, then turned square left. We continued along it, past a huge barracks for the M.V.D. guards, and to a large gate that was closed, with a concrete guardhouse on each side of it and an M.V.D. officer with a submachine gun in each post.

We continued on around the wall and out to the far end of it, anchored in the western ridge that closed in the cove. By the time we got back it was nearing midnight and Vissarion told me he would have to leave me. We went into his château through the courtyard, and he took me to his duty officer, a Colonel Boroslav, who had sat at the general's left during dinner. This Boroslav was about my own build and a little younger, and he made no effort to hide his hostility.

171

"Colonel Miles is here at the invitation of Marshal Beria and myself and is to receive all co-operation," the general told him. "He will visit various guard posts and speak to the guards. You will kindly see that his wishes are satisfied. When his tour is completed for the night, please see that he is taken to bedroom C and that he is properly cared for."

"Very well, my General," said Colonel Boroslav.

"You understand," the general said to me as an afterthought, "that there is no question of entering the Generalissimo's premises tonight or tomorrow until Marshal Beria emerges?"

"I understand, my General," I said. "Good night, sir."

He went off up the grand stairway, and I stood in the hall below, beside Boroslav. This great hall was the command post of the headquarters, and Boroslav's desk was in the center of it.

"Well, where do you wish to go?" he asked.

"I noted from the outside that there are guards in the towers," I said. "Perhaps we could visit them."

"That's a damned far climb," he said nastily. "Wouldn't you like to wait until daylight?"

"I'll go up there now," I said, just as nastily. "You lead the way, Boroslav."

The sea-front tower on the west side was the third one we visited and it confirmed my most optimistic hopes. It overlooked even more of the Stalin beach and terrace than I had estimated, and I noticed on my way up that through several of the narrow slits of windows in the tower wall that spiraled up with the stairway the Generalissimo's portico was visible. These windows would prove ideal for scouting before I had to take care of the guard on top—if I ever got that far. I took in the scene from aloft in a fast glance, said a few brief words to the guard, then started down. Boroslav followed me.

"How long is that guard on duty?" I asked when we emerged from the tower door at the third-floor landing.

"Eight A.M.," he said. "That's the change of guard. Why?"

"No reason," I replied. "I'll make whatever statements and explanations that are necessary to General Vissarion."

We exchanged sneers and then he asked, "Well, what next?"

"I presume you have special men on your communications setup," I said.

"That's right."

"I'll look it over," I said.

"It's down below, on the first floor," he replied. "That's a highly secret operation."

172

"So is my mission here," I said.

He led me to a back stairway and down the two flights to the hallway which connected his command post in the Great Hall with General Vissarion's conservatory office in the beach wing. We came out a door and went some fifteen feet down the hallway toward the command post, and entered a large mahogany room with two switchboards and a couple of short-wave radio transmitters in it. One short-wave man was sitting by the door. The two switchboard operators had their backs to the door, and the fourth was at a transmitter and loudspeaker receiver by a window. The short-wave operators also had headsets and telephone transmitters on their chests and evidently received all of their orders by phone.

I looked the men over quickly, then turned and started out. Boroslav closed the door after me.

"I presume that that's where your general alarm would originate from," I said.

"What general alarm?" he demanded.

"Why, in case of some dire emergency," I said.

"There will be no dire emergency here," he stated with grim assurance. "Our system is ample for all our needs, and we require no improvements." He started off down the hall to his desk, muttering, "General alarm! What nonsense!"

I followed him, and after he had cooled off somewhat, I told him I would retire for the night. He made no effort to hide his relief.

Boroslav put me in the hands of a sergeant, and I was escorted to my bedroom, which was on the top floor, on the side away from the Generalissimo's palace. After he had left I went on down and out to my car. Boroslav scowled at me as I passed his desk in the main hall but made no comment. There were too many guards around for him to worry about me.

I opened the door of the car on the side away from the guard at the palace entrance and, after determining that he was not watching me, I slid underneath and removed the gun bag. I pushed it out to the side of the car, then scrambled from under, dusted my clothes, banged the car door shut, and picked up the bag. I carried it on in and was well by Boroslav when he called to me.

"What have you got there?" he asked.

"Overnight bag," I said. "Why?"

"What's in it?" he demanded.

"My toothbrush," I said. "If you have any more questions,

173

you take them up with the general and Marshal Beria in the morning. Good night."

I walked on, expecting almost anything, but nothing happened. I must have had a good fairy sitting on my right shoulder.

I went up to my room, assembled the rifle, made a final check that all the guns were properly loaded, then placed them under my mattress and slept on them. I can attest that they were not comfortable.

This was about four in the morning. I slept for five hours, woke up, and smoked a couple of cigarettes, then dozed fitfully until noon. There was a mess boy standing in my room when I opened my eyes the last time, and I told him to get me eggs and coffee. I had no private bath and I didn't want to leave my room, so I just shaved and washed my face. Then my breakfast arrived and I ate it off a small table by the window which overlooked the Black Sea, but on the wrong side. I chased the boy out when he started to make up my bed.

I got back into bed after breakfast and sat up and smoked and wrote myself a couple of passes and orders in the marshal's hand. According to all information that Bureau-X had been able to dig up on the subject, 1:30 P.M. was the hour that Joseph Stalin most generally arose.

When that hour arrived I got up and I strapped one of the pistols around my thigh with adhesive tape (I had several rolls of it in with the guns) and then put the other pistol in my side pants pocket. I put the Maxim silencer in my coat pocket, then I shoved the muzzle of the Mauser down my pants leg, tightened my belt around it, and put on my coat over it. There was quite a bulge, but I didn't expect to be under any close observation.

I opened the door of my room and took a long look out in the hall. There was no one stirring. I walked out as quickly as I could with the interference of the rifle, and went around a couple of corners to the door of my tower. I opened it quickly, ducked inside, closed it, and stood there. There was no sound of anyone stirring. I took the Mauser out of my trousers, screwed on the silencer, then started my climb upward. It was a narrow circular stairway of stone, and the regularly spaced machicoulis gave plenty of light to see. I stopped at the top window that overlooked the Stalin castle. This was some twelve feet from the tower platform. There was no door over the exit to the tower top, but I was well hidden there so long as I made no noise.

174

On Stalin's terrace a table was being laid by two serving women, and there were several figures on the beach. One was a woman, probably Stalin's daughter, Svetlana, and four men. None of them was Stalin. I recognized Beria and Molotov.

Five minutes passed. Ten. Fifteen. Twenty. Thirty. Then those on the beach started up toward the portico, as though from a signal by someone out of my view. Five minutes more. Ten. Fifteen. The five were standing behind their chairs, and they were joined by one more from inside. There was still no one at the chair at the head of the table, which faced me. Then a group of eight dark-suited secret police suddenly came on the scene from inside and took up positions around the table, each with his back to it.

I crawled on up the stairs, a step at a time, hearing my own heart beat. As I neared the top I saw the legs of the guard. He was standing looking down at the Generalissimo's terrace, with his back to me. I moved forward and upward two steps. I raised the Mauser and coughed. He turned quick as a cat, and started to bend toward me. I shot once, but the only sound, with that silencer, was a click. He fell toward me and I snatched the cap from his head, put it on, and quickly stood up in his place. I looked around casually and saw the guard from the tower in back of mine watching me. He seemed satisfied, after a moment, and turned his attention elsewhere.

I held the rifle between my legs, the stock resting on my foot, and looked over the parapet at the Red dictator's breakfast party. He was just moving out to the table, walking slowly and saluting his guests with upraised hand. He was about five hundred yards from my turret, and when he sat down he would be a perfect target.

I rested the rifle on the tower edge just as he started to sit, hiding it as much as possible from the other tower observers with my body, and quickly got Stalin in the cross hairs of the scope sight. I caught his face first and saw his walrus mustache, then I lowered it to his heart. I squeezed the trigger. There was another click.

I dropped quickly to my knees, took off the cap, and put it back on the head of the dead guard. I propped him up so that the cap could be seen from the other towers, then started toward the stairway and down.

175

38 The next place I had to get to was the communications center on the main floor. Knocking that out would give me my only chance to escape. If I couldn't, it was my death warrant. I figured I had no more than a few minutes before those surrounding Stalin would collect their wits sufficiently to determine the cause of his death and to give the alarm. That alarm would come only to the communications room, so far as I had been able to determine, and from there it would spread to the fortress, to the guards, to the Crimea, and to Russia and, eventually, to all the world. But not to the world until the Russians got ready to give it out.

I carried the rifle with the silencer down the stairs and out to the third-floor landing. I had three bullets left and I needed them, but more than anything else I needed the silencer. I hid the rifle as best I could under my coat.

I took the back stairs down and landed in the hallway on the first floor without meeting anyone. The hallway was empty. At the command post I could see the side of Boroslav's head as he sat at his desk. He did not turn my way. I crept the fifteen feet to the communications-center door, watching his head all the time, then opened the door quickly, ducked inside, closed it, and started shooting.

I shot three of the four men in there—the two manning the telephone switchboards and the one by the window on the short-wave set. The one near the door, I clubbed with the rifle barrel. He had started to rise and make a grab for his pistol. I pulled out my knife and cut all the wires I could find on the radio sets, severing speakers, phones, and mikes, then went to the switchboards and sawed through the trunk cables. What saved me there was that they were not sheathed in metal. I left the rifle there, got my pistol into my coat pocket with my hand on it, and walked out. It had taken no more than three minutes.

As I closed the door behind me, General Vissarion emerged from his office and came down the hall. I took my hand off my gun and saluted him.

"Good morning, my General," I said.

He nodded to me. There was a worried, preoccupied look on his face. I was wondering if he would comment on the fact that I had just emerged from the communications room, but he walked on without taking notice. I followed him into the com-

176

mand post and on to the door to the courtyard. I held the door open for him and we went down the steps together. "Have you found your man yet?" he asked me.

"No, my General," I said. . . . "If the General has no objection, I will drive into Simeiz for a few hours."

"That is highly irregular," he said, turning and scowling at me.

"There was a young lady who came down with me," I said.

"Highly irregular," he repeated. He hurried away toward the path to Stalin's castle. I got into my car as fast as I could without attracting attention from the two guards by the exit gate, backed around, and headed out. The guards gave me a salute.

As soon as I got past them and around a bend, I turned on my red searchlight and eased the throttle down to the floorboard. About a quarter of a mile from the first gate, I started the siren going, and I saw the gate being swung open with maddening slowness. I had to brake away down to keep from hitting it. The armored car was parked alongside the guard post.

"Emergency," I yelled at the guards. "There's been an accident. Keep these gates closed and don't let anyone through! All communications are out!"

I sped on, winding up to over eighty before I started slowing down for the second gate. I started my siren again, but I had to skid to a stop. The gates did not open. I jumped out quickly and waved excitedly at the guard.

"There's been an accident!" I yelled. "All communications are out!"

"We know that," the guard replied, standing there stolidly, with his submachine gun pointing at my feet.

I pulled out my papers, and among them the special pass dated August 18 which I had written out that morning in Beria's name.

He examined it with great care. Off in the distance from which I had come, I heard shooting. It was small-arms fire, and there might have been one machine gun. Then I heard the high wail of a siren, very faint but unmistakable.

"I am in a great hurry," I said. "As a colonel of the M.V.D. I am not in the habit of being delayed this way."

The guard raised his expressionless eyes to mine. "I am a colonel too," he said.

He handed me back my papers and I leaped back into my car. The other guard started to open the gate. He swung one

177

side back and had just started to move the other when the wailing of the pursuing sirens suddenly reached us loud and clear. He stopped swinging the gate. I stamped on the gas pedal and leaped forward with a screech of tires. I hit the guard a glancing blow and, knocking him ten feet, rubbed the edge of the gate along the entire side of the car. It sounded as though the body were being ripped off. Then the submachine gun started to chatter. A couple of bullets went through the windshield at the height of my head, but just off to the side. Then I was out of range, again traveling fast.

There were no further incidents until I neared the Simeiz airport. About a hundred yards from the airport entrance the motor conked out. I let the car coast into the driveway and stopped it in the middle when it began to slow on a grade. I opened the door and jumped out. I went around the back of it on my way to the operations building, and noted that there were a score of bullet holes in it. Some of the shots must have punctured the gas tank.

As I reached the door of Operations I could distinctly hear the wail of sirens. Maybe others did not hear them yet; I know that my ear was attuned to them. I walked as fast as prudent through the office and out a door to the airplane ramp. A twin-motored light bomber, with engines idling, stood off to my left, and I headed for it. An M.V.D. man who had been lounging near the wall started toward me, calling for me to stop.

I stopped. The wail of sirens was much more distinct.

"Where are you going?" he demanded.

"To my plane," I said, indicating the bomber. I pulled out my papers fast and flashed the Beria pass at him. "I am in a hurry," I said. "Do not hold me up."

He started to study the pass, then began looking through the other papers, one by one. I stood there, jittering for the first time. The sirens were getting very loud.

Arbat 3 saved that situation. He ducked under the wing of the plane and called to the guard.

"Do not delay the colonel!" he yelled in a surprisingly loud voice. "Come on, Colonel, we must hurry!"

I grabbed my papers from the hand of the guard and ran. I didn't look back at him. I ran around the wing, and Arbat 3 gave me a boost through the door. I ran up to the cockpit, sat in the pilot's seat, and jammed the throttles halfway down. I swung the tail around and taxied across a newly planted grass plot to the nearest runway and headed down it. There was a

178

wind sock hanging limp, so I didn't have to worry about a cross-wind. I gave both engines full power, looked at the oil gauges and manifold pressure, hoping for the best. Everything seemed to be working. I took that crate upstairs in a run of not more than 200 yards, retracted the wheels and started a tight turn to the south. That was a mistake. Every damned antiaircraft battery around that field opened up on me.

I straightened out fast, leveled off, and then let down to within fifty feet of the ground. I kept it low and in a gradual turn, straightening out over Simeiz and hopping over a couple of buildings. Then I was out over the Black Sea, doing about 400 miles per hour with everything wide open. I turned around and looked for Arbat 3, but he was not in evidence. I continued on for about fifteen minutes, then went up a couple of thousand feet and put it on automatic pilot. I went to the rear and found Arbat 3 lying by the door, bleeding his life away. There was a huge hole in his chest, made by a 40 mm. at least. There were four holes in the plane through the door and fuselage.

I bent down and looked at his wound. He was done for, breathing his last. He mumbled something unintelligible, then lay quiet. I felt for his pulse. There was none.

I went back to the greenhouse and took over control of the plane and descended again to wave-top. I was approaching the Turkish coast and I didn't want to be picked up by their radar if I could avoid it. I was keeping a close watch up and back, and just about the time I sighted the coast I saw the first two Soviet MIG's start their dive on me, from about 7,000 feet. I counted three—not a very long three—throttled down, dropped my wheels and flaps, and slowed down to a walk. The jets overshot me, passing over the coast and swinging in a wide turn to the left. I saw antiaircraft open up on them and I headed for that place, taking up my wheels and flaps and pouring on all coal.

I passed over Cape Ince Burun and was within sight of the port of Sinop when the second two jets came down on me. They riddled my fuselage, smashed my instrument panel, and set my port motor on fire. I was too low to have any wide selection of a landing spot, but I got within range of the antiaircraft batteries before I crash-landed in a cultivated field.

I opened the emergency hatch when I hit and sat there riding it out for two hundred yards. Then I scrambled out of that hatch and ran like hell across the field. I was sixty yards from the plane when it blew up, and I was knocked flat on my face into the dirt.

179

But I was all in one piece, in an Allied country, with my assignment carried out.

Joseph Stalin, the Red Tsar, had been "executed."

39 It seemed like years since I had seen anything quite so welcome as those Turkish Army uniforms that came swarming toward me from their American command car, which they had stopped on the road a quarter of a mile from the field where I crashed. I stood up and waved to them, then looked north and saw the four jets buzzing around madly out over the Black Sea, beyond range of the Turkish antiaircraft. They were smoking symbols of Soviet anger.

My captors came up to me with various brands of riot guns pointed, but I could see no menace in them. These were my friends and my allies and I grinned broadly at them and began trying out several languages on the officer who was in command. He brightened up when I spoke German, and I explained in carefully chosen words of few syllables that I was an American who had just escaped in a stolen plane from Soviet Russia and that I would be pleased to accompany him to his commandant and explain all. He gave me a fast frisk for weapons—missing my last pistol strapped to my thigh—and ordered me to accompany them. I marched back to the command car and got in the back seat. A couple of them left us to examine what was left of my plane. My guards kept their guns at ready, even though I had appeared unarmed, and the driver gave us a fast, rough ride into Sinop and through the town to the military barracks, arranged in a huge quadrangle which overlooked the bay.

I was taken into the commandant's office, and the arresting officer remained to interpret. The commandant was a tall, bronzed gent with huge black mustachios that were carefully brushed and waxed into magnificent points, and he gave me a careful going over with jet-black eyes.

I repeated my earlier statement that I was an American who had escaped from the Soviet Union by stealing one of their airplanes, and my captor translated.

The commandant made a short speech, and I was asked for my papers.

I explained in detail that all I had with me were Russian

180

papers, which I had used while I was in that country; that I had nothing to show who I actually was, or to prove that I was an American. I handed over my Russian documents, and the commandant, after a brief glance at them, handed them over to an aide, who took them out—presumably to be translated.

Then I made another speech. I told them that it was imperative American authorities be notified immediately of my presence in Turkey; that I was on an assignment of the utmost importance to my country.

The commandant asked me if I was a spy, and I replied that spying had not been my primary duty. Then he asked me my name, and I told him the name I was using was John, or Jan, Miles.

It was all very slow and deliberate, and I was beginning to become impatient, when the aide came back with my papers and had a long confab with the commandant. After that he made a brief statement to me, which was translated as follows:

"Your papers show you to be an authentic officer of the Russian M.V.D., so we are forced to discount your story entirely. We are placing you under arrest."

"What will you do with me?" I asked.

"Tomorrow we will send you to Ankara," was the reply.

"Tomorrow," I said, "will be too late. I will warn you of this: that the Russians will go to any lengths to kill me. I presume that Turkey has not yet declared war upon Russia; I know that America and the Atlantic Pact nations are involved. But if you keep me here in Sinop, the Russians will be back in just a matter of hours and they will either make a landing and try to capture me that way, or they will destroy your entire city and your military post by bombing."

This took a long time to convey, with halting translation; and I doubt that more than half of it was made clear. The commandant listened patiently, then said in a quiet voice:

"The Russians will not dare to bomb Sinop."

"They will dare," I said. "I will give you good odds that before the night is over they will explode an atom bomb right over this headquarters."

He shook his head and smiled when that was translated to him. I argued for another fifteen minutes, but I could not budge this stubborn man. I was finally taken to a guardhouse on the north side of the quadrangle, and I was locked up in an ancient cell on the ground floor which was furnished only with an iron cot with straw mattress and a bucket. Its small barred

181

window looked out on the square and its steel door opened to a hallway that had a half-dozen cells on each side. The entrance to this hallway was by another steel door with a big old-fashioned lock on it.

It was about 6:30 P.M. when I was locked in the cell, and I sat on the cot and began figuring my chances. I decided that my thought about the atom bomb was a much better inspiration and a much more likely move on the part of the mad Russians than even I had at first considered. It was easy to arrive at. I just put myself in their place and figured what I would do under the circumstances. If I were Beria, for instance, I wouldn't let anything in the world—declarations of war and a shortage of atom bombs included—stop me from killing this Jan Miles.

So I had to get out of Sinop, and I had to do it before many hours of darkness had covered the land. I got up from my cot and I surveyed the quadrangle from my cell window. I had a good view of it and could see out to the main gate. There was one soldier on guard duty there, and I noticed that he gave only perfunctory salutes to vehicles entering and departing; that he stopped none of them and examined none of them, nor their personnel. What a difference from the fear-ridden Russians!

There were vehicles of one kind or another parked all around the quadrangle—jeeps, command cars, weapons carriers, bicycles, motorcycles, and even a U. S. Army duck of World War II vintage. I watched several vehicles drive up and their people get out, and I watched particularly if there was any evidence that any of them locked the ignitions and took keys with them. So far as I could see, none did. They would shut off the motors, but there was never a gesture of a key being put in a pocket, either in or out of the cars.

Just as it started to get dark, a guard came across the compound carrying a huge pot in one hand and a ladle in the other. It looked like dinner, and I ducked down, took off my pants, and got my last pistol from the inside of my thigh. My skin was left raw from the adhesive tape, which was a special Russian brand that takes most of the hide with it. I got to the side of my door and waited for the guard to enter the hallway and open my door. He had set his pot down on the floor, and when he opened up I grabbed him by the front of his tunic and pulled him inside. I put the gun on him and informed him with gestures that he was to undress. He demurred and I put the gun to his temple. So he complied.

When he was undressed I tore up his shirt and bound his

182

hands and feet with the sleeves. I made a gag with the rest of it and put it in his mouth, being careful so that he could still breathe. Then I quickly put on his pants and tunic. They were a bit tight, but not as bad a fit as I had expected. I took his keys, locked my cell door and opened the outside door a crack. There were several soldiers about, but none of them was looking my way. I slipped out, leaving the keys in the door, and walked purposefully to a weapons carrier I had spotted about fifty feet away. I climbed in, started the motor, and drove out, not too fast and not too slow.

Coming in from my crash landing, I had noticed a highway curving southwest, and I figured this was undoubtedly the main road to Ankara, which should have led somewhere in that direction. I drove through the town and found what seemed to be this main road and took it. There were road signs, of course, but they were all in Turkish, which was beyond me.

I was less than an hour out of town, climbing through a range of hills, with a black, moonless night folded over the land, when the sky behind me was suddenly lit up as though the sun had exploded. I stopped the weapons carrier in the middle of the road and waited. In just about a minute I heard the blast and felt the earth rumble with it.

I had called that one right. The Russians had dropped an atom bomb on Sinop. (If you remember reading about it, now you know the reason why.)

I started up again and kept going, hoping that I was on the right road and, more important, that I could find a properly understanding ear in the Turkish capital. Shortly before midnight, after a drive of around two hundred miles, I came to the outskirts of the city. My gas gauge read "empty," but I figured I still had a gallon or so in the tank and I kept going, through narrowing streets and increasing throngs of hurrying humanity.

Word had reached the capital of the atom bombing about two hours before, and had been spread by radio broadcast. Turkey was in the war against her traditional enemy, Russia, and the excitement was contagious, even though I could not understand a word of these yelling people.

I stopped my weapons carrier on an avenue that seemed to lead somewhere important and got out and hurried with the rest. I finally found myself in the main business district of the city and saw a big sign on a corner building advertising "Air France." I went into their offices, which were still open, and asked a clerk in French if he would be good enough to direct me to the American Embassy.

183

The clerk asked me, "What?" and I repeated my question. He nodded. He replied in Turkish, a long, unintelligible collection of gibberish.

"Do you speak French?" I asked.

"But of course, Monsieur," he said. "I am a Frenchman, so naturally I speak French."

"Well, then," I said, "answer me in French, if you don't mind. I speak no Turkish."

"But Monsieur is a Turkish soldier!" he exclaimed.

"Look," I said, "all I want is a simple answer to a simple question. I want it in French, for reasons which we will call my very own secret. Do you know where it finds itself, this Embassy American?"

"But of course," he said, looking at me as though I were an idiot. "It is five squares straight down and one to your left. That is what I told you in the first place."

I walked out and five squares down and one to my left. I rang the bell of an imposing mansion in white marble and stained-glass windows, with the familiar Great Seal of the United States on the door, and I was confronted by a butler straight out of a Noel Coward play.

"Yes," he said.

"I wish to see the ambassador," I said.

"Have you an appointment?"

"No," I said. "I didn't have time to make one. Very sorry about that."

"This is no time to be calling on the ambassador," he said severely. "What are you doing in that uniform? Are you a Turkish soldier?"

I pushed him aside, walked into a graceful hall with curved stairways coming from two sides of a huge balcony, and closed the door after me.

"Here!" he demanded, "what are you doing?"

"Stand aside," I said. "Go and summon someone in charge —anyone. I am an American officer and I am not going to be held on a doorstep while you ask silly questions. Move."

He moved. I've always been able to get action with that tone of voice. What I got this time was a male secretary with hostile pince-nez shining at me and a mincing walk.

"What is all this?" he demanded.

"For your purposes," I told him, "I am John Miles. I am a commander in the U. S. Navy, on detached duty. I have just completed a hazardous mission and I am here to request asylum

184

and also that a message be sent immediately to my command, informing them where I am."

"Your identification?" he asked loftily.

"I do not happen to carry identification," I said.

"Then I shall be forced to notify the police," he said.

"You make one move to notify anyone without my say-so and you'll be a permanent cripple," I said. "What the hell sort of a place do you people run here? Who are you to question me or ask for identification?"

I was really steamed at this twerp, and I guess I did a good job of conveying it to him because he turned a couple of shades of white and started to bite his lip.

"I'm sorry, sir," he said, finally. "We just have to take normal precautions . . ."

"Forget it, sonny," I said. "Take me to your ambassador and all will be forgiven."

"You do talk like an American," he conceded.

He led me to a study at the rear of the building, which overlooked a garden, and told me to wait there and that he would call His Excellency.

I waited about fifteen minutes and the ambassador came in. He apparently had been given a complete briefing on this tough character in a Turkish Army uniform, and there was a look of frank curiosity on his face. He went to his desk in a corner of the room, and I got up and closed the door, which he had left open. Then I walked over to his desk.

"I am John Miles," I told him. "I don't expect the name to mean anything to you, but I have just come out of Russia after three years with the M.V.D. I hold the rank of commander in the U. S. Navy, and I was on assignment by an Allied organization with headquarters in New York. It is vital to me and to my organization that they be notified at once that I am alive and that my mission has been completed."

"What is your organization?" he asked.

"I can't tell you that, sir," I replied. "I can only give you the name of an individual and an address where this message is to go. There will be nothing official-sounding about it. I'll have to ask you to take all of this on faith."

He sat back in his chair and looked at me. He was what you might call a typical American, with a keen, sharp face and an alert, efficient manner. He showed that he was interested; also he showed that he was skeptical.

"I understand that you have no identification," he said. "You sound like an American, and I am much inclined to believe your

185

story and to comply with your request, but I should like to know more about it."

"What is your intelligence rating?" I asked him.

He gave me a four-figure number. That number indicated what manner of classified—secret—material he was permitted to know and discuss.

"I can tell you this," I said. "I am the most wanted and right at this instant, the most hunted man in the world—by the Russians. The atom bomb that was dropped on Sinop a couple of hours ago was dropped for the sole purpose of killing me. If the Russians should find out that I am now in this legation they would be over here within an hour, with another atom bomb. There are no lengths to which they will not go to wipe me off the face of the earth. That is the solemn truth."

That impressed him. "You sound as though you have just assassinated Stalin," he said.

I shrugged. "Who knows whether Stalin is not dead?" I said.

"All right," he replied, "I will send this message. Write it out and I will pass it along."

"Oh, no," I said, "not that way. I will encode a message for you, and then you will have your coding clerk use your own top-secret code to scramble it again. Instructions must be sent in your code that it will not break into a clear message. The only thing I can write for you is the name and address."

I don't think he followed me—but it wasn't important. He knew none of those details.

"Do it as you wish," he said.

I borrowed a Bible from him and went to work on a table in the center of the room. I gave him a group of twenty words and numbers, the name "Mugwump," and an address on Washington Street, New York City. Then I wrote out, "Message will not break in clear," under the address and gave it to him.

"If you will expedite that, then I will be off your hands in a matter of hours," I said. "They will send for me."

He looked at it, scratched his head, then pushed a button on his desk. The pince-nez'd secretary came in, and the ambassador gave him the message and instructed him to have the coding clerk go to work on it immediately. "It is to be transmitted as soon as it is coded," he said.

When the secretary had left he asked what else he could do for me.

"A bath and some other clothes," I said. "I hope you will mark the fact that I am not a bit reticent about making my wants known."

"And supper?" he asked.

"The last time I ate," I said, "was around noon, sitting in a bed in the château of General Vissarion, on the Black Sea, between Simeiz and Alupka. Yes, I would love some supper."

He called in the butler with another press of a button and told that worthy to take me up to a guest bedroom, prepare a bath for me, and then find me some civilized clothes. "After that," he said, "see if you can rustle up a supper for the commander."

I followed the butler aloft and discovered that he was a friendly and reasonable type; that one just had to meet him on the proper level. He loaned me a gray flannel suit of his own (I sent three of them back to him a month later), and a shirt, socks, and underwear. I was wearing Russian boots and I wanted to keep them. They were a beautiful pair, made of glove leather—my only souvenirs of the Soviet Union.

While I was eating in the breakfast room an hour and a half later, the ambassador came in and told me he had just received a phone call from Washington.

"My caller told me to give 'my guest' everything he asks for and tell him that they are sending a plane for him," he said. "He told me I was entertaining the most distinguished man in America."

"Thank you," I said.

He sat down at the table beside me. "Just what did you do?" he asked. "That was the President himself who called me."

"You'll find out sooner or later," I said. "I did assassinate Stalin—just as you speculated."

40 I spent six hours in an embassy bed and was awakened by the butler, who informed me my plane had arrived at the Ankara airport and was waiting for me.

"The ambassador told me to tell you they are in a hurry," he said, "otherwise he surely would not have disturbed you."

I bathed again, shaved, and put on the butler's gray flannels. I went below to a breakfast of ham and eggs, which tasted better than anything I had eaten in a year and twenty days. Then I was taken to the airport by the ambassador himself and boarded a B-36 after a fond farewell. There was a good man to have on your side.

187

I was flown directly to Washington and spent the next two weeks talking to all the high brass of America, from the President and the Joint Chiefs of Staff down to the Intelligence organizations of all the armed services and a few extra. I was shocked to see the damage the Russian A-bomb had done to the Capitol and some of the other government buildings, and I finally got permission from my keepers to take a tour and learn the full story. I was shot at once, walking along Connecticut Avenue, and one of my guards, a Bureau-X man by the name of Bill Casey, was wounded in the shoulder. My assassin was killed by Casey.

That ended the sightseeing, and I was hidden away in the Bethesda Naval Hospital, up at the top, in a room guarded by a squad of Marines. That place was picked because they said I needed a checkup, and I lasted it out for about five days, when the whole situation suddenly got too thick to bear. What I mean is, there was still Dorothy Janus.

I made a deal with the guy in the next room to borrow his clothes and get the hell out. He was a big, friendly ex-naval officer and he was a congressman from Idaho, or some such. The way I put it up to him, he figured it would be a good joke on all the stuffed shirts who had me in tow, and he readily agreed to swap rooms, beds, and ailments with me so that I could get away. I didn't bother to tell him how hot I was.

"Besides," I told him, "there's a girl I've got to see, up in Rye."

"That I can understand," he said.

He had a suit in his closet, a more somber sack than I would have chosen, but it covered my limbs adequately, and although his shoes were too loose, his hat fitted fine. Also, his bankroll of some $150 fitted fine. He was a real gent.

I strolled out of there in those loose shoes around 4:00 P.M. of September 3, and I took a cab to a shoe store on Fourteenth Street, then another cab to Union Station and a train to New York.

I got into a phone booth at Penn Station and called a number that I could never forget, and a girl answered.

"Miss Dorothy Janus," I said.

"This is she," she said.

"This is the guy you met on a train that time," I said.

She drew in a deep, audible breath. "Which one?" she said.

"Everything happens for the best in this best of all possible worlds," I said. "Remember?"

There was a long silence.

188

"Where and when?" she said finally.

"Now," I said, "and here, in New York."'

"I'll drive in," she said.

"Go by the northwest corner of Fifth Avenue and Thirty-fourth, slow," I said. "I'll hop in. What are you driving?"

"Black Lincoln," she said.

I killed an hour walking the streets and then I was waiting across the street from the corner I had named, watching all the cars that went by slow. Most of them were cabs. Then there came a black Lincoln with a girl in it and it went by very slow, then turned West on Thirty-fourth and started around a couple of blocks. There were two women standing on the corner and two men. Neither man was looking at anything in particular, and I watched them. The Lincoln came by a second time, and they still stood there. The women had moved on. I saw the car turn the corner to go around again, and the men also turned and looked at it. I walked up Fifth to Thirty-sixth Street. The Lincoln came down the block and stopped for a light, behind a cab. I waited until the light changed, then walked over to it, opened the door and climbed in.

"Go straight over Thirty-sixth," I said. "Make a left on Madison, a right on Thirty-eighth, and another left on Park. Keep on going up Park to Fifty-seventh, then turn east to the bridge. . . . This wasn't such a good idea."

Dottie didn't look at me. She did as she was told and we kept moving slowly until we came to Park. I was looking at her as she drove, and getting a happy feeling. I noticed a large emerald ring on her left hand, engagement finger.

"Now step on it," I told her. "Get uptown as fast as you can and head out to LaGuardia."

"Where are we going?" she asked.

"Back to Washington," I said. "I'll get some dough there and another car. We may pick up a lot of company, but anyway we'll drive up to Elkton."

"Isn't that where people get married?" she asked.

"Uh-huh," I said. "That's the idea."

She pulled over to the curb and she stopped just on the other side of the Grand Central ramp.

"You big lug," she said, "you stop giving orders and you kiss me and you ask me nice! Who do you think——"

I kissed her and I stopped further conversation for some moments. Then I asked her nice.

So now Dottie and I are living on this island, which is a very beautiful island in the Pacific, but I'm not permitted to

189

say any more about it than that. Actually, I'd like to give its name and its location, including ship and air schedules, because, living as we do in the midst of our colony of former Bureau-X people, there's no such thing as fear. That's because were living among friends. In friendship there is all the protection that anyone needs.

Someday, perhaps, the Russians may find that out. I hope they do.

THE END

www.ingramcontent.com/pod-product-compliance
Lightning Source LLC
Chambersburg PA
CBHW020635180626
46816CB00003B/985